Air in the Paragraph Line

Air in the Paragraph Line

Issue 12

¶|

Paragraph Line Books

Denver, CO

Air in the Paragraph Line

Issue 12

ISBN 978-0-6151-6314-7

Cover art and interior illustrations by Matthew Pazzol.

For more information, visit ParagraphLine.com

PL-100

91107214

Contents

Introduction

BY JON KONRATH

Hello and welcome to Air in the Paragraph Line #12!

Those of you who tuned in for the last issue will remember that it was the first themed edition, discussing all things good and bad related to work and employment. I always enjoyed the old *Dishwasher* zine, and I figured others had a good yarn to spin about their past underemployment. Everyone seemed to dig that project, and when I started preliminary work on this issue, I immediately wanted to find another theme.

But what? Love? Sex? Death? War? Food? Drugs? Dreams? Or maybe I needed to dig deeper for a really weird conceptual thing, like an entire issue about NASCAR or the price of candybars when we were young. (That jump from 30 to 35 cents damn near killed me.) I thought of esoteric themes that would draw almost no writing, or simple themes that would pull in tons of the most generic and unpublishable essays from hacks and idiots. And as the editor of this thing, it's my job to find the best, most interesting, and on-track writing, but also manage to collect enough stuff to fill the pages and turn out the issue in less than five or ten years.

While complaining about this to John Sheppard, he was on some weird Richard Nixon fixation, publishing links to YouTube videos of Tricky Dick on his blog to the point where I had to ask him if something was wrong in his personal life. He came back with the idea that the issue should be themed "Weird, Paranoid", and I threw in "Insane" to round it out a bit. And that stuck.

An editor throwing out an invitation to write about insanity to the MySpace crowd is a lot like a frogdiver strapping raw meat to his junk and jumping into a sea of frentic great white sharks. I think many people believe that crazy means "I drank a bunch of Diet Coke and went bowling at three in the morning", but I was looking for "I knew a dude who took PCP and put his head through a reinforced steel cop car door."

Luckily, a few people knew what I was talking about, and came up with some great stories.

I'm also happy to report that this is the first time in a while I had an artist to do the cover and some interior art. The last time I had someone else do the cover was for issue #9, which came out in like 1938, and since then, I've had to scrounge together the covers myself. I hope you dig what Matt threw together as much as I do. And I also hope any of you prospective artists get in touch, because after this issue hits the presses, I'll be begging for art for #13.

As always, some of the writers in this issue are AITPL regulars, but there are a half-dozen new people, some published, some brand new to the game, and all excellent. Please do them all a big favor and check out the web sites, blogs, and books mentioned on the contributors page at the end of the book. There's lots of good reading out there from these authors, and my hope is that this journal gets them all some exposure and new fans.

And please, if you enjoyed any part of this issue, tell your friends! It's always tough trying to promote this kind of anthology, and every blog mention or referral to a friend is a godsend.

Next issue is lucky #13, and I think the theme will be bad luck, superstition, and the like. If you're interested, drop a line and stay tuned to the web site for updates.

As always, if you want to get in touch, or read any of the old issues on the web, check out our new site at ParagraphLine.com.

Stay weird, paranoid, and/or insane,

—Jon

P.S. You may have noticed this issue is now published by Paragraph Line Books. This is something I'm starting, with the help of John Sheppard, to publish some books of ours and others. Our first non-AITPL title will be John's *Tales of the Peacetime Army,* which I'm very excited to be publishing. We're also looking for other books that fit the style of AITPL to publish, so get in touch if that sounds like your cup of tea.

Uncle Bud,

Chaos
Superstar

Rebel
Star
Hobson

When my Uncle Bud was thirteen, he fired a shotgun at the front door of the family shack, and shot my Uncle Jerry in the leg. Jerry waited in the emergency room of Parkland Hospital in Dallas for 24 hours before receiving medical treatment. By that time, gangrene had set in, and he became my one-legged Uncle Jerry. He had it coming. He was pretending to be a coyote at the time of the shooting, and scared the shit out of Bud. Everyone knew Bud didn't think before acting. That's what made him interesting.

In the seventies, Bud met a trio of sisters named Ruby, Chuck and Barbara. He dated and smoked speed with all three of them. After months of partying, he decided to marry Barbara. She was manic-depressive, and therefore, better suited to deal with Bud's insanity. They set up house in Ft. Worth, living in the home Barbara had won in the divorce settlement with her first husband, a famous dance instructor. Barbara and Bud had a baby named Angela, grew pot in their backyard, argued, and smoked speed for days on end.

When Bud's increasingly erratic behavior and poor attendance caused him to lose his job, he became a professional car thief. He was very good at it. He stole my parents' car as part of an insurance scam they were attempting. The scam fell apart when the girl he lent the car to got pulled over, and my disappointed parents had their car returned. My dad was so scared of going to prison, he was pasty and sweaty for a month.

Bud would often come to our house to hide out when the police were on his trail. One night, he came in a limousine stolen from a local funeral home. He charged inside the house and began devouring everything in sight. I saw him chug an entire jug of milk, prompting me to ask, "Mommy, what's wrong with Uncle Bud?"

After he finished eating, he collapsed onto the couch and slept like a rock for three days.

When my cousin Angela was five, Bud got pulled over in a stolen car. During the vehicle search, the police found a large quantity of speed in the console. He was sent to prison. While serving his sentence, he received word that his daughter had been sexually abused. Bud vowed to kill the man responsible when he was released from the state prison. True to his word, his first act as a free man was to purchase a pistol. Unfortunately for everyone involved, his second act was to buy and smoke speed. Fuzzy on the details, and whacked out of his skull, he hunted and shot the wrong man. He was not as accurate with a pistol as he was a shotgun, and the man survived with a relatively minor wound to the shoulder.

Bud went back to prison for attempted manslaughter. After serving his second sentence, he quickly went back for a third time for failing his parole mandated urine test.

Upon the completion of his third term, he pledged to live life on the straight and narrow, stop guzzling vodka straight from the bottle, and smoking speed. He came home, got a job, a little house, and brought his daughter to live with him. He did well for several months, until he became seriously ill. He was taken to the county hospital, where a series of tests were run. The diagnosis was not good. The doctors told him that his years of drug and alcohol abuse had taken a toll on his liver, and he was suffering from an advanced case of cirrhosis.

"We'll be surprised if you make it another six months," the doctors said.

Bud came home, quit his job, and moved into my grandmother's one-room shack.

Cirrhosis causes your liver to shut down, leaving you unable to urinate. There is medication available that spurs your liver into action, but it is taken by the quart. Bud hated the thick, chalky liquid. He refused to drink it most of the time.

"That stuff tastes like liquefied shit," he would yell when reminded it was time for his dose.

When the body is unable to expel urine, ammonia builds to toxic levels inside the body. Eventually, it begins to affect the brain, causing psychosis. We called it "the piss crazies". When Bud got piss crazy, his behavior became extremely erratic.

One day, I was at my grandmother's, watching television while Bud napped. My cousin and chief tormentor, Jereme, came over to make himself a sandwich. Jereme and I were talking, when Bud bolted upright from his bed. He glared at Jereme.

"It's not green, motherfucker," Bud yelled at him.

"I didn't say it was green, motherfucker," Jereme replied.

This seemed to agitate Bud, and he picked up a chainsaw that was stored by the front door. He began to approach Jereme, pulling the cord . On his third pull, the chainsaw roared to life, filling the room with the odor of gas.

"I said it's not green, motherfucker," he yelled over the buzz of the chainsaw.

Jereme 's eyes got huge. He ran towards the door and yanked it open.

"I'm getting the fuck out of here, this motherfucker is crazy," he yelled.

Bud followed, hot on his heels. I went outside to stand on the porch so I could watch the drama unfold. He chased Jereme around the yard, continuing to scream about green, while Jereme cried and begged me to get his mom. I stood there laughing, and refused to get help. The chase finally ended when Bud collapsed from exhaustion, and lay in the yard, kicking his feet, until my grandmother came home. Later that day, Jereme cornered me and punched me in the neck as revenge for laughing at him.

When Bud's ammonia levels were high, he had to be taken to the hospital so his bladder could be drained. It was not a good idea to drive to the hospital with an unpredictable psychotic in the passenger's seat, so we called the ambulance to ferry him. The ambulance drivers were not allowed to take him if he did not agree to go, but if his family could wrestle him into submission and force him into the vehicle, they would slam the doors and speed off. When Bud saw the ambulance, he would become violent, throwing things at us in an effort to escape. It usually took four people to get him into the ambulance, and we were always left with bites and scratches, souvenirs of our battle.

Two years into his illness, he became gravely ill and slipped into a coma. The doctors said the end was near, because his liver was failing. During an exploratory surgery, they discovered stomach cancer. We were called to the hospital to say our goodbyes. They told us that he would die within four hours. Six hours later, he popped out of bed and demanded to be unhooked from his IVs.

"I'm going down stairs to smoke me a cigarette, and see if I can't find me a barbecue sandwich," he said.

The doctors told him that he had cancer.

"It don't matter anyway," he said "I'm already a walking dead man. Give me something for the pain and let me go home."

They gave him a prescription for Oxycontin and released him that afternoon. The addition of Oxycontin to his system made him act even more irrational. Never a believer in taking a prescribed dosage, he popped a pill, or pills, whenever he wanted. He would lay down to take a nap, only to get up and cook in his sleep. The pills seemed to make him ravenous, and to remove any care he had for safety or cleanliness. My grandmother woke in the middle of the night to find him burning hamburgers in a skillet, sprawled naked across the dining table. He opened cans of beans and slung them onto the ceiling, and smeared potato salad all over his face.

"I can't get this goddamned potato salad out of my ears," he yelled the next day.

He never had any recollection of these nocturnal adventures.

Sometimes, he would head to town to go to the grocery store, have an attack on the way there, and disappear for days. We would spread the word throughout the surrounding counties, and would inevitably receive a phone call that Bud was at The One More, our local bar, trying to stab someone with a broken pool cue, or was seen wandering the gravel pits, naked and gathering brush to start a fire. We would retrieve him, have the ambulance battle, and pick him up from the hospital, restored to rationality.

Six weeks after his cancer diagnosis, he found out his daughter was pregnant. Ecstatic about his future grandson, he agreed to receive treatment for his cancer and to put his name on the organ transplant list. The cancer was put into remission, and he set about spoiling the little boy that bore his name. He faithfully went to the hospital every week to take the required drug test (only upstanding citizens are eligible for transplants) and to see if any matching livers had been found.

He went to his daughter's house to visit on the last weekend of every month. On his way home from a visit, he had an attack and disappeared. When he didn't return that night, my mother became hysterical. She called all the hospitals in a hundred mile radius. When she didn't find him in the hospital, she called all the police stations. After ten days, he was discovered at my cousin Bubba's house, smoking crack. He was again taken to the hospital for treatment. When they did his weekly drug test, he was positive, and kicked off the recipient list for six months.

The setback sent him into a spiral of insane behavior. He started taking his pills by the hand full. He hid vodka bottles all over the tiny, one room house he shared with my grandmother. She would not admit that he should not be allowed to drive, and refused to take his truck from him.

"He's a grown man," she said, "he's gotta have his freedom."

One night, high on pills and drunk, he went to visit a family friend, Burke Burnett. Upon his arrival, he convinced Burke to go out on the town with him. They sat in the dingy bar and drank until it closed. Bud declared that he was more capable of driving them home safely, and Burke agreed. As they made their way home, Bud's truck spun out of control and landed in a cornfield. The back half of the truck was left in the road. Instead of waiting for help, they left the vehicle and started walking. A woman driving home from the same bar hit the truck, and flipped it over, totaling both of the cars. Oblivious to the trouble he had caused, Bud and Burke returned to the bar to picked up Burke's truck. Bud was again able to convince Burke of his driving capabilities, and they headed for home. Bud made it two miles past the scene of the original accident, before slamming into a light pole and knocking it over. It landed across the hood, and totaled Burke's truck. They walked the rest of the way home.

Bud was eventually put back on the waiting list for a new liver. He was at the hospital to have x-rays done, when the doctors found a dark mass in his brain. After a biopsy, it was determined to be brain cancer.

"This time, the diagnosis is real. This brain cancer is a death sentence. Get your affairs in order, because you're going to die within six months."

"You motherfuckers keep tryin' to kill me, but I just won't die. Take me off the list."

Two years later, Bud was driving down a curvy farm road, on his way to pick up my cousin. He was full of Oxycontin. He reached down to change the radio station, and missed a curve. His car slammed into a tree at 70 miles per hour, decapitating him. Witnesses said his brake lights never flashed. I wouldn't have expected them to.

Richard Fucking Nixon

Jon Konrath

I listen to a lot of metal. We're talking about a huge collection of extreme metal, from rare import CDs and unreleased demo tapes from Dismember, Cradle of Filth, and Anal Cunt, to more underground stuff like Inverted Bitch Fister and Nuclear Winter. I also dig the classics: Hendrix, 'Zeppelin, 'Sabbath, and 'Priest. But I also listen to and enjoy a lot of music that, by all other standards, sucks. I mean, owning one Journey album could be written off as a fluke. Having a couple of Blue Oyster Cult discs laying around is pretty questionable. But having every Mariah Carey album released to date, and not only that, but having all of the imports, the remixes, the 12" DJ wax, the *Glitter* soundtrack, and knowing the words to all of the songs, well that's a stomping offense in some circles. From the first Winger album, to the Grim Reaper discography, and all of the Chick Corea Elektric Band CDs, a lot of my music collection is kept under wraps, especially when dealing with extremely straight-and-narrow metal dorks who think not being "true" or "supporting the scene" are much worse offenses than living their entire lives in their mom's basement.

Another secret that not many people know about me is that I spend a lot of time hanging out with Richard Nixon. I don't mean I know some other dude named Dick Nixon, or that I read his books, or watch that horrible movie where Hannibal Lechter plays him; I mean I actually party with Richard Milhous Nixon, 37th President, 36th Vice-President, and a huge fan of grindcore and death metal. And yes, he's still alive. The whole cerebrovascular blood clot death thing in 1994 was an elaborate ruse created by one of Clinton's stooges to draw heat from an intern sex scandal that got buried by the funeral news.

Tricky Dick is still rockin' out, hanging out in a two-bedroom condo in Hoboken, doing some minor mob boss enforcement work in Jersey, and working on his fan tribute site to the movie *Point Break*, one of his favorite flicks. "I love that shit," he told me, "especially since *The Fast and the Furious* totally ripped it off, but it had some great car chases, and there's a scene where you can totally see side tit on Jordana Brewster, which is pretty hot. Also sometimes I like to wear one of those Nixon masks like the bank robber, because that's a freaky little bit of irony for you to wrap your head around."

Every now and then, Dick swings by my pad to chill out with me. I hooked up with him years ago when I was trying to unload some Ronnie James Dio tickets, and after many nights of beers and record collection comparisons, he started writing reviews for my old death metal zine, *Xenocide.* We developed a friendship from there, based on our fondness for extreme metal and Vietnam war movies. (He's a HUGE *Apocalypse Now* fan.) Sometimes I'd take the PATH train out to his place in Jersey, and we'd go to the Apple Store in Shorthills Mall and change all of the computers' desktops to some random anal fisting JPEGs. He also had a crash pad in Queens, close to the strip clubs in Long Island City, where he'd hide out on weekends, shoot coke, and make prank phone calls to the DNC.

Tricky Dick swung by most Saturdays with a cold case of whatever was on sale, usually to borrow my Nakamichi high-speed-dub tape deck and make copies of whatever death metal promos showed in my mailbox that week. He always had plenty of high-quality blanks with him, because he apparently struck an endorsement deal with Maxell in Japan, where he's huge, and they did a lot of tongue-in-cheek Watergate-based commercials over there.

We never talked about politics, because after he had a few beers, he got pissy, melodramatic, and downright paranoid about the Kennedy family and any of a thousand other political enemies, and I found it to be a topic best avoided. The one time I indirectly asked him what he thought about something Clinton did that week, he threw a Rolling Rock bottle out the window, narrowly missing my head, then went on this 45-minute screaming tirade about how every person in the Democratic party is a dumb fucking Jew cocksucker and the country would be better off if we found a children's charity for the mentally retarded and let them run the country.

But I'll tell you what: Big Dick knows his fucking metal. He's been banging his head since way back, and he's got an impressive collection of vinyl, tapes, and zines in the same vault that he uses to keep his personal copies of the White House tapes and private correspondence. I mean, this dude used to trade tapes and write with Cliff Burton back when he was still in Trauma, years before he joined Metallica. And while some people might be able to tell you that Metallica covered some Diamondhead albums, this guy had a copy of the original Earmark Records pressing of Diamondhead's *Lightning to the Nations,* signed by the whole band. A conversation about metal with Nix usually weaved all over the place, and involved frequent consultation with a half-dozen music dictionaries and web sites to resolve disputes like, say, if Ron Keel formed Keel before or after Steeler (after) or if Cozy Powell played drums on that Whitesnake album with Steve Vai. (No! He was on the road with Gary Moore then!) I doubt if there is or will ever be another American President that can name all of the Black Sabbath singers aside from Ozzy and Dio (Ian Gillen, Tony Martin, Ray Gillen, Dave Walker, David Donato, Glenn Hughes, and briefly Rob Halford, when Dio pussied out in the middle of a tour), and that always makes for an interesting evening of shooting the shit.

One Saturday night, while I was playing some *Grand Theft Auto* and trying to decide between Domino's and crap Chinese, I got a call from Nixon saying he wanted to stop over before he hit the titty bars later. Within a few minutes, Dick showed up at my place in one of those goombah track suits, with a six of Schlitz tall-boys, looking a bit older and thinner than famous photos when he was in office, but still with the ski-jump nose and sunken jowls. He wore a thick gold chain with a gold-plated cassette tape dangling from it, like he was some obscure hip-hop star. He told me once he gets a lot of weird questions about it, not because an ancient dude is wearing bling, but because "nobody under the age of thirty knows what the fuck a cassette is anymore."

"Hey Johnny, how's your god damned video game? You kill all of the Haitians yet?"

"Working on it. How was that Twisted Sister reunion show last week?"

"Fucking sucked," he said. "Christ, Dee Snyder looks older than me. Actually, they weren't bad, but they had like 19 opening bands, and they all sucked shit. I taped it though."

"Christ, you tape everything."

"Speaking of which, can I use your deck and dub that new Carcass tribute album? Man I love these guys — did you know my dad was a butcher when I grew up?"

"Toss me a blank, I'll get it started."

Dick threw over a C-90 from his endless supply, and I got the synchro-start going on the Nakamichi. Meanwhile, he crashed on the couch and snagged my PS2 controller. He immediately typed in a cheat code to get a flamethrower, and started mowing down pedestrians with fire.

"Die you fucking Vietnamese! Napalm!" he yelled at the TV. "Hey, put on some fucking music!" he said. "You got anything new?

A stack of CDs I got at Virgin earlier in the day sat next to the changer, one of which was Dokken's 1985 effort, *Under Lock and Key*. Now, I'm a huge closet Dokken fan, and Richard's really into their stuff for many of the same reasons. We both listened to much heavier metal back in the mid-Eighties — I mean, that's the same year Slayer released *Hell Awaits*, Iron Maiden put out *Live After Death*, and SOD started out with *Speak English or Die*, just to give you an idea of the climate back then. (Nixon always mentioned how he wished he could have blasted that SOD song on the Air Force One when he first visited China.) But I've always liked Dokken, even back when Voivod's *War and Pain* was the much cooler thing to be listening to. I threw in the CD, and tried to guess what his reaction would be.

Dick cracked open his Schlitz master cylinder as the synth-gong sounds at the start of "Unchain the Night" started. Before the first drum beat, he said "Fuckin' Dokken! It's been a while since I heard this one."

"Yeah, I just picked it up on CD," I said. "I had a dub on tape, but it's practically worn through."

"This is their second-best one, I think." he said, before slamming back the rest of his beer. (It's worth noting that Nixon could easily down an entire six-pack of 24-ounce cans before I could finish my first.)

"You like *Back For The Attack* more? That's blasphemy."

"No, no, *Tooth and Nail*, you shithead. Everything before that sucks, and then they nailed it. Shit, 'Alone Again'... ten seconds of that song and I'm back at Camp David with the whole world against me, everyone trying to indict me for just a couple of tape recorders and break-ins, I'm crying like a little bitch, and even Kissinger isn't taking my phone calls." He paused the video game, cracked open another beer, and took a hit. "*Back For the Attack*, it's not bad, probably their last listenable one, but Neil Kernon spent too much time thinking about it. He produced this and 'Attack, you know. But he didn't have his claws in this one too much. They took too long recording 'Attack, and it got too sterile, too many overdubs."

"I think Kernon spent too much time around Queensryche and wanted to give Dokken the same clean prog sound, and it didn't fit."

"And we all know how that ends," he said. "Your singer and guitar player spend forever wagging cocks at each other, and after a too-long tour and a piss-poor live album, both of them split up and start crappy solo projects that can't sell out a McDonald's during a lunch hour. Then grunge shows up, and Don Dokken is sucking dick for crack while George Lynch is selling car insurance door to door."

"And ten years later, Neil Kernon is producing Hall and Oates albums."

"No shit? I never knew that. Probably out of someone's garage. I'd guess Oates's."

"I still don't see how could you like *Tooth and Nail* better than this," I said. "Dokken's singing is nowhere near as good — he sounds way too saccharine sweet. Every line is like a cliche. And the guitars are buried."

"At least you can hear the drums over the fucking guitar!" he said. "You know, I did some producing back in the day, when I put a band together."

"Was that The Plumbers?"

"You mean the Ass Plumbers? Ha, ha. Well, it was me, John Mitchell, John Dean and Bob Haldeman. Gordon Liddy wrote most of the music. After Dean squealed like a fuckin' stuck pig, we replaced him with Ehrlichman, who couldn't play worth a shit. And the acoustics in the White House bowling alley really aren't what they should be. We had this spook from the NSA helping us with the recording equipment, one of those big Ampex tape decks, and he insisted on doing all of the producing. We had Brush — Bobby Haldeman — on this Ludwig five-piece, a really tight kit, but this dude was totally mudding up the drum sound. I managed to kick him the fuck out of there and redo the board when we recorded 'Daniel Ellsberg Was a Nazi', though."

"Why didn't any that album get released? Conflict of interest with the office?"

"I'll tell you," he said. "Back then, the record industry was run by Jews, godless Communists, and faggots. I wanted to unleash HUAC full-force to crack some skulls and maybe get some honest, god-fearing Christian Americans in there to help us release some unholy Satanic death metal, but it didn't happen," he said. "And there were so many other problems. Dick Cheney was our manager back then, and we thought he'd get us a good record deal, because he had some Yale connections, but then he started getting all of these DUIs, and a deal never came out. And then someone accidentally erased a section of our master tapes..."

"Oh, speaking of buried drums, on this track..." he got up from the couch. "Here, gimme the fucking remote..."

He snagged the clicker, jumped up a track to "In My Dreams", and hit the volume.

"Listen to this shit. Where's the snare? Where's the FUCKING SNARE? It sounds like he's thumping on a down pillow with a wet cucumber. On 'Bullets to Spare' or 'Heartless Heart' it's like 'BAM', 'BAM', 'BAM', explosive, like they had it wired to a trigger, except this was way before everyone went MTV and started triggering their drum kits, except maybe Frankie Goes to Hollywood or something. And forget about the bass — you can't even hear if it's there or not," he said. "Also, what's with this harmonized shit? They taped Donny singing every line five times and looped it back on itself. He sounds like Cher or something," he said. "'Aaaah! Aaaaah! Ah-ahhh!' What a douche. I do like this solo, though."

The perfect fretwork of George Lynch screamed over the top of the band, probably Dokken's one redeeming quality. These guys weren't entirely a "hair metal" band, but danced with a slightly more technical and produced sound, more like a prog-rock band than a Poison or Cinderella. I think that eventually killed them, though, because they tried to sell to that teenybopper crowd and couldn't, but the tough guys wouldn't go for it, either.

"Oh, let me look at the CD book," he said. "I want to see if they look like fairy whores or not."

"Just what I was thinking," I said. I opened the CD booklet and almost spit beer upon looking at their photo. All four guys had that Samantha Fox feathered, permed, and frosted hairdo from the 80s, sported way too much eye makeup, and wore leather pants so tight you could confirm if each member was Jewish or not.

"It's like a fucking Clairol commercial," Dick said. "You could replace any of the guys in this picture with Lita Ford and not tell the difference, except maybe the tits. What the fuck were they thinking?"

"Sluts?" I said. "Money? They're too wimpy to do drugs. I don't know, it was a weird time."

"Speaking of latent homosexuals, here's their big ballad," he said, as "Slippin' Away" came on.

"This isn't bad," I said. "It's the same stupid ballad every band back then wrote, but, I like the acoustic guitar over the top of the slow, reverb base."

"Yeah, Lynch is a madman. He's always been a great player. I keep meaning to check out the new Lynch Mob stuff, but I can't get Elektra to send me a review copy. Being allegedly dead makes it damn near impossible to get free shit from the record companies."

"Check out this solo" I said. Two minutes in, George Lunch pushed the slow distortion of his ESP guitar and strolled through a near-perfect verse, the kind of power metal ballad fretwork far superior than the more mainstream stuff you saw back in the eighties on MTV.

"He's got a good tone here," Dick said. "Back when Johnny Mitchell was playing guitar for us, he could always hit a perfect sound like that. Bill Rehnquist used to jam with us when we were first getting together. He was really into 'Sabbath back then, and totally had a hard-on for Grand Funk Railroad. He had this really heavy chordwork, like what we'd call 'stoner metal' now, but his tone was all over the place, just fuzz and chunky volume. Me and Johnny were more into Deep Purple, that old Ritchie Blackmore tone, classic Zappa, and Captain Beefheart. I remember during the Indo-Pakistan war, me and Yahya Khan used to listen to *Trout Mask Replica* over and over. Used to drive Spiro nuts. Anyway, Bill Rehnquist got into that Gilbert and Sullivan shit, and we knew he wouldn't be a good fit. But Johnny — his sound was always so exact, we used to call it the Mitchell Effect. Get it?"

"No. What's the Mitchell Effect?"

"God damn it, what are they teaching you fuckers in school these days? Look it up. Anyway, about Rehnquist, turns out he's distantly related to Nicke Andersson, the old drummer from Entombed."

"No shit?"

"Yeah, Bill's grandparents were Anderssons — they changed their name when they got here from Sweden. They're cousins a million times removed, but he plugged his shit into FamilyTreeMaker during a court recess and found the connection. 'Course he didn't know that FamilyTreeMaker is run by the Mormons, and him and his whole family tree got missionaries showing up at their door like cockroaches in a New York apartment. Anyway, Bill got into death metal after that, big time — always used to go to Sweden, started detuning his guitars, wearing leather pants and one of those bullet belts under his robes, the whole deal. He was pretty tight with the guys in Entombed, Dismember, Grave, all of those Swedish death metal bands. Not Unleashed, though. For some reason, he never got along with Johnny Hedlund."

"I could see that — all of the Tolkein shit probably threw him."

"Yeah, Bill hated that Hobbit shit. I remember one time he beat the living shit out of his son Jim with a gavel because he caught him playing Dungeons and Dragons. Hard-core porno, a little reefer, Rehn didn't give a shit about that. But one twenty-sided die under the bed, he would thrash you within inches of your life. He played hardball."

"Sounds like."

"Hey, these lyrics aren't bad here," Nixon said. "I mean, they aren't as doubled up as the other songs. But man, on *Tooth and Nail* they sounded so perfect..."

"Here's the good shit," I said. "Lightning Strikes. This is a little more prog-rock than if you think about it," I said.

"Yeah, listen to this and Queensryche's *Rage for Order* back-to-back, and you'll wonder why Geoff Tate didn't sue them for royalties. Hell, if I wasn't disbarred, I'd take the case for him, pro bono." he said. "Hey, what's the second-to-last song? They always put the slow one there," he said.

"'Will the Sun Rise'." I punched up to track 9.

"He's got really clean guitar tone here," Dick said. "And I like the acoustic stuff over the top. Gives it really good texture."

"He actually did that with a synclavier guitar," I said. "All of these pads are put together digitally, or with a Roland 707 or something."

"No shit? Sounds like something Zappa would do. This is around when he was doing *Jazz from Hell* and all of his other Synclavier stuff. That's also around the time that bitch Tipper Gore was giving him so much shit with the PMRC. Christ, you'd never see Pat pulling that kind of shit when I was in office."

"Did you know Zappa had a full-time tech move in with him just to wrangle that thing? Like when Elvis had Ampeg build him a reel-to-reel VCR in the Sixties, and it took a live-in engineer to record his football games and keep it running."

"I ever tell you about the time I met Elvis in the Oval Office?"

"About a hundred times. Dude, I think everyone in the free world knows that story. That picture of you two shaking hands is more famous than the one of Neil Armstrong stepping on the moon."

"I met him too, you know."

"Yeah, I know," I said. "I saw the moon rock endtable at your condo."

"Man," he said, "this solo's hot, too. I can't believe the sound he gets out of his rig. This is way before you could just punch this shit up on your digital POD or whatever. That's as sweet as the sound of a wing of B-52s heading in to Cambodia for a low-altitude napalm run."

"He's like an audio testimony to those old Marshall Super Leads," I said. "He can just start it screaming and then back off like it's a human voice or something."

The song faded out. "Last track," he said. "It's their fast one. Too bad Dokken's singing. This track should be as good as 'Turn on the Action', that last one on *Tooth and Nail.*"

"Yeah, I like the car crash effect they used, with a weird filter," I said.

"You ever listen to that with headphones? It's got a really weird panning effect, it really sounds like the car's going across the road or whatever," he said. "Oh shit, cover your ears — Donnie's going to try to hit a high note."

"Oh man, that's bad," Dick said. "He's squealing like John Dean at a Senate Committee. And it could use more drum. Check out this ending though."Don Dokken shrieked out an "AAA- A A AAAA!" in the worst, most falsetto voice imaginable outside of a King Diamond record.

Dokken repeated the chorus, whined the last notes, then held it for the big "da-dum" finale. Then as the drums crashed, the song ended, the cymbals hit, you could hear Lynch's Marshall amps humming, shorting, spitting like they couldn't take anymore.

"Man, I am fucking starving," Dick said. "Any 24-hour places around here where we can grab a bite?"

"Sure, there's the Neptune. Let me guess — poached eggs and corned beef hash?"

"My view is that one should not break up a winning combination. Now gimme that tape dub and let's get some fucking food."

I shut down my audio rig, hit the lights, and we headed for the cheap Greek diner for some food and grease.

"You see that Redskins game Monday?" he asked. We walked in the darkness of the Queens neighborhood, down a side street filled with garbage and bombed-out auto carcasses.

"No, I don't watch football."

"Is your TV broke, or are you some kind of Communist? I mean, I know they bent over, grabbed their ankles, and took it from FedEx when they moved to Maryland, but come on — it's the Redskins. Vince Lombardi. Joe Theismann. Jesus Christ, are you sure your parents weren't French or something?"

A second later, three punks came out of the darkness and surrounded us. They were the typical wannabe thug kids that hung out in the neighborhood, smoked bad dope, and stole car stereos to pay for their atrocious Scarface t-shirts. They all brandished straight razors in one hand, and cheap fourties in the other. All three of the punks wore Yankees caps and oversized Derek Jeter jerseys that hung to their knees like dresses.

"Yo, hand over the chain yo," said the main goon. "And all your money, son."

I kept my hands in view, but Dick didn't really look scared at all. "Derek Jeter?" he asked. "Is he a pitcher or a catcher?"

"Yo, son, he's a shortstop, cuz." The three goons laughed. "Homie thinks Jeter's a catcher, cuz."

"No, I didn't mean his baseball position," he said. "I was referring to the fact that he's a pillow-biter, and I wasn't sure if he wore a dress for his husband A-rod, or if Jeter assumed the male role in the relationship, or maybe they took turns, like on road games, Jeter was the bottom, and then they switched off for home games. Or maybe they both grab their ankles and have the entire 40-man squad from the Boston Red Sox run a train on their asses, while they both took turns blowing Theo Epstein. Either way, the three of you happen to be wearing his jersey in celebration of your own alternative lifestyle choice, right? I mean, it can't be because you like how that lazy, overpaid piece of shit doesn't field worth a fuck. Or maybe you're just fans of his cologne?"

"Shut the fuck up, cholo! What the fuck? Jeter's not a faggot. He dated Mariah Carey, yo."

"I rest my case."

"God damn it, hand over the shit before I have to cut you."

"You guys want to see some real gold?" Dick pulled a gold-plated Colt .45 pistol out of his running suit. Two of the wannabe gangstas took off running, but Dick fired off six shots into the main thug, and he hit the deck. The kid sprawled across the dirty sidewalk in shock, gurgling through a sucking chest wound. Richard whipped out his cock, and took a nice long beer piss right into the injury.

"Colt 45, works every time," he said, zipping up. "Did I ever show you this? It's the gun Elvis gave me."

"What the fuck are you doing?" I yelled. "We have to get the fuck out of here!"

"Don't worry, nobody's missing this guy. Besides, Jerry Ford pardoned me of all, crimes, remember?"

"God damn it, I keep telling you, that pardon only goes up to the day of your resignation! We can go back to my apartment and look it up online if you don't believe me."

"Don't believe that stuff," he said. "The internet's all run by Jews. And if Al Gore invented it, I would trust a damn thing on there. Now let's go get some dinner."

"Christ, you didn't tell me this was a Greek diner," Dick whispered to me, as we sat in a booth, paging through the menus. "Spiro's family could be running the place."

"I'm sure they only have ties to the Greek mafia, not him."

"Well, we know he wasn't handling their finances. I mean, they haven't been shut down for tax evasion, right?"

The waitress came over, a dark-skinned, top-heavy Mediterranean beauty with a thick accent and a no-bullshit attitude from too many nights on the midnight shift. "You guys ready?" she said, pulling a pad and pen from her apron.

"Hi there, sweetie. How about three poached eggs, corned beef hash, cottage cheese, don't forget the ketchup, and a Pepsi, no ice."

"And you sir?"

"I'll just have a grilled cheese and fries."

The waitress walked back to the kitchen to hand over the green and white order ticket to the cooks.

"Man, did you see the rack on that one?" he said. "You know who would love to get on that shit, is Gus Pinochet. That man loved his jugs. One time he was in DC for some CIA coverup thing, and me, him, and Richard Helms went to this titty bar out on M street. This was before I fired his ass and sent him to rot in Tehran, but when we had visitors from out of town, Richie liked to party. But Jesus Christ, Gus went nuts, and just buried himself in giant mammaries. I swear I didn't see his face for the first hour we were there..."

"Dick, I'm a little worried about what just happened back there?"

"The cottage cheese and ketchup? I know it sounds horrible, but you should try it."

"No, I mean that kid you shot back there."

"Lighten up, it's not like I shot Ben Bagdikian or something. It was some half-assed punk, probably selling dime-bags of oregano and stolen iPods out of the trunk of his Camaro. He won't be missed."

"But what if he lives?"

"First of all, he won't. But if that son of a bitch lives, he's going to go through the rest of his life telling everyone that Richard Nixon capped his ass and pissed into the wound, and not a single person is going to believe him."

"Sometimes I don't know how you sleep at night."

"Good question. Easy answer." He rooted through a pocket of his tracksuit, and pulled out a square white prescription bottle. "Dilantin. Good stuff, I've been using it for years. Here, take this one, try it out. I've got a whole closet full of bottles at home, I've got a great croaker, an old RNC buddy, out in Jersey City that sets me up with anything — Viagra, HGH, THG — he's even got a stash of pharmacy-grade PCP from some Parke-Davis lab in Eastern Europe."

"Thanks, I'll give it a try," I said, stuffing the bottle into my pocket. "Any side effects?"

"I used to have a couple of rocket-fuel Mai Tais at night — you use Bacardi 181, great stuff - and then drop some Dialntin, or maybe some Placidyl, or both, and then I'd get a call at three in the morning from Kissinger, whining that some airport got bombed by terrorists or whatever, and I'd tend to say crazy shit. One time that Nazi fucker calls me at four in the morning to tell me that some NBA/ABA merger failed during labor talks, and I told him to load up 75 B-52s with tactical nukes and take out J. Walter Kennedy's house in Stamford, Connecticut. So yeah, if you're going to mix rum and anticonvulsants, get an answering machine and shut off your ringer."

The waitress appeared with plates in each hand, and laid out the spread on the booth table. "Thanks much, honey," Richard said. He turned to watch her ass as she walked away, then immediately launched into his food. Watching Nixon eat was a spectacle, because he'd practically inhale everything, make all of these slurping and chomping noises, and continue to talk through the entire meal. Add to that the fact that he ate some downright gross combinations of food — I mean, who the fuck puts ketchup on cottage cheese? It was a wonder I could even stomach my grilled cheese while he was slurping down the yolks out of his poached eggs.

"God damn it, I hate the Yankees," he said, mid-yolk. "I wish I would have put on that Slayer song, 'Angel of Death', and did a double-Uzi drive-by on Jeter and A-rah."

"Why, because you think they're gay?"

"No, I really don't care about what he does off the field. Hell, if I got paid $21.6 million a year to be a piss-poor shortstop, I'd be fucking all sorts of things people haven't even thought of yet," he said. "It's just I fucking hate George Steinbrenner. The prick gave me money when I was President because he thought it was going to keep him out of trouble, then he starts blabbing to the whole world, 'I think he's going to get impeached. I think we should impeach him. He's about to get impeached.' Whatever. It's real fucking hard to successfully run a team when you've got a quarter-billion dollar payroll and can buy every single player on the planet that's worth a shit. I'd like to see him run a secret war in Cambodia with no public support."

Nixon completely finished his food before I got through the first half of my sandwich. "Honey, can we get the check here?" he said to the waitress. "Christ, you eat slow. Don't ever join the military — I swear, in the Navy, we used to have to eat that slop in five minutes flat, or you didn't eat."

I shoved the rest of my sandwich in my mouth, as Dick studied the check. "What the Christ? This place is robbery. Maybe Spiro did work here. $3.99 for a scoop of cottage cheese? And they called me a crook." He pulled out a huge roll of cash, and dropped a $2 tip on a $28 check. "Let's get out of this hellhole."

I gave up on my food, and we went to the front register, where Dick peeled off a couple of bills, then proceeded to put an entire bowl of dinner mints in his pocket. "These are free, right?" he asked the casher, who clearly wanted to slap him. "Come on, let's hit the fuckin' road!"

On the way back, half of the street was taped off, as a dozen cops dug around the crime scene, their cars parked with flashing lights waking up the entire neighborhood.

"Fuckers are probably just looking for something they can pawn to keep up their meth habit," Dick said. "I don't even know why they're here. The last time I called in a shooting, the cop laughed and hung up on me."

"We better cut over to the next street. I don't want you to start killing cops a block from my house."

"Ah, I would never kill a cop. I mean, not tonight. I might steal that car that's running with the door open, and then run it into a Dunkin Donuts at high speed. But why shoot them, when someone else will eventually anyway, right?"

We cut down an alley, and stopped again so Richard could take a piss. (On a building, not someone's body.) Richard's car, a '67 Eldorado with limo-tinted windows and a jet black paint job, sat at the curb outside my place.

"I think I'm going to head over to Scandals and see who's dancing tonight. You interested?"

"Nah, I've had enough excitement for the night."

"Fine, you pussy. Can you play that PlayStation game and whack off at the same time."

"Thanks for dinner. And let me know if you want to go to that GWAR show on the 22nd."

Nixon hopped in the Caddy, and fired up the Carnivore song "Jesus Hitler" in the CD player. He then leaned out the window, gave me the double-V-for-victory salute. "Get a good night's sleep and don't bug anybody without asking me!" He hit the gas and took off into the night.

Inside, I found my GTA game paused, people running down the road on fire like that famous Vietnam picture. Tricky Dick. I wiped off as many fingerprints as I could, cleaned up the empties, and called it a night.

Boogerlove

Yuppie Rockwell

Sometime in the Mid-21st Century

His real name was not James Boogerlove, but it was a convenient alias for the time being. He was Head Chairman of Camp Bowie Scavenger Squad #9. He got the job after former Head Chairman Smokey Drugsford was killed in a hail of police gunfire. He had been smoking a cigarette in a Non-Smoking Zone, which was most of the City of DalWorth, TX these days. Cigarettes were only to be smoked in certain Smoking Zones. The only problem was there were fewer and fewer of these around since The Lawsuit Brotherhood had hit town 10 years ago.

James sometimes would flavor his boogers with tobacco, but for the most part preferred a mint or spearmint flavoring. He was trying to kick the nicotine habit. After 6 months in DalWorth Nicotine Rehabilitation Center #189, he thought it was time. It was at this rehab that he actually began the habit of booger consumption and thus gained the nickname/alias: Boogerlove.

Chewing gum, alcohol, drugs of any sort, salt, sugar, fat, and all meats were illegal. In fact gasoline was illegal except for government or state vehicles. The few private vehicles still in existence either ran on ethanol, butane, propane or electricity. Paper was even heavily rationed. This was mainly because half of the world's forests were gone at this point.

Thus was the need for the Scavenger Squads. If you formed a Scavenger Squad under Freedom Ordinance 4445555986749399-NMU7645204949 of the Permanent Rationing Code, you could trade bodily organs or large sums of money for the banned substances legally. For example: 1 kidney or 25,000 PY (Peso-Yen, $25,000) = 10 beef steaks or 10 marijuana joints, with your Dalworth Scavenger Card of course. Viable human organs were a big business these days since disease was so rampant. It was rare anyone lived past the age of 50 by the Mid-21st Century.

However, despite all the above listed substances being illegal, guns and weapons of all sorts were not only legal, but non-ownership of at least 1 machine gun, 1 handgun, and 1 hand grenade by all persons over the age of 10 was a crime punishable by up to 5 years in prison or death, depending on the discretion of The Roving Judge Syndicate. Since it was perfectly legal for defendants in these cases to carry weapons into the various secret court rooms, it was hard to keep judges or find people for the job. The Cyborg/Robotic Judge Project was still in it's infancy by the Mid-21st Century, so there were not many of these non-humans around to judge cases. So far the whole Project only consisted of 100 units in The North American Union (formerly Canada, Unites States, Mexico).

The killing of a machine carried the same penalty as killing a human judge – none. There was simply not enough prison space to house the lawbreakers. Since there were 50 million currently in prison what were the judges suppose to do, let out filthy low lives caught freely smoking and selling cartons of cigarettes? Of course not! Thus because of this logic, lawlessness ruled the day despite there being more laws in the North American Union than in any other civilization in the history of humanity. For example: the North American Union had 100 million more laws than the now defunct State of California or The former United States of America.

The main reason for so many laws was because of the various guilds, institutes, mafias, syndicates, groups, clubs and organizations that existed in the North American Union. The Union itself did not have one single law authored in its name by the Mid-21st Century. All laws came from the above-mentioned guilds, institutes, mafias, syndicates, groups, clubs, and organizations. For example: in New Havana, Florida smoking cigars is perfectly legally everywhere, including hospitals and gasoline/ethanol stations. However cigarette smoking is completely illegal in Dalworth, TX (except for the few Smoking Zones). In fact, New Havana possesses no Smoking Zones. As you can imagine, this causes for a plethora of nicotine activity as was well as many explosions. This makes for a robust fire department. In fact New Havana, Florida's Fire Department is the best in all of the North American Union.

President Zeus is head of the North American Union. He has no real power since law is controlled by the above plethora of organizations, though his cyborg image makes for an easy symbol of authority for the people to identify with. In fact he gave at least one speech daily, lasting roughly 5 to 10 minutes, and every video screen had to carry it on all frequencies. This even included the popular M (micro) sets.

James Boogerlove sat in his locked apartment as one of President Zeus' speeches aired. Even if your visual devices were turned off, they automatically came on when he gave his speeches. His speeches always happened at random times. One day they would be at 0200 hours and the next day they would be at 1824 hours. It was unpredictable.

"Dear North American Union citizens, I come to you tonight with a heavy heart. As you are well aware, we have had 2 small nuclear attacks this week in Choville, Iowa and Cyborg Tech IV, Baja California. I have attended both memorial services for the roughly 20,000 that died at each tragedy. However, I will not let this deter me from my position of pushing my New Nukes Legislation that will let every man, woman, and child in our great Union over the age of 10 and with proper security clearances of course —now just for 20 PY at any of your local WalFarts - to own their own personal nukes to defend themselves. Now many in the Fraud and Graft Judicial Chambers want to keep these weapons banned. But if they are banned, only the criminals will have them! Nukes, nukes, nukes to defend the homeland"

Loud prerecorded shouts and cheers erupt in the empty room where President Zeus is speaking.

"Thank you. Now as you know insect collection is close to my heart. I like water bugs, spiders, and bees in particular. In fact my lover Mike and I were sitting around the other day looking at my collection when I burped. The burped tasted like mayonnaise with lead in it. I was thinking it might be the water but then Jesus told me lead doesn't exist. That lead was made up by devil lovers like deviled eggs. I never eat those either. I got a demon once when I was 12 from a deviled egg..."

From that point President Zeus trailed off into very low toned mutterings and was escorted off from his speaker's podium by the Secret Service. Just another typical speech. It was illegal to say that any President was mentally ill. The acceptable words were: 'The President drifted into a Transcendental Jesus State for the good our Great Union'. The video screens always went blank for a few seconds at this point, then regular programming continued.

Boogerlove had a flashback to Counselor Dickey Shrub, The chief interrogator at the Nicotine Rehab. Shrub paced back and forth in his casual golf club attire, swinging a golf club back and forth over the seated Boogerlove.

"Aight muthafucka"

Began Shrub in his best black ghetto accent, though he had never lived in a black ghetto he liked to fancy himself a former resident because he was banging a black/Viet chick by the name of La Kisha "Agent Orange" Nguyen. All the women in her family for the past 100 years had been born with 3 breasts because of the use of Agent Orange in The Vietnam War. This fed well into Shrub's strange sexual fantasies.

"Speak up muthafucka"

Shrub said again prancing and angrily swinging his golf club, hitting Boogerlove in the knees. Boogerlove bent over in pain.

"Say you love Jesus. Say you love Jesus!"

Shrub said over and over hitting Boogerlove in the knees, finally fracturing one kneecap.

"You swine, you muthafucka traitor. You Anti-Zeus bastard! You love me don't you? You think I'm cute. You want to fuck me in the ass!"

"NO"

Shrub hit Boogerlove again in his knees, fracturing the other kneecap for his insolence.

"Ah baby, you know you love me. You know you want to nail me where it's pink and puckered. You queer ass muthafucka!"

Boogerlove remained silence and flashed back to reality. He was in his locked apartment. The encounter with Counselor Shrub was a bad memory from over a year ago when he was in the Nicotine Rehab. Thanks to Mid-21st Century gene therapy, there was no permanent damage to Boogerlove's kneecaps. Gene therapy, however, was considered a sin in the North American Union and only allowed on torture victims to cover up "incidents". Sin and Crime were synonymous with each other by this time in history. He took many illegal sleeping pills and passed out. Tomorrow was another day.

Tomorrow arrived and Boogerlove looked out his window at the hazy Dalworth skyline. He dressed and stepped out into the sauna heat. He took a long walk over to Camp Bowie Scavenger Squad #9 to check in. At the door as usual was Judge Farley. Farley had lost his judgeship because of multiple wounds and since cyborg science was still new, his artificial heart, pancreas, and legs did not function well enough for him to keep his traveling judgeship. He was let go with no benefits or severance pay. Benefits and severance pay were against the law in the North American Union. He soon joined the Scavenger Squad after his dismissal. Almost all Scavenger Squads had a former judge in them, which came in very handy when dealing with the multitude of laws.

"How ya doin' judge?"

"Oh, Okay, got busted for a cig the other day, but the cop recognized me as a former judge and let it slid for 100 PY. I'm broke now, but free."

Boogerlove just shook his head, dug out a slimy booger, and savored it between his cheek and gum. Once inside he saw only 6 of the 20 member squad sitting around the meeting hall. The meeting hall was an abandoned old Taco Bell. This struck Boogerlove as strange since this was a regular meeting and all 20 members were required to be there. He saw Nero Jones standing there with a sad look on his face.

"What's up?"

"We're shut down, that's what's up"

"What? But we've been making all our payoffs, following all the rules..."

"BOOGERLOVE! Man, you never have gotten it! DalWorth Authority can shut us down anytime they like for any reason. The whole Scavenger Squad Program has always existed in a legal gray zone from day one."

Boogerlove paced the floor trying to regain his cool.

"So what's the reason?"

"Well to boil it down from all the legalese," began Nero, "It amounts to the fact that DalWorth claims we've been short on our Operational Fees for the past 2 months."

"That's bullshit; we paid them every peso of the 5000 PY they want each month."

"Well, there was a memo. They wanted 5010 PY a month starting 2 months ago."

"I didn't get it."

"NO ONE DID, BOOG! That's when the electric grid was off most of the time and more stringent paper rationing went into effect so there was almost no other means to receive it other than electronically. In fact, 2 guys had been given the memo in paper form to carry over to us but were arrested for violating Paper Rationing Code #4996903890-60009939839-RTYN and are now in lockdown for the next year.

Boogerlove just sighed and began pacing again. He grabbed a hard, crisp one from his nose and began to nibble. Nero remained silent and chewed on his fingernails. The other 6 in the room quietly got up and left. Soon Boogerlove and Nero did the same.

As soon a Boogerlove entered his apartment, the telescreen flashed on.

"This is President Zeus. I have decided to shutdown all The Scavenger Squads Union wide. What at first seemed like a good compromise in this troubled world of ours has proved to be nothing but a hotbed of corruption. It seems that most of the government liaisons to these Squads have been using them to line their own pockets. Since this kind of corruption can not go unchecked, they are now officially closed. The penalty for violation for this new law is still being worked out since we are now running out of numbers and letters to name them with. But this, my fellow Unionists, is the price for freedom!"

President Zeus' image disappeared from the screen. Boogerlove stared off into space. He laughed to himself about the speech. There was always corruption and always a new law made to deal with that corruption or sin or violation which again caused yet another law and another to be made. Ad Infinitum. I'm sure if it weren't for Paper Rationing, all these laws printed out would reach the moon.

Boogerlove began to cry in frustration at the anal stupidity of modern life. He had read in banned books that things were not always like this. In fact as late as 70 years ago, people could freely walk down the street smoking a cigarette and legally buy a drink in a bar. No one was arrested for having too much paper. You could have a much paper as you liked or could afford. Also people didn't have to sell their bodily organs for money to live. Talk about the good ole days!

Boogerlove sat on his couch with his gun in his mouth. He pulled the trigger but nothing happened. He remembered then that he had no bullets. He had to trade them for a loaf of bread last week. He cried again and vowed to kill himself just as soon as he could come up with the 50 PY ($50) for more ammo. Of course, he knew he didn't have The Corpse Disposal Fee, but he really didn't care. Fuck those bureaucratic morons! Maintenance could take out his dead carcass like everyone else and put it in the Human Disposal/Recycle Bins.

Death from disease, war, and suicide had become so common that they had special bins everywhere for those who couldn't afford The Corpse Disposal Fee. This included 90% of the population since this fee was $100,000 PY ($100,000). These bins had razor wire fencing and cameras around them since stealing and selling human organs had become a big business. Only maintenance men with special licenses were allowed in and out of these bins. Corrupt maintenance personal made millions of Peso Yen on the sly selling an eye here, a heart there, etc.

Suicide was actually illegal under Freedom Institute Ordinance #9998888855559-YNRGFSHIO-67849399C389583959-RTYYTC-44444988483999DFRR79038RJK86 of DalWorth, TX. A year later James Boogerlove violated this ordinance, writing a short but simple suicide note on an illegal piece of paper. It read: FUCK THE WORLD.

Effortlessly Hitting A Vein

Keith Buckley

Dr. Calder Bingley regretted accepting his uncle's dinner invitation the moment he opened the kitchen door. The stench of boiled turpentine singed his nostrils, immediately informing him that the Variolas' absent-minded cook, Pedro, had once again ruined the pesto by leaving the pine-nuts in the oven too long. Why don't Uncle Dirk and Aunt Evy fire the worthless little troll, Calder asked himself as he caught sight of his aunt and the careless Guatemalan cook tangled in a furiously writhing mass beneath the butcher block table. And how in the name of God had Aunt Evy so firmly wedged her left hand in the shrieking Pedro's rectum?

Better find some canapes, Calder decided. I am starving and dinner's obviously going to be delayed once again!

Just as the young abortionist was trying to tip-toe out of the kitchen, Evelyn Variola called out, "Calder! What a dear! You've come to rescue me. Be a lamb, would you, and whip up a batch of hollandaise for the asparagus— I daren't trust Pedro with open flames again this evening. The butter and eggs are right by the stove!"

"My pleasure, Aunt Evy," Calder lied. The gas jets on his aunt's ancient Amana range usually ran hotter than the engines of a 747, and he feared for his life should he curdle the sauce.

Trying to ignore Pedro's tortured cries of agony, Calder dropped two quarter-pound sticks of butter into a double boiler and silently perused the impressive array of surgical devices glistening, like freshly gutted lawyers, on the marble countertop. He quickly scanned the entire kitchen, but there wasn't a whisk in sight. "Improvise, then," he quietly muttered, and selected an open-bladed steel speculum. Nice to work with old friends, Calder thought.

Almost as soon as he started beating the melted butter into a rich yellow froth, the five Demerol tablets he'd chugged a few hours ago with a tumbler of 18 year-old MacAllen lost its edge. His right knee almost buckled as the nerves throbbed to life. Painfully shifting his weight to his good leg, he casually announced, "Aunt Evy, if I'd known I was going to be put in charge of the hollandaise sauce, I might've considered the orthoscopic procedure Dirk suggested to me last month."

"We can probably find you a step-stool to sit on while you're stirring the sauce," Mrs. Variola said. Before she could tell him to move the children's corpses out of the walk-in refrigerator so he could find the lemons, however, Pedro performed a clever forward somersault.

Although the cook managed to free himself from his doughty employer's hand, he also broke at least three bones in her wrist. Calder guessed that Evelyn Variola did not appreciate such bold initiative amongst the help, and ducked out of the way as his aunt jammed a food processor cutting blade in the screaming cook's face. He hastily elected to retire from the kitchen for a few minutes, as he could not abide a waste of good food— Mrs. Variola had inserted almost half a batch of freshly prepared pesto into the Guatemalan's gushing wounds along with the razor-sharp blade.

While Calder was well aware such acts of sudden and unprovoked violence were commonplace at the Variola residence, he nevertheless thought prudence and the state criminal code required him to bring his uncle up to speed concerning the latest atrocity committed on his property. Getting information as to his host's whereabouts, though, proved to be tricky business indeed. Many of his fellow party-goers had already quaffed heavily of the mysterious, cloudy blue fluid in the massive crystal punch bowl on the buffet, and a large number of the smartly appointed revellers were having difficulty breathing, much less responding to Calder's urgent queries. After half an hour of dodging the truly impressive streams of projectile vomiting which inevitably greeted his inquiries, Calder finally happened upon Pamela Oleander, Dr. Variola's latest secretary. Although she too ignored him for a minute or two (intently engaged, as she was, on smashing the bevelled glass panels of a large walnut vitrine so she could begin demolishing Mrs. Variola's collection of rare Lladro statuettes), she at last wheeled around and slurred something about "the old bastard and his two little pet bastards are in the study, getting shit-faced." A racking cough shook the petite blonde, and as her dull ocher eyes momentarily brightened, she begged Calder to perform upon her biological acts frowned upon by adherents of most Judeo-Christian traditions. Calder gave the proposition a second's grave consideration, but memories of Pedro's pesto-laced injuries brought him to his senses.

Calder finally found Dr. Variola standing in front of a large rolltop desk with his back to the door of his study, laboriously translating a 19th century German monograph on fetal decapitation while his two current residents, Dr. Dennis Witkop and Dr. Wu Wei Yaw, took turns urinating on a stunning bougainvillaea luxuriating beneath a sun lamp on the opposite side of the room. Calder, always the poet at heart, spent a few minutes pondering this curious tableaux and attempted to compose a sonnet commemorating the scene. He at last abandoned this whimsical exercise, as he couldn't think of a word that rhymed with "ureter."

Calder stepped forward and tapped his godfather on the shoulder.

With his barrel chest, grizzled white beard and betel-stained lips, Dirk Variola was often mistaken for Ernest Hemingway until even the casual observer noticed his tiny eye sockets sat less than half an inch apart, separated by a crooked blade of bone. This singular physical oddity frequently frightened newer patients beyond compute, and the sight occasionally unnerved Calder. As Dr. Variola wheeled about to face him, Calder reminded himself of the countless hours in his godfather's office during the last fifteen years, the orthopedic wizard studiously crushing and reshaping his deformed ankles with a rock hound's mallet. The harrowing memories steadied him, and he said, "Trouble in the kitchen, Dirk."

"Oh, fuck," Variola growled, tossing aside the sheaf of stained antique parchment. "Don't tell me Pedro's ruined the standing riboast! I had to pay the cytology lab fifty dollars for that torso!" Witkop and Yaw spun around, zipping up their trousers. The Chinese resident whispered a high-pitched curse, having ripped apart the tender flesh of his prepuce.

Calder allowed himself an evil smirk. "No, but I think the Guatemalan Embassy might be filing a complaint against you in the next few days."

The doctor blanched and gasped, "Oh, dear sweet Jesus. She didn't take the cleaver to him, did she?"

"Nothing so dramatic. He will need some pretty extensive plastic surgery—as far as I could tell, Auntie Evelyn did a fair number on his nose and lips with a Cuisinart chopping knife. Is that the way she's accustomed to dealing with the domestic staff?"

Variola chuckled and draped an athletic forearm over Calder's shoulders. "Hasn't anyone ever told you? Your Aunt Evelyn's parents were missionaries in Borneo during the Japanese Occupation. When Evy was five years old, the damn Japs tossed her mom and dad in the Baleh River, tied to her dear father's pump organ. Left her in the jungle for the kraits and crocodiles. Tribe of Dyaks saved her and adopted her. They were still head hunters during the Forties, y'know. By the time she saw another pale-face, she'd become quite the little savage. Something of a terror with the old parang. You have children, don't you, Calder?"

Calder lowered his head and mumbled a few unintelligible words.

The doctor smacked his forehead with his free hand. "Forgive me, boy. That was truly insensitive. Forgot about that nastiness with your ex-wife and the sperm bank. The judge let her take the twins with her to the state women's prison, didn't he?" Calder solemnly nodded. "Well, believe you me, son," Variola said, "we could all learn a thing or two about child-rearing from your Aunt Evy. One good swing of the arm, and she's straight through a bull's neck. You wouldn't believe how a child will think twice about talking back or complaining that he doesn't want to take a bath after he's seen a few siblings' heads go bouncing across the floor. Jesus, man! Your Auntie Evy gets hold of a machete or scythe, she'll teach you the meaning of 'amok' before you can say 'just a few inches off the top!'"

"But the cook, Dirk— " Calder said, desperately trying to refocus his godfather's train of thought.

"Don't give him a second's worry," the doctor chuckled. "I knew how Evelyn loves to lord it over the kitchen when I hired that dolt . . . made him sign a tidy little waiver my attorney drew up. Just the same, though, maybe we'd better do a little reconnaissance."

Calder headed for the door, but his godfather held back to make a professional observation. "I say, Calder," Variola murmured, "I do believe you're limping again. Is that knee still giving you trouble?"

"Knee? Knee?" Yaw chirped like some sort of trained bird.

Calder grinned apologetically. "You always did know best, Dirk. Yes, I should've had the operation."

"What's this about a knee?" Witkop hissed, a feral gleam brightening his swarthy face.

"Partially torn anterior cruca," Variola muttered out of the corner of his mouth as he fumbled through the pockets of his tweed jacket. "Look here, Calder, I've got just the thing to take your mind off it, if only I could find my kit." He rummaged through every pocket, producing only an ampule of beige liquid. "Damn me, I've got the solution, but I can't locate my gear. Dennis, Wu, do either of you happen to have the, ummmm, proper accoutrements?"

Before Calder knew what was happening, Witkop had produced a hypodermic set, and Wu had unbuttoned his shirtsleeve, tying off his left upper arm with a cocoa Jutta Neumann belt. "This will definitely put you in the mood for your aunt's cooking," Variola giggled, effortlessly hitting a vein in the crook of Calder's arm.

As his godfather pushed the plunger to the bottom of the syringe, Calder felt a soothing warm sensation, like hot raspberry syrup, seeping down his spine. "Now that is wonderful," Calder whispered. "What the fuck was it?"

Variola smiled, gently withdrawing the needle. "My own special blend," he said. "A bit of dilaudid, a pinch of Halcyon, just the teeniest drop of belladonna, a whopping dose of THC, and a tincture of gonadotrophin from a black rhino in full rut. Perfect for this type of formal affair."

"How so?" Calder sang as the surgeon and Witkop dragged him out of the study.

"Well, the dilaudid, quite plainly, is telling your brain that the torn ligament in your knee isn't worth noticing. The THC ensures that you'll have an appetite, in spite of the synthetic morphine, and I throw in the belladonna because I really can't stand the way opiates mess with the smooth muscles of my large intestine and gives me constipation, can you?"

"Hell no," Calder laughed as Variola steered the group in Pamela Oleander's direction. "And why the rhino gonadotropicals?"

"Gonadotrophin," Yaw said, correcting him. "Dilaudid make major league detumescence. Rhino juice give you hard-on like aluminum baseball bat."

"How thoughtful!" Calder babbled. "Then by all means, Dirk, seat me next to your glorious secretary! You would not believe what she asked me to do!"

"She did, eh?" Variola said. The four men had halted among a dense patch of fallen guests, and the doctor watched his secretary as she methodically destroyed the contents of the vitrine.

Calder tried to nod, but his head flopped from side to side instead of up and down. "Couldn't figure out why she'd need me to do that," he said.

"Oh, it entertains the ponies. Keeps them from fleeing the rancid stench," Variola replied.

"I wouldn't run away," Calder eagerly admitted.

The doctor grimaced. "Then you haven't had the pleasure of tasting Miss Oleander's dubious charms," he said. "One of the most vicious and, ahem, obnoxious cases of fungal vulvovaginitis I've ever met. The horses run screaming into the night, believe me, if she doesn't have an assistant to distract them." He glanced at his residents. "Speaking of assistants, gentlemen, could you hold up my dear nephew here while I take care of some pressing business?"

Variola freed himself of his godson and marched towards Miss Oleander, who was just picking up a small figurine of a girl standing beside a well. "Not that one, Pamela," he snarled. "It belonged to my mother."

The intoxicated blonde swivelled to sneer at her employer, then hurled the fragile ceramic heirloom against the wall.

"This will not do," Variola grumbled. The doctor pulled a pair of Felco pruning sheers out of his breast pocket, grabbed the woman's right hand and began snipping off her fingers.

"In case you wanted to know," Witkop told Calder, whose lower jaw had fallen to his sternum, "Doc puts the Halcyon in his little cocktail so you'll forget anything your brain can't deal with."

Only then did Calder find the ability to nod, and said something he hoped sounded like, "Good job!"

By the time he'd finished removing all five digits from his secretary's right hand, Variola was spattered with gore. He allowed Miss Oleander to sink to the floor, and returned to his residents and godson. Mopping the larger gouts of blood off his tweed jacket with a handkerchief, he casually said, "Wu, she really isn't any use to me as a typist now, so if you could send her along?" Dr. Yaw smiled brightly, and let the surgeon take his place under Calder's left arm.

"Yaw's the best I've ever seen!" Variola proudly told Calder.

The Chinese resident walked past Miss Oleander, who was now kneeling on the floor, loudly mourning the loss of her fingers. Yaw searched through the wreckage of the vitrine. In a matter of seconds, he'd found what he was looking for— a long, slim shard of glass. Tearing a piece of cloth from the dress of one of the many unconscious females spread across Variola's living room, Yaw wrapped his makeshift handguard around the jagged sliver. Quick as a wink, he grabbed Miss Oleander's head, pushed it forward, shoved the glass spike up under the base of her skull and twisted it three times.

"Isn't he amazing?!" Dirk exclaimed to his awestruck godson. "I've seen Wu pith terminal cancer patients literally twice his size! Just a word of advice," the doctor added as the quartet entered the dining room. "Don't let the little devil get behind your back with an icepick or a screwdriver! Now then, where's the damn ribroast, eh?"

Pills

Kurt Eisenlohr

I've long had a fondness for pills. It started in high school. It was real easy to get pharmaceutical speed back then, back then meaning nineteen seventy-eight. There were these older guys who sold them by the football field; yellow jackets and black beauties, for the most part. But they often had valium, and I liked those better. They calmed me. They calmed me so much that first hour math class seemed interesting. I'd glaze over like some feeble-eyed savant and the hour would pass before I was even aware of it having begun. You could buy three valiums for a dollar, and for the next few years, that's where my lunch money went. I graduated high school and pretty much forgot about pills, aside from the occasional handful of Quaaludes while drinking. I never went to college.

When I was nineteen, I started seeing a shrink--and that's when all hell broke loose. I could get just about anything I wanted from this guy, and after eight years in his care, I was a walking pharmaceutical wreck. I got off that shit, after much difficulty, and swore I'd never touch the stuff again.

And for the next seven years, I didn't...

It was work related.

There was this guy, a regular, his name was Marcus. He had a wife and three kids and a nice little house in a nice little neighborhood near the bar where I worked. He was only in his early forties but he had a bad back, some slipped disks and an arthritic spine, and it fucked with him pain-wise and every other way, so he was on disability and trying to be a stay at home dad and a husband and a fledgling songwriter and a full blown prescription drug addict as best he could. His kids were all in school and his wife worked a lot, so he was often at the bar, scribbling in his notebooks and nursing a beer. His standard uniform was a cowboy hat, Hawaiian-print shirts, shorts, and a pair of mirrored sunglasses worn at all times.

"I put something special in your jar," he told me one night.

The place was just about empty so I reached into the tip jar to see what he'd left. I figured it was joint; he was often generous that way. I pulled out a wadded up piece of toilet paper.

"Thanks a lot," I told him, but he was already out the door. I unfolded the wad of toilet paper and found four blue pills inside, tiny things, along with a wee bit of notebook paper with the word MILK written on it.

MILK?

I took one with a glass of wine. I took a shower and fed the cats. I started to feel good. Then I started to feel very good. Then I began digging around the apartment for my copy of The Complete Guide to Prescription and Non-Prescription Drugs, H. Winter Griffith, M.D. 1995 Edition. The book had a section full of color photographs and I soon found a match.

Dilaudid--See NARCOTIC ANALGESICS 592.

I remembered reading a biography on Lenny Bruce. Somewhere in there he was quoted as saying that taking Dilaudid felt like "a sunflower opening up in my belly." I don't know about sunflowers, but it did feel good. It made me feel like butter, loose, happy butter.

What drug does:

*Blocks pain messages to brain and spinal cord.

*Reduces sensitivity of brain's cough control center.

Time lapse before drug works:

30 minutes.

Don't take with:

Any other medicine without consulting your doctor or pharmacist.

I had another glass of wine. Then I gathered my keys and some change for the bus. The Brian Jonestown Massacre was playing at Satyricon that night, and I wanted to take some pictures with the new camera I'd recently gotten in trade for a painting I had made years prior. Taking pictures was going to be my new thing. I needed a hobby. On the bus, I took another Dilaudid. The driver saw me do it. I raised my camera and took his picture.

"Take my picture again and you'll be walking," he said.

The next day, I dropped my film off at a one-hour photo place on Northwest Burnside. I went into a nearby bar to wait. I had two or three drinks while staring into space. I put a dollar into the jukebox and listened to some Lee Hazelwood and some Motorhead. Then I went and picked up my photos and headed back to the bar to look at them. They were pretty good, but I couldn't remember taking most of them. When did I climb up onto the stage? I kept flipping through them. Some of them were great, shot from slightly above and directly behind the band. You could see the hair and the sweat of the band members and the twisted, blissed out faces of the crowd. I kept flipping. I came to a shot of a drunken looking girl with blue hair and black lipstick posing on an unmade bed. She had her top off. I had never seen her or the bed before. I ordered another drink. The place was dead. It was just me and the bartender and the stale afternoon air and the nicotine stained everything. I played some more music.

I kept staring at the topless girl with the blue hair and black lipstick. She wasn't bad looking at all. She had pale blue eyes that matched her hair, big pink nipples, and a sexy smile. I wondered if someone else's pictures had gotten mixed in with mine. The bartender turned up the volume on the jukebox. "Some velvet morning when I'm straight," Lee Hazelwood sang. I felt kind of weird, like a panic-attack was on the way. I lit a cigarette and killed my drink, then got another one. An old bag lady walked in and sat down on the stool next to mine. She ordered a can of Hamm's. The bartender gave it to her and she payed him in dimes and nickels and pennies which she pulled one by one from from a little rubber change purse. The topless girl was still sitting out in front of me on the bar.

"Cute picture," the old lady said. "Is she your sweetie?"

"No," I told her. "I don't know who that's a picture of."

"I have some pictures. Would you like to see them?" She had a giant ragdoll looking white wig tied to her head with a rope. It went right over the top of the wig and the ends were knotted together beneath her chin.

"Sure," I said.

She pulled a stack of dog-eared photos from one of her plastic bags and spread them out over the bar--a dozen or so shots of a naked brunette dancing around a 1950s livingroom, full bush, in black and white.

"That's me," she said, "before I got old and ugly."

"Christ, you look like Betty Paige."

"I looked better than Betty Paige."

The bartender walked over and took a look. "It's true," he said.

"Goddamn right," the old lady told him.

"Goddamn right," I said. "Barkeep, I'd like to buy Betty Paige here a drink."

"I'll have a vodka and soda," she told him.

We toasted the air, nothing in particular.

"My name is Vera," she said.

"Nice to meet you, Vera."

I tucked the blue haired girl into my pocket along with the rest of my photos. I wondered who she was. I wondered who I was.

I knew who the bag lady was. Her name was Vera, and she had once looked like Betty Paige.

Here for this
Joshua Citrak

"Congratulations, you've successfully worked the system," I was told, as I came up next in line, about to say, 'present' and get a paper pillow.

There was a green star by my name written on the dry erase board at the door. Hobbs drew a fat line through it and then, carefully with his index finger, rubbed it out.

"Your ride is right over there," he said, pointing to a dented Mobile Assistance van and to a driver who was angrily asleep.

Hobbs grabbed me by my elbow.

"You see where I'm pointing? Right there."

I shouldered my duffle bag and crossed the street.

"Ok," I heard Hobbs say, flipping open his clipboard and addressing a bunch of drunks blown over onto the sidewalk from their own velocity. "We just got ourselves another success story. There he goes onto a new and hopefully productive life. Who's next? I need to see a voucher or a twenty dollar bill for his bed. It's a lucky bed, I'm telling you guys the god's honest truth. Hey, hey you… put your pants back on."

It was one of those fifteen passenger vans, but it was empty except for the driver. He wore those big giant sunglasses that covered half his cheeks and eyebrows, carried his keys on a monogrammed shoelace tied around his neck. I tapped on the window to wake him up.

"Well, it's not like I got anything else to do," the driver said to me, sliding himself upright in the seat and reaching around to unlock the sliding door. "I mean, I am getting paid, ha, yeah, that is, you know, I just hold the money for my baby's momma."

I sat all the way in back. The driver started the van and drove us to building four of the Cecil Williams Housing Project.

"I gotta run in for a sec," he said, jerking the front tire onto the sidewalk. "Lie down 'cross the seat in case my supervisor drives by."

The van was upholstered like a child's car seat or something that could easily be hosed off after being pissed or puked on. The floor was worn, corrugated sheet metal, the ceiling was black foam rubber picked and scratched with the names of men who had nothing left but their own devices. There were no handles or latches or interior dome lights that could be screw-drivered off and sold on the street. It was empty and institutionalized, like those of us whose charge it was to shuttle from street to hospital to shelter to halfway house.

I was glad to be on the final leg. Sayonara to the Civic Center Drop-In, where I loitered through a period of three foggy months until eight o'clock each night. At eight, Hobbs and his band of pathetic social workers would open the doors to the shelter, dish out the cots and fold us into a hot meal. Meal? Fuck. Hot was about all you could say. We were supposed to get counseling during the day, but those of us who weren't crippled by lack of a hit or a drink ran errands for Hobbs and his underlings, who spent most of their time with their feet propped up onto something, watching TV and sipping pep drinks from shiny cans.

I knew the Chinese bookies. Where to get the best corned beef sandwich. I was useful, which is why it took nearly three months to get transferred to a real home. I had to train my replacement, Indian Bob, who wasn't an Indian at all. He was Mongolian, I think. He had long, jet black straight hair and wore lots of beads, which he used to pay for half pints at Punjabi's Liquor Store, because they were real Indians.

"You do good and sometimes they tip you a dollar," I told Bob, coming back from Yu's. "Many wampum's."

"The only thing you get by working for the white man is fucked, man," he replied.

Now, the driver was back, yelling some promises up to a window and we took off again.

"You know they have them tracking devices installed on these things?" he said.

I sat upright and didn't reply. We went West, past the Freedom Projects and the Lilia Mae Housing Units going on towards the real neighborhoods, where they claimed life wasn't such a self-defeating struggle.

"We can stop at some store," the driver said. "You maybe need to get some things. Toothbrush. Maybe some soap. I dunno. Something."

I told him I could use some cigarettes.

"Nope," he said, shaking his head in the rear view mirror. "It's a law. I can't let you smoke in the van."

"But this van fucking stinks, man," I said. "Why not?"

With his index finger, he flicked a pine tree shaped airfreshener hanging on a stereo knob.

"How 'bout now?"

"I've waited three months for this," I said.

"Don't worry," he said. "There'll be plenty more things to wait for."

Nearing the University, we pulled into the driveway of a Victorian or Edwardian, whichever looks like a tiny castle. In the top of the spire a window was open and a tiny lady, who looked nothing like a princess, peered down at us.

"This is it," he said, offering up the shifter to park.

We were met by my caseworker, Sharon Meadows, a woman who thought socks and sandals were a good match. I closed the sliding door and held onto my bag with both hands.

"Looks like we've got an even swap," she said, wearying of an enormous guy squatting on the front stairs.

The guy was on the stairs looking sullen, twisting and knotting up a sweatshirt in his giant hands. Next to him was a paper grocery bag packed with all his shit. The handles were ripped off, so when he held it, he had to hug it to his chest because even comfort can be cheap nowadays.

They asked him to get in the van.

"I called you people like an hour ago," McKinney, another caseworker, said to the driver. "Where've you been?"

The driver shrugged and glanced at me.

"I dunno man, I was waiting, you know. I gotta finish one thing before I start another."

The man on the stairs stretched out and played dead.

"I coudda been the first in my family to go to college," he said.

The driver of the van and McKinney hoisted the big man like an really long stretcher and tried to fold him into the front seat as if he were an oversized blanket, but he was too heavy and his shoes kept popping off.

Ms. Meadows ran in circles, directing them.

"Watch his head! His head!"

McKinney and the driver huffed and strained, but still couldn't get him in the van.

Suddenly, I heard,

"Admit you are powerless!" yelled down from the top floor. The little woman asserted half her body out the slid open window and tried to spit, but it was carried away by the wind. "You're a slave to yourself and a brutal master!"

The driver of the van and McKinney became exasperated. They dropped the enormous man on the sidewalk and walked in circles with their hands on their hips.

"I'll show you this!" the man screamed, coming to his knees, throwing wild haymakers toward heaven. "Get me some shoes. I can't run anywhere with just one sock on my feets!"

"He's not riding anywhere in my van! Hell no! I only carry mace," the driver said.

"Well, watch him, make sure he doesn't go anywhere," McKinney said, going back into the house. "I only got one of his shoes."

"He can do whatever he wants. I ain't fuckin' with him."

Ms. Meadows suggested that we also go inside. We took the middle door that led up to the middle floor.

"Who was that?" I asked.

"I'm not sure," she said. "I'm carrying a full load as it is. Just obey the rules and you won't end up like him. Top of the stairs, first doorway to your right. I forgot your file out in the car."

I supposed that dude was my roommate, but he was being put into a cop car now. I opened the right door to a bedroom that had three beds, one all made up with clean sheets. A real bed. It was nice. I lay down on it, clasped my hands behind my head and crossed my legs. I breathed in the flowery scent of the sheets, looked out the window and all I could see was the curve of the sky. I relaxed a little, for the first time in years. It was nice.

There was a quiet knocking on my door as it was opened. Ms. Meadows came in with McKinney. I could hear people talking out in the hallway. New guy, they said. Fresh from Civic Center. Five days max.

She closed the door, handed me a copy of the 'house rules' handbook and ran down its finer points. McKinney just stood there with his arms crossed.

"We realize there's an adjustment period," she began. "But here's the thing- this is only a twenty-eight day program."

I knew what she was getting at. Because this wasn't a sleazy homeless shelter downtown. This was a real house in a real neighborhood populated by normal people who expected normal things at normal hours of the day. But normal is just a gratuitous label, because people don't understand what they're striving for. Ok, yeah, I wasn't stupid. I knew that she meant if I had to piss I couldn't do it on someone's doorstep.

"There's always someone on duty," she said. "For any crisis. Off hours try to keep it minor, though. Remember that they're only grad students."

"Uh huh," I said. "I can do that. I practically helped raise my baby sister."

"Ok, great, so you know what I mean."

We weren't free to come and go, she continued. But we could come and go as often as we liked, as long as it didn't interfere with group meetings or mealtimes and as long as we checked in and set a timetable for our return. But after curfew, which was nine, there weren't any exceptions.

She handed me a paper bag that rattled.

"These are for you. From Doctor... who did you see?"

"I know how to swallow," I said.

"It's part of the program," she said, slipping a paper stuffed day planner from her bag.

"I know, I know," I said, looking both of them in the eye. "I'm here for that. They told me. Everyone told me."

"Well then," she said, itching her toe.

There were a lot of rules here. They weren't halfway about anything. I thumbed through the pages of the handbook. Once you were here long enough, they let you out and gave you a handshake and that was what I was going for. No way was I going back to the streets. At the shelter they threw out my sleeping bag and blankets because they had bugs.

"Ok," I said, nodding over across the room to the other made bed. On it were folded clothes arranged neatly by color. "Who's the other guy?"

"McKinney will tell you everything else you need to know," Ms. Meadows said, threateningly.

She stood up to leave piling her papers and folders and bags in her arms like a kindergarten teacher I had once who taught me how to draw turkeys by tracing my hand.

"Look, we're not about God here," McKinney began. "Not using that name, anyway. Whatever you want to call Him or Her or It is fine with us. In the manual it says, 'Higher Power', I think that's pretty unobtrusive and definitely open to any interpretation you may give it. Although, It isn't a dog or a sandwich or anything like that. Think greater and more omnipotent than yourself."

McKinney had a degree from somewhere, but he use to be just another junkie. In school they taught him about guilt and god and no matter how far we run from it or him, we can be redeemed by an about face and twelve steps. The grad students just crawled out onto the fire escape smoking cigarettes and talking on their cell phones. They knew there was nothing they could do for us. But there was a light in McKinney. A hope fueled by the things he must have done when he was using and his desire to ultimately shed them from his memory.

"The clocks are running late on the first floor," McKinney said, holding open the door in such a way that I understood I was supposed to walk through it.

After dinner, I stood out in the backyard waiting for someone

to come out and light up a cigarette. I was hoping to bum one. There was a tall fence enclosing the tiny yard that looked as if it had been erected over the course of two or three generations. Some of the wood was fairly new, other parts of the fence had been chipped and repainted various shades of white. One supporting beam was at an odd angle, so I pulled on it, but it seemed set in its ways. I bent down on my knees to examine a six inch square notch cut out of the bottom of one of the boards and wondered if it was for a cat that no longer lived here. The next yard over was much larger and better taken care of, that was for sure.

"Whatcha lookin' at?"

I looked up to the third floor balcony. It was the woman I'd seen hanging out the window earlier in the evening. She claimed her name was Janie.

"I was looking to bum a cigarette," I said.

"From who? A ground hog?" she laughed, which brought on a terrific coughing fit. She leaned over and spit a translucent gob that caught the wind and sailed like those baby spiders do when leaving the nest.

She was unattractive, missing teeth, a black eye. Her frizzy hair was pulled up tight to the top of her head.

"I quit," Janie said. "Everything. They made me. I'm pregnant."

"Oh," I said.

She jabbed her belly. "We live in California. They've got laws against this type of thing."

Janie turned off the outside light, went back inside and said,

"Now all I have to do is find its damn father."

In my room, Marlon, my roommate, was already in bed. He was a sweaty, middle aged guy who came across as someone you needed to be cruel to.

"This is a great place, you're lucky," Marlon said, watching me undress, the covers pulled up to his chin. "They could've sent you to that farm up in Sonoma. I heard that's the equivalent of hell."

McKinney popped in and slapped the lights off. I crawled into bed. It was then that I realized how tired I was.

"Everyone's real cool here. They make it easy for you. I mean, look at me. I was the hardest case there was. Hard core. Nothing could make me quit."

I shifted onto my stomach.

"And now? I'm feeling better than I've felt in years. Amazing, not that I want to milk cows or anything," he said through the darkness, unable to care whether I was asleep or awake.

"I'm on this new medication, Remeron. It's basically a tetracyclic anti-depressant with a little histamine thrown in to help me sleep. My mother died twelve years ago and I've been a mess since then. But I owe a lot to McKinney. He showed me how I'd been carrying that around with me for all these years. He taught me how to grieve."

"There're chicks here," I said.

"You better forget about that. Rule Eight. All the rules are for our own good. The women live upstairs, besides. You only see them during group or other supervised activities. My advice is just to concentrate on yourself. Once you get better and clean, there'll be someone here to tell you so."

"If you say so."

"It's in the Steps," he said.

We said nothing for awhile, but I couldn't fall asleep. It was too still, too quiet. I could hear no sounds of traffic, or street noise, no whispering or snoring of men lined a hundred to a room in cots too small to turn over in. I could sense Marlon in the night. It made me uneasy to be in this small room, alone, with him, with the door closed. I wondered what he was doing over there. What a man like him, over fifty, balding, the very picture of a loser among losers, dreamt about on such a timid night.

Suddenly, Marlon groaned, shot up out of bed and hurried down the hall and out to the back yard.

"Oh, god," he cried and began violently dry heaving. He coughed and gagged, straining to calm himself.

Soon, he was attended to by one of the grad students asking if he was ok.

"You're going through the toughest part," I heard the student say, as if he knew, as if he could say it was going to get better.

Next morning I was woken at seven. I showered and sat down to breakfast with the rest of the group. After breakfast, I participated in my first group meeting in which, encircled, we followed each other in clockwise fashion with our stories, our weeping lists of self-inflicted atrocities. After group was individual counseling and lists of chores to be done. Our daily routine was organized down to the minute.

"I think I'm going to get along here," I said, hand drying a stack of plates. "I'm feeling glad to be here today."

"You don't have to ass kiss," Janie told me, handing me cups. "This isn't group."

"I mean it," I said. "For the longest time I've felt like I wasn't concerned with what happened to me after I woke up each day. I worked my ass off to get here. Now I'm going to make the best of what I've got left."

"I've got some bright idea's of my own," Janie said.

"I've been in and out of shelters for three years. I'm really glad to be here. The food is better too."

"Hmm," Marlon said, wrinkling his chin. "It's donated."

"I'm not gonna gush about opportunity," Janie told me. "Because to me, this is just another state sponsored stop on my route through life. They owed me something, but put me on Antabuse and Welbutrin instead. So here I am."

After the next group, we had some free time. A bunch of people were going walking out in Golden Gate Park. Janie asked me if I wanted to go.

I liked Janie and sympathized with her cynicism, so I said, sure.

We left the house and had to go slow. Janie had asthma and walked all hunched and bent over like she was used to going down for the things she needed. They call women who use themselves like credit cards whores. But that wasn't all it. There was a beginning somewhere. Janie probably didn't drink enough milk as a kid either, but right now, childhood was the least of our problems.

Once we got into the park, our ragtag group split up and went their separate ways, some house members wanted to go see the buffaloes, others to the reflecting pool. McKinney admonished us to be back at the house in an hour.

It was evening and the fog was rolling in. I gave Janie my coat and let her lead. We traveled in a slow arc away from the vicinity of the rest of the group, past the lush lawn bowling courts and an acre of empty jungle gyms until we came to the end of the park at the mouth of Haight Street.

"How did we end up here?" I asked. This was the first time I'd really ever been to Golden Gate Park.

"Hey, you know, I got this friend," she said. "Sometimes he hangs out just down the Haight a little ways. I'd really love to go and say hi to him."

"Shouldn't we be getting back?" I asked.

"Well, how 'bout down to the store and back? Don't you still need cigarettes? You shouldn't have to quit everything at once."

"Yeah, ok, I'm not wearing a watch, but," I laughed, nervously. "It's only my second day."

"Just to there."

Janie paid for my smokes and put two behind her ears. We left the store and she continued walking down the street, away from the park.

"Hey," I said. "I didn't sign up for this."

"Admit you're powerless," she said.

"I got that. From last night."

"Say it," she said, taking my hand.

"Ok, yeah. I'm powerless. Step one."

Janie dropped my hand and looked longingly down the street. I knew what was going to happen next and I was glad that it wasn't happening to me. Across the road, in front of a used clothing store, a dreadlocked hippie kid stood up onto a garbage can and began singing earnestly at the top of his lungs,

"Jane says, I'm done with Sergio. He treats me like a rag doll... but if he comes back again, tell him to wait right here for me, oh, I'll try again tomorrow."

A bus drove up and stopped. Some short Mexicans in colorful ball caps looked down at us. A few young people got off, strapping their burdens to their backs and hauling them into the evening.

"Yeah," she said, watching youth walk away from her for what I supposed wasn't the first time. "So am I... powerless... I gotta find my friend."

Later that night, I was afraid and in my room clutching the house rules book, reading aloud so that my room would be filled up with all the rules in the world that were for my own good. Forever I would carry them with me, with my new feelings of peace and helplessness, so that if I saw Janie again, I could pluck those words right out of the air and hand them to her.

Out in the driveway, a man slept in a dented Mobile Assistance van and there was a paper bag packed on the stairs waiting to be taken away from here.

Bright Guilty World

John Sheppard

As a child, I was a typical, overfed, pasty and underexercised american with a lower-case "a," with little interest in anything beyond the tip of my nose. The Army, with a capital "A," remade me using its not-so-subtle methods.

Standing in my new attic home that I'd only just rented hours before, fresh home to the world, peering into an oval, full-length mirror, I saw a scarred beanpole with eyes that could bore a hole through a plate of depleted uranium. "Get right, soldier," I told the reflection. He glared back at me with scorn—Civilian.

Some of those little scars in my face came from my old battalion XO, a major who'd snapped at us "troopers" out of the side of his mouth like an old-timey movie gangster. He'd told us not to pick up anything that looked out of the ordinary maybe an hour or two before he died. We'd swept into Iraq earlier that day and were ready for adventure. "Anything could be boobytrapped," the major had told us. "Anything at all. With a capital 'A.'"

Less than an hour later, amongst a pile of Iraqis we'd just killed from afar — poppity, poppity-pop with our impressive little arsennel of small arms — the major stooped over to pick up an AK-M, which is an AK-47 with a wooden stock. And, ka-pop!, off went his hand and face in a pink puff of smoke. Magic! He was dead, just like that. He fell, gently, onto his side. I was about ten meters away and little pieces of metal and officer face chunks and hand bones lodged in my arms, legs, face and hands. Nothing debilitating, mind you. Body armor saved my torso and ESS goggles my eyes. The major took the brunt.

I saw a man killed, a superior officer, and my reaction was surprising, even to me. I thought, That was pretty cool.

The major who replaced him, two months later, was a reservist from Sheridan, Wyoming. He was a dog trainer back in the world and offered winning advice for dealing with newly freed Iraqi personnel. He told us what he told all of his clients back home in bumfuck moo-cowland: "Don't make eye contact. Walk into any situation as if you're the alpha male, and that will make you the alpha male." It was sound advice for dealing with dogs.

He wasn't the only one who had a theory. All of our superior officers, from the generals on down to dippy second lieutenants, were encumbered with theories and books. I'd never seen so many books. The books were going to tell them how to pacify our new Iraqi friends.

In the meantime, we were living inside our vehicles and swallowing great dry gulps of desert sand. The heat and sand came slamming down from above and up from below and whipped around our heads and got inside our ass cracks. The people from back home sent us baby wipes and congratulatory letters. "Dear Soldier, I don't know you but thank you for saving my freedom."

Whatever, man.

I killed a man one day on a street crowded with angry, hungry people. I picked the guy out at random and shot him. Ka-pop. It was not cool. "You sure know how to end a riot, Dugan," said a second lieutenant right after I'd zapped the dude.

"Check your theory book. Page 19, second paragraph, sir," I said, not looking at him, all alpha-male-like, my hands shaking, as people screamed and ran away from me, down the heat-and-dust-clogged street.

"Har-dee-har-har," he went.

Smoke came out of the dead man's wound. He was maybe twice my age and his family, or people I assumed were his family, came and dragged him away later. A boy, a girl, a woman.

We dug in, eventually. Sandbags and concertina wire. Guard towers. Eventually, the cans came. They were little sleeper compartments. And then showers. And then air conditioning. And, much later, soft-serve ice cream in several ambrosial flavors. And contractors to serve the soft serve. And delightful dining facilities in which to consume the soft serve. And plasma TVs and the Armed Forces Radio and Television Service, where we learned every day that we were winning, always winning. More importantly, we also learned who was leading the points standing in NASCAR and which college football teams were doing well.

After winning the war on a daily basis, I rotated to CONUS. Then I rotated to Korea. Then I rotated to Iraq. Then I got blown up and went to Landstuhl Army Hospital in Germany and, later, Walter Reed Army Hospital in Washington, D.C. And then I left the Army with a capital "A." Sort of.

I sat down on my bed and watched the world through the little round window, the sun sparkling through the green, green leaves. When it became dark, I curled up and fell asleep.

I dreamt that gunmen had taken over my mother's fake New England fishing village in Florida. I woke up, grabbed my wallet and tiptoed downstairs. I could hear the tenants growling and grumbling their way through angry sleep.

I pulled a calling card from my wallet. On the front of it was a picture of a G.I. in the nicest desert you'd ever seen, the sun sparkling high in the blue-yellow sky above him, and him on a payphone that had miraculously popped up out of that desert, his head bowed, calling home. "Hi, Ma! Hi, Pa!" "Oh, Sonny Boy! How is the war going?" "We're winning, Ma! We're winning, Pa! Everything's super! How's Sissy? How's Sparky? How's our swell mutt Jasper?" "Everything here is peachy keen! Biggest economic expansion in human history now that you've secured our freedom and protected our country." "That's swell!" "It sure is swell!"

Whatever, man.

I punched in all the appropriate numbers. The receiver emitted its buzzing noises. Nothing unusual there. The mother picked up.

"It's your brother," said the mother.

"Hi," I said. "How's it going? Whatcha doing? Is anything wrong?"

I picked up a plastic gin bottle on the floor and took the last swig, tossed it into a nearby wastepaper basket.

"It's four in the morning," she said. "You haven't called in three weeks," she said. "Maybe everything is going wrong. You wouldn't know, would you?"

My Catholicism sickened me, along with the leftover gin. "It is 4 a.m. I guess I must finally be going nuts, like you know who."

"Don't mock your brother," she said.

"I think you should call him right up. Invite him over. He can tell you about his Doppelganger from the red universe who's having all the fun, while he's stuck in this universe working his ass off like a sucker."

"I don't have to call him. He's here."

Chess was out of the nuthouse. Free. I thought about running down to the front door and locking it, as if that would do any good. A vision of Chess with a fire ax chopping down the balsa wood door floated into my head. "Oh, that's just swell. Is he taking his pills?"

"We both take our pills at the same time in the morning."

"If you don't mind, I'll start carrying a tazer with me. Just in case."

"You're too hard on your brother. He's your twin. You two should be closer."

"If we felt each other's pain, I'd be hitting myself in the ass with a board all the live-long day. A board with a nail in it."

"That's a terrible thing to say."

"Yes it is."

There was always something wrong with my brother, some little kernel of not-right. Chess knew it. And he knew that whatever was wrong with him didn't apply to me.

Being a twin is supposed to mean never being alone. We dressed alike, were crammed into the same room, shared the same bolus of DNA, but were always, both of us, alone. I took it better than Chess. Chess was twitchy and filled with violent fury. I was merely twitchy.

"Stop being afraid of me!" Chess shouted one time, when we were little. We were in a vast, dandelion-covered field near our house in Nebraska. Chess had come outside to play Red Rover with the neighborhood children. I was part of the group. They all stopped, the children, stunned voiceless in the presence of Chess' rage.

"I gotta go," an undersized kid said. He had the look of a boy with a career in accounting in his future. He wanted to become that accountant. He ran off.

"I'll show you," Chess said to me. He practically whispered it, but the other kids heard and involuntarily backed off a step. Then, voluntarily, they peeled away one-by-one until only Chess and I stood in the field. Chess stood close enough for me to feel the anger pouring out of him as heat. He looked everywhere but my eyes.

"You," he finally said, staring, trying to will a hole in my forehead. Chess turned on his heel and stalked off, leaving me standing alone in the field.

By the time the family moved to Florida, I had given up on the idea of friendship, mostly.

"Hello, big brother," Chess said through the receiver.

Our cancer-stricken mother had surrendered the phone to him.

I was older by ten minutes. If you believed the reports.

"So you beat up a dying old lady and snatched the phone away from her," I said. "Good for you. Who needs a job when you have 'not guilty by reason of insanity' in your back pocket?"

"She waved me over and handed me the phone," he said. "Did you know she had the movers bring my weights over from the old house? I'm setting them up in the garage."

"That's comforting. When you stop taking your pills, you'll be twice as hard to restrain. How's your double in the red universe doing? Still taking all your vacation days?"

"Look, I'm trying to be civil. Quit it. This is what you wanted, isn't it? For me to sit with Mom until she croaks?"

"Okay. Calm down. It's ten after four in the morning and you haven't had your pills yet."

It's an all-night party over at the Dugan Compound, I thought.

"Fuck you," Chess said, in an almost civil tone.

The phone clicked dead. I stared at the phone a moment, and then hung up. They didn't even ask where I was. Not interested, I guessed.

"Quiet out there!" one of the angry boarders shouted through a closed door.

Exsanguinate.

This is what my shrink at Walter Reed told me came out of my mouth over and over when my dinged-up corpus was delivered to

Landstuhl Army Hospital in Germany. I'd survived the golden hour, the hour after I'd been blown up by an IED. Then I was magically swept out of good ol' Iraq.

So I'd been patched up and flown out of Iraq before I knew what hit me.

I was in Landstuhl, in that wretched old Army hospital, rolling down an aisle watching the acoustic tiles above me. Here a yellow stain, there a yellow stain. Florescent lighting, yellow stain. The hospital was oozing.

And me: "Ek-SANG-win-ate! Ek-SANG-win-ate!"

A little prick of something to calm me down, but still more: "Ek-SANG-win-ate! Ek-SANG-win-ate!"

Two years before I joined the Army and two-and-a-half years before Chess had gone so obviously insane that my mother had no choice but to sign the commitment papers, my father had taken us four kids in the family truckster over to the Ringling Museum of Art to tell us all about how he was leaving Mom.

And us, for that matter.

When we came in the front door, through the glass behind the ticket counter we could see the open courtyard. The museum formed a big U around it. A bronze cast of Michaelangelo's David stood in the elements with his dick hanging out. My father paid for our tickets and we made our way out there.

My father wasn't one for the arts, though he had a rough appreciation of Andy Warhol's work, for the swindling aspect of it.

He brought us there because the museum had guards. If Chess took a swing at him, he had a small army of guards at his disposal. He sat us down on a bench out in the courtyard near a sculpture of a woman getting fucked by a swan and stood in front of us, all nervous and twitchy, wringing his hands and trying out his salesman's smile. My father had an unshakable faith in his ability to convince just about anyone of anything, save his family, to whom he'd preached the wisdom of not being the sucker. And now, he had to make us suckers as his final gesture as head of household.

"So how are you kids doing today?" he asked us.

"Tip your waitress," Chess said. His hand tap-tap-tapped on his knee, which was rapidly popping up and down. We were 17, identical twins who didn't look a damn thing like each other, who couldn't stand the sight of each other.

My hands were laced, shoved between my thighs, my head down, staring at my Doc Martens.

"What's going on?" Magda asked. She was so tiny then. My mother did her hair in rag curls. Her feet swung, not reaching the ground, patton-leather Mary Janes gleaming in the hellish Florida sun. In high school, she became an artist, painting portraits of circus people and illustrating her homemade children's books.

"This is it, isn't it?" Chess said. "You're leaving."

He slowly rose to his feet. My father was not a big man. Guile, craft, wit and illusion were his weapons.

We were about 5-foot-11 by that time. I was thin. Chess was ripped. He spent his afternoons mowing lawns and lifting weights that he'd bought with the lawn money. While I lounged around reading and trying to listen to the Smiths in our room, I could hear Chess in the adjacent garage growling and clanking his cast-iron weights, a boombox blasting out CD's full of Black Flag and the Angry Samoans. A picture of Henry Rollins in full fury, his eyes blazing and neck tendons popped out, adorned the underside of my bunk so that Rollins would be the first thing Chess saw when he woke up in the morning.

"Now, son," my father said, his hands raised up, pasty palms out. He was afraid. We were all afraid of Chess, except for Magda. She admired him.

"C'mon old man, let's hear it," Chess said. "Shine us on." He was inches from the father, his fists balled up like he was going to knock his teeth down his throat.

"I'm your father," he said pleadingly, half in a whisper.

Chess was confused for a moment. He stepped around my father like he was a pile of dogshit and stomped over to the vulgar statue and kicked it. If he hadn't had steel-toed work boots on, he'd have broken his toes. He leapt back from the statue, like the statue had attacked him instead of the other way around.

"Go to hell!" he shouted at my father, and ran off.

My father stood frozen and sweating, staring off toward Chess as he flew out of the courtyard.

I stood up and took my sister by a hand. "We'll be by the car," I said.

My father pulled a wad of keys out of his pocket and handed them to me. I shoved them in my pocket with my spare hand.

"Get it cooled down," my father said.

I felt sweating drizzling down my back. My father walked in the direction of where Chess had run. He sped up to a trot and disappeared around a corner.

"Anyone want to see some paintings?" I asked my sister.

"What's happening?" Magda asked.

"Remember that lady we saw him with at his office?" I asked her.

"Yeah," Magda said.

"He's taking her with him," I said. "Now he'll start a family with her, just like he started a family with Mom after he left the lady he was married to in Ohio. And he'll forget Mom and us the same as he forgot the lady in Ohio and those kids."

"You're lying!" Magda said. But she didn't believe it.

"Nobody likes the truth," I said. "You want to take the car and get some ice cream? We can go to the mall, too."

"Daddy'll get mad," Magda said.

"Who gives a shit?" I said.

"Yeah," Magda said. "Who gives a shit?"

I didn't feel good, and hadn't felt good in a long time. It was not physical. But I did feel like throwing up. I didn't eat much because of that. I walked and I walked.

The town. The leaves on the trees. The placid green. The quiet. The lack of suspense. The tiny, well-kept houses and pleasant howdy-do's and the yapping dogs and the sprinklers shooting cool water at my feet.

Everything seemed so fucking normal. It made me sad. Normalcy was sickening, if I paid any attention to it. Normalcy was vulgar.

The chaos I was used to — the dust and the rage and the exoticism — had a hard, true edge to it. That's why I didn't fight going back to Iraq the second time around. That's why I was thinking of going back right at that moment, even though I was considered broken by the Army. I was 75-percent disabled, and I knew they'd take me back in the length of time it would take to sign another contract. The Army was that hard-up.

The squawking boxes filled with simulated combat in the video games section at the Buy and Bye down the street, and the movies section and the home theater section — they were combat made normal.

But there was nothing normal about actual combat. Actual combat was the sound of a sucking chest wound coming from the guy you were sharing fuck fantasies with at the D-Fac over Thanksgiving dinner.

"When I get home..."

Shit yeah.

When I get home, when I get back to the world, when I get home, when I get home.

And then you get home and it's fucking bullshit.

A Brief Tale of Great Integrity

Tony Byrer

All this happened a long time ago and thank God it did because if I had to go through this shit now I'd just go suck off a shotgun and put myself out of my misery.

I used to be an assistant manager at Hardee's, the most thankless, pissed-upon job I've ever had in my life. Talk about being exploited! Those pricks could suck the green out of a dollar until you were left with nothing but a transparent piece of parchment that would disintegrate in your hand leaving no trace but a wishful, wistful longing for something better. I'd regularly work seventy, even eighty hours a week serving fatburgers to whining, spoiled customers who seemed to expect five star service for their measly $3.98 Big Deluxe combo purchase.

Like this one time I was running the drive through because once again my entire fucking crew either called in at the last minute or they just didn't show up. Some guy came up to the speaker and placed his order. Well, it was just me and one other guy running the grill in back, so it was taking us a little time to deal with the rush. We thought we were doing a pretty good job all things considered, but when this prick got up to the window, the first words out of his mouth were, "God damn it, what's wrong with you fucking idiots?"

I'd had enough even before he showed up, so my response was less than diplomatic. "Don't cuss at me, bitch, I didn't do anything to you!" I took his money and gave him his change while he sat there muttering to himself, his face growing redder and redder.

"Next time, I'm going to McDonald's!" he said as I handed him his order.

"Good," I said.

"I'm never coming back here," he threatened.

"Good," I repeated. "We don't want you."

He muttered something to himself and sped away.

John, one of the crew leaders, came up from the back where he'd been running the grill and assembling sandwiches. "I heard that guy bitching at you over the speaker," he said. "I spit a big green hawker on his sandwich. That burger's going to be extra chewy."

I gagged a little. "Thanks, man," I said. "Now let's go smoke a joint."

That's how we handled stressful situations at that hellhole. Every chance we had, we'd go into the freezer and smoke some pot. By the end of my shifts, I was usually wrecked. We were all potheads, even the other managers. We'd found that the gauge or regulator or whatever it was on the helium tanks made a damn fine pipe. It eventually disappeared. Someone took it home with him to use there. Then there were no more balloons for the kiddies' birthday parties.

So John and I went into the freezer to smoke a joint. While we were passing it back and forth, the bell sounded in my ear, signaling another car had just driven up on the drive through pad.

"Thank you for choosing Hardee's," I said. "Would you like a combo?"

"Yeah," some vapid gum chewing teenage voice said. I didn't pay any attention to what she said next. She rattled off some long complicated order that I didn't want to have to deal with. "...and a Diet Coke," she said.

I exhaled a lungful of God's sweet smoke. "Would you repeat that, please?" I asked.

She sighed and started going through the whole thing again. "Uh, wait a minute," I said.

I took another long pull off the joint and waited while I listened to the girl sighing and chewing her gum.

"Okay," I said between chuffs of marijuana smoke. "Would you repeat that, please?"

She repeated the whole thing while I rolled my eyes at John. "Okay," I said. "That's a Big Deluxe combo with curly fries and a Sprite, two chicken fillets with no mayo and add tomato, a Big Mac combo with a brownie and Miller High Life, and two scratch off lotto tickets." I had no idea what she'd ordered. I was stoned and John was thrusting the joint at me again.

"No!" she said. "Were you even listening to me? Lotto tickets? What are you talking about?"

I took another long pull on the joint and keyed my mic. "Thank you. Please drive through."

"You didn't get my order right!" she wailed. "I want a bacon cheeseburger..." I tuned her out and concentrated on smoking this big joint John and I were sharing. It really was a big honker of a marijuana cigarette. Man, I was stoned. I looked at John. His eyes glowed bright red and drooped half closed. Yup, he was stoned, too. The girl at the drive through cursed and drove off. "Good riddance," I said to John. We both laughed.

Another car drove up to the speaker. "Thank you for choosing McDonald's," I said. "Would you like to fuck off and die?"

"What?" some outraged voice shrieked.

"Excuse me," I said. "We've been getting interference from CB radios all night long. Would you repeat that?"

"Oh," said the voice. "I'd like a chicken fillet sandwich, no mayo, and—"

"Wait a minute," I said. It was going to be a long night. John and I finished the joint and emerged from the freezer. There was no chance any customers would wander inside the store. I'd locked the doors over an hour ago. I hated it when people came inside the building. It was bad enough they drove up to the drive through all night long. I decided to turn out the lights, too. Maybe then they'd leave us alone.

"Hello?" said the voice from the drive through. I'd totally forgotten someone was out there. "Hello?"

"Aw, shit," I said to John. "How long do you think it'll take for this bitch to drive away?"

"Too damn long," he said. "Just ignore her."

"You're right," I said, unclipping the drive through beltpack from my waist and removing the headphones. "Enough's enough. Let's clean up and get the hell out of here."

John laughed. "It's only 9:00," he said. "We're supposed to be open until eleven."

"Fine," I said. "You run the whole joint if you want. I'm getting the hell out of here."

"Are you closed?" asked the voice.

"Goddamn right," I said as I started flipping switches. One by one the banks of lights went out. "Turn off the equipment," I said. "We don't want the place to burn down overnight." I considered what I said.

"Check that. We want it to burn down, but we don't want it to be our fault."

"I have coupons," said the voice. John and I both cracked up.

"Oh, shit!" John shouted. "She has coupons! That's better than a note from your mother!"

"On that note," I said, "I'm leaving. You have a good one."

"Hello?" said the voice.

"How much weed do you have left?" John asked.

"Enough for me," I said. "You gotta get your own."

"Bullshit!" John said. "You had a whole quarter and we only smoked three joints out of it! You have enough to spare me a joint."

"I don't see you offering up any money," I said. "This shit's expensive, you know."

"You know I don't have any money," John said. "All my money goes for diapers and baby formula."

That was true. John was only seventeen and he was already married with a baby. He'd gotten his high school girlfriend knocked up and now he was trying to work full time, finish high school, and support a baby and a deadbeat wife. On top of all that, he was a pothead. A broke pothead.

"All right," I said, feeling a bit of pity for him. "I'll give you a little bit, enough to maintain your buzz a while longer, but you have to stay behind and turn off all the equipment."

"Are you closed?" the stubborn damn drive through customer asked. I couldn't believe she was still sitting out there. I snatched up the drive through headset.

"Yes, goddammit!" I shouted into the mic. "We're closed! Now get the fuck out of here!"

"Yeah," said the voice. "I wanna fish sammitch, a two-piece chicken dinner...."

"Unbelievable!" I said, throwing the headset aside.

John shook his head. "People are addicted to this shit," he said. "It's not even good shit. It all tastes like shit."

"Speaking of shit," I said, holding up the baggie. "Are you gonna stay behind and shut off all the equipment?"

"Yeah, I guess," said John. "If you'll get me high again."

I gazed at him. Through my bleary eyes he looked like walking death. He had dark bags under his heavy red eyes. His cheekbones stuck out through his flaccid skin. To me, he looked like a skull covered loosely with flabby skin. "Man," I said, "you must have a real problem. I'm stoned as fuck."

"I wanna get more stoned," John said. "It's the only way I can go home and deal with a screaming baby and a bitching wife."

"All right," I said. "Let's go back in the freezer." I reached over to the electrical box and shut off the power to the drive through. If that insane bitch wanted to sit out there all night talking to a dead speaker, then she could damn well do it without bothering me.

We ended up smoking two more joints that night and by the time I left I was utterly wasted. As we walked out the door I peeked around the corner. "She might still be sitting there, man," John said. I high-fived him before I climbed into my truck. I always act like a fool when I'm thoroughly wasted.

It was only a ten minute drive across town to my house, but it took me twenty. I was creeping along at half the speed limit, only a little faster than a fast run and I still kept running up over the curb. It was like the street kept changing directions on me, skewing off to the right or left as I was trying desperately to go straight. And I had this peculiar tunnel vision. I could only see straight ahead for maybe fifty yards. Everything else was dark amorphous shadows twisting just beyond the range of vision. It reminded me of an old Betty Boop cartoon I saw once. She was creeping through a dark forest. The trees behind her were leering and dancing, reaching out to grab her. I saw it when I was a little kid and it scared the hell out of me. The thought of being grabbed by a tree was more than I could bear. What would a tree do with a little kid? I imagined it would stuff me down its woody throat and I'd be trapped inside it forever having to drink rainwater and eat bugs while everyone wondered whatever had happened to me. The memory sent a chill down my spine just as I bumped over another curb.

I jockeyed the truck left and right, dodging curbs and trees and the occasional amorphous shadow that detached itself from the riot at the edge of my vision to dash across the street in front of me. I knew there wasn't really anything there, but once or twice they fooled me anyway. I stomped on the brakes to avoid them even as they dissipated before my eyes. Luckily nothing real ran in front of me. Neither did I run across any cops. If I'd been pulled over, I would have been toast. My eyes were glowing brightly enough I didn't need headlights to illuminate my way home. The baggie of marijuana in my pocket would only have complicated matters.

I was able to park the truck in the driveway at a reasonably straight angle only from long practice. I sat a moment inventorying my pockets to ensure I had all my possessions. Store keys, check. Cigarettes, check. Lighter, check. Pot, check. Carefully I surveyed the lawn and the surrounding area for prowlers, boogeymen, and cops. No one was present. Good. Next I studied the house itself. All the lights were off except the small fluorescent light over the kitchen sink. That meant my wife was already in bed. Good. I had the rest of the night all to myself. I could get as stoned as I wanted.

I swung out of the truck and nearly shut the door before I realized I'd left the keys in the ignition. Feeling relieved I hadn't locked the keys in the truck, I leaned in to pull them out and walked carefully to the back door. I only weaved off course once when my sense of balance abandoned me for just a brief instant. If anyone was watching me, they were doing it from behind their drapes and I didn't see them. That's okay, I told myself. I'll be in the house behind locked doors long before any cops could get here.

Once inside the house, I locked myself away upstairs in my computer room. I kept myself busy for a while preparing my pipe and logging on to the internet. Once I'd found my favorite chat room, I fired up a big bowl and leaned back into the chair. This was the way to live, I thought, exhaling a large cloud of fragrant smoke.

A car went by on the street outside and I leaped to the window to peek out through the blind. I didn't see anything, so I vaulted to the other window and lined my eyeball up with the gap between the shade and the sill. Still nothing. I saw no reflections of red shouting lights, so I sat back in my chair and tried to get involved in the conversation online.

The talk was moving too fast for me to keep up, so I just leaned back into my chair and smoked some more weed. Lots of weed. Too much wasn't enough. I'd finish a bowl and ten minutes later fire up another. Birds were twittering in my head and everything at the edges of my vision was writhing in sinuous hairy figure eights and ovals and every now and then some awful primordial reptilian head would leer at me from under the desk or from behind the baseboard along the wall. I contemplated smoking more. The argument ran in tedious circles in my head.

Smoke more, I urged myself. No, I thought, it's too late. I have to get up in the morning and go to work. I glanced at the clock. It was nearly 4:30 a.m. I had to get up at eight to be at work by nine. Smoke more, I thought.

I reached for the pipe. Silverish tinkling voices chimed in the air above my head. Sometimes a deep rumbling voice would mutter something, but the tinkly voices paid no heed. I couldn't hear what they were saying, but the tone sounded reasonably friendly. I filled the bowl of my pipe and glanced at the clock again. I have time, I decided, and fired it up.

The marijuana did nothing for me. I was already so abysmally stoned, all the smoke did was make my chest burn. My throat was full of snot and I'd been coughing steadily for a couple of hours already. I wanted a cigarette, but there was no way I could handle the harshness of it. I sat slumped in my chair staring absently at the screen. It was nearly five o'clock by now. I thought I could get by on three hours sleep.

I logged off and staggered as quietly as I could downstairs, peeling off my reeking clothes as I went. I missed the last step and twisted my ankle badly. I heard the pop of the joint stretched beyond its limit, but felt no real pain. I limped to bed, my ankle feeling hot and loose. Who cares, I thought, falling into bed next to my sleeping wife. I watched the darkness swirl above my head and listened to the pretty voices until I passed out.

I was still stoned the next morning when I arrived at work, still stoned from the night before and stoned even more from the joint I smoked on the way to work. My boss Sharon was outside the restaurant sweeping. From the grim set of her jaw I knew something was wrong. "Good morning," I sang to her as cheerily as I could given the strange feeling I had in my head, like dirty cotton balls had replaced all my brains. She attacked a bit of mud off someone's tire tread like that bit of mud was the author of all her misery.

I shrugged and opened the door. None of the employees would meet my gaze. I wondered what I'd done that was so bad. Then I realized I'd forgotten to drop some Visine into my eyes before coming in. I probably looked like Mr. Hyde fresh off a five day bender.

I shambled into the office, limping on my painful ankle, and glanced at the schedule. My name wasn't on it. "Damn it," I breathed. Sharon was always doing that to me. She'd make out a schedule and because she didn't know yet what she wanted me to work, she'd leave my name off and just tell me from day to day when to come in to work. I hated that. I could never plan anything.

Then my eyes fell on a fresh write-up form with my name on it on the desk. Great. I was being written up again. I searched the spotty database of my mind for any misdeeds of the previous few days. There were plenty. On Sunday I was scheduled to work 5:30 a.m. to 5 p.m. I'd come bopping in around eleven, then called Mark, a strange little toad who was always asking for more hours, to come in and cover for me. I'd left right after lunch. I always closed early and I ignored most of the drive through customers. Not to mention I always locked the doors around six or seven at night. Seems like I'd been caught.

Sharon came into the office and shut the door. "What the hell happened last night?" she demanded.

"What do you mean?" I asked, the very personification of beatific innocence.

"When we came in this morning, the freezer was off and there were marijuana butts all over the floor."

"Shit," I said. "Did you save them?" I thought I could roll them into some potent roach weed joints.

She sighed and picked up the write-up form. Then my vision cleared and I saw it wasn't a write-up form at all, but a termination form. I was being fired.

I laughed. "So I'm being fired, huh?"

"What else do you expect me to do?" she asked, a hitch in her voice. Her furious façade was crumbling. Sharon liked me.

I shrugged. "I don't know. Hand it over. I'll sign it." She thrust the form at me and I signed it without reading it. Suddenly I was free. No more of this tedious, infuriating fast food restaurant crap.

"If you hated it so bad here," she said, "why didn't you just quit? Why put yourself through all this stress?"

"I'm stubborn," I said. And it's true. I'm far too stubborn for my own good.

She grabbed me in a hug. "I'm going to miss you," she wailed. I let my hand slip down to her shapely ass. Sharon was, among many other things, as hot as a house fire. I felt her breasts pressing into my rib cage. Mmm mmm mmm.

She slapped my hand away. "Be good," she said. "Don't let my last memory of you be ugly."

"Okay," I said. I smiled at her. "Take care of yourself. This is a horrible place to work."

"I know," she said. "But it's all I've got."

There was nothing more to be said. I turned and trudged out of the office. I didn't speak to any of the morons working the morning shift. As I pushed out the door I noticed for the first time it was a bright and glorious day. I smiled up at the clear and guileless sky.

I felt very tall.

Tomato Lust

Joseph Suglia

Dedicated to Joseph Suglia

I. Birthday Love Tomato Cyclone

What would I like for my birthday? A massive white blender that stands 400-feet tall. Towering above the railroad tracks, it is visible within a seventy-mile radius. Surrounding the massive blender are tangles of foliage, a whispering grove, and a landfill teeming with fire ants. Flashing orange lights radiate upon the annular rim of the blender. Its blades are 20-feet long and sweep around at 1,000 miles per hour. They are capable of reducing whole herds of cattle to mucky gore and cow-hair.

The blender looms. It dominates. It engulfs space.

The gigantic blending machine is to space what the sexual act is to time.

The blender normally only operates at 24% of its capacity. It consumes enough electricity to power 2,000 homes. Yes, yes, yes, yes.

The siding of the blender is made of ivory, distilled from the tusks of elephants. Over 4,000 elephants were slaughtered to construct the siding of the gigantic ivory blender.

Pygmies come with baskets fastened to their heads, baskets full of tomatoes. They ascend a 450-foot ladder that reaches to the pinnacle of the humongous ivory blender. To the music of Philip Glass, the pygmies empty their cargo into the abyss.

Out of the grove parade the dancing women, dark-skinned, Josephine Baker-types bearing 100 tons of zebra shit in knapsacks slung around their backs. The dancers will ascend the ladder and pour the zebra shit into the giant blender.

Matthew Barney will film this event. The work, which will be screened at the Museum of Modern Art (MoMA) and subsidized by the National Endowment for the Arts (NEA), is called Tomato Cyclone.

II. The Lake of Tomatoes

In Western France, twenty miles East of Nantes, is a lake known as "The Lake of Tomatoes" (*Le Lac des Tomates*).

As the name suggests, it is ravine overflowing with tomato sauce.

1.1 miles in length, 1.3 miles wide, it is the world's largest known tomato lake.

The Lake of Tomatoes is approximately 21.5 feet deep.

Do not swim in the Lake of Tomatoes.

Its piscine life is variegated.

Minnows and tadpoles bloat and marshmallow; their skin grows porous and spongy.

Eels slither and swim through the warm eddies of red.

Standing on the pier, fishermen angle for reddish trout.

Half-devoured tomato carapaces bounce on the foamy surface of the lake.

On a raft with my beloved, I steer through the thick tomato sauce.

The pungent musk of decomposing tomatoes fills our nostrils.

A saurian lunges at us as the raft passes.

The eels ripple through the tomato sauce like galvanic currents.

The Phantom Coalition

Grant Bailie

1.

I was drinking a brandy beside a strange fireplace, the snow still on my shoulders, while my impromptu host regaled me with a long and loud car trouble story of his own.

I looked into the fire and wondered when the tow truck would arrive.

The host was finishing up; as far as I could tell, it was just a story about how his car stalled once, but he told it with such detail and animated glee that I had felt obligated to look up repeatedly while he was going on to say things like: "That's something," and "You don't say."

At least it was warm by the fire. I had walked two miles to get to this part, passed nothing but blank white fields and dark woods before finding this one house, half hidden in a grove of gnarled trees.

The house was old, and the fireplace was massive—far too big, in fact, for the room itself, which was smallish and otherwise unadorned. On either side of the fireplace's gaping hearth where two stone figures, with strange black eyes. The figures were men, but there was something brutish in their features that made them seem just as close to some other primate. Above these two stone ape-men, a set of stone wings formed the top of the opening.

That was the fireplace; the rest of the place was small and drab. Nothing on the walls. No furniture save a fragile looking chair in the corner. There was a doorway into the next room, but the door was closed. It was the doorway my host had gone through earlier to call the tow truck, and to fetch us the glasses and something to drink by the fire.

"It's an interesting place you have," I said, when it was clear there was nothing more to be drained from the subject of car trouble.

"Thanks," he said, finishing off the last of his brandy and smacking his lips. "Been in the family for years. Drink up."

I took a few sips, just to be polite. I am not a huge brandy fan. But it made a warm line going down, and after the long cold of the walk, at least that was something. That and the roaring fire.

I looked at the flames again—watched them dance around, pieces of it arcing from one ember to another, tongues of fire forming into figures that danced around, leaping from log to log. The figures in the fire were familiar to me but it took me a moment to realize that they were like the stone ape-men on the fireplace itself.

"Hmm," I said. I think I actually meant to say something, but for some reason or another it only came out as "hmm."

"Yes," my host said. I looked up. His face was enormous. There were beads of sweat on his upper lip the size of raindrops—like raindrops beaded up on the freshly waxed hood of a car—not my car; I hadn't waxed my car in ages.

"Is everything all right, young man?" the man asked and his voice sounded like both a howling wind and the hissing of a burning log.

I took a step back from the fireplace. Maybe it was just the heat of that starting to bother me. That and the brandy.

"Fresh air," I said—and again. I had intended to say more, but that was all that came out. I took a few steps toward where I thought I remembered the door being. The steps did not go as smoothly as I had planned. There was something wrong with my feet. They were tied together, or stuck in an invisible mud or fused together by heat like a wax doll left standing on a radiator. I kicked out, trying to break them free of whatever was holding them. It didn't help. I lost my balance and fell slowly to the ground, so slowly that I had time to think things over a little on the way down. I'd been poisoned, of course. My host was probably the member of a satanic cult and I would wake up in a dark basement cavern strapped to a stone altar with some high priest or priestess marking off the bits of me to cut with a paintbrush dipped in goat blood. A hell of a thing, I thought, as I continued to fall. I don't even like brandy. And all because I was too cheap or careless to keep up with the regular maintenance on my vehicle. Would an oil change or a better grade of gas have helped, I wondered. Would a new air filter have saved my life?

2.

I woke up in a garish room—not at all like the dank, subterranean cathedral I'd been expecting. The walls were blue and gold, with paintings of saints and cherubs ascending. I was on a couch—if couch was the right word for that museum piece. It creaked under my weight, crackled like it was stuffed with dry grass—unless it was that had been stuffed with dry grass. It was hard to know for sure.

With some effort, I sat up. A few seconds later, my brain sat up with me, and we both looked around the room, more or less in unison.

Aside from the couch and the paintings on the wall, there were about a dozen other bits of expensive looking furniture and objects, mostly marble statuettes, silver clocks, porcelain boys fishing on dark wood tables with curling legs. On the table directly in front of me was the bronze statue of a colt rearing up on its hind legs. I picked it up. It was heavy and seemed like it might be useful for breaking down doors or bashing in heads. It had a price tag.

I stood up, found a door, found that it was not locked, and walked through it and into another room—the front room of an antique shop. I was still holding the bronze colt and there was a little old lady at the front counter, dusting off a collection of majolica ashtrays. She looked up, smiled at me without animosity. She reminded me of a nun I knew once, but without the cruel glint in her eyes.

"Would you like to buy that, dear," she said.

I looked down at the horse statue in my hands. It was reasonably priced—it might even look good on the windowsill of my study. I reached into my back pocket and was happy to find a wallet there.

"Yes," I said. "I would."

"It's not really bronze, you know," she said.

"Oh no?" I said.

"No. Some sort of alloy. And the right hoof is slightly misshapen."

"That's OK," I said, handing her the money.

She put the horse into a plastic bag and handed it to me with my change. I walked out of the store like that: without stealth or violence.

And outside was an ordinary looking winter day, in a town I had never seen before in my life.

I zipped up my coat, put the horse under my arm and thrust my hands into my pockets to keep warm. That's when I felt it: a piece of paper folded into quarters. I took it out, opened it and read:

"Dear Mr. Baillie,

We are sorry for the inconvenience. We thought you were kith of a certain mystical bloodline---but never mind all that. It was all a stupendous mistake on our part. Our research department will be appropriately chastised, we assure you. We trust we have not inconvenienced you too very much. Please forgive us. As a token of our guilt, please find one train ticket back to your town, a long with a little traveling money. You will also find your car repaired and waiting for you in your driveway. We have even topped off the tank. That's how bad we feel about this whole thing.

Sincerely,

The Phantom Coalition"

I checked my inside breast pocket and sure enough, there were train tickets and a small handful of cash.

I hailed a taxi and had him take me to the train station. I had a few hours to kill before my train left, so I went into the diner attached to the station and got a cup of coffee. The coffee was good and I was beginning to feel human again. I asked the waitress what the special was. She told me it was gruel.

"Gruel?" I asked. "Your special is gruel?.

"It's making a come-back," the waitress told me.

3.

I was standing on the platform waiting for the train that would take me home. The platform was old or just made to look that way; iron lampposts with large clocks faces were set every hundred feet apart.

Porters in the classic uniform walked back and forth checking their pocket watches.

A man in a gray jumpsuit was mopping the far end of the platform. This struck me as a questionable thing to do in the winter, but there he was, dipping his mop into a bucket, and sloshing the slop-water around.

A light snow was just beginning to fall. It looked like soap flakes or maybe frosted cornflakes. The man with the mop looked up, squinted, held out his hand to catch a few flakes, then returned to his mopping.

The train pulled up with a cloud of steam. It was an electric train, but still there was a cloud of steam, obscuring half the platform in a white cloud while a whistle blew. I found out later that it had a special pipe for pumping out steam just for the dramatic effect of it all.

A man yelled: "All aboard."

I climbed the steps into one of the cars, handed over my ticket and was shown to my seat by the window. The snow was getting heavier and a strong wind was blowing. It felt good to be inside, in the warmth and safety of a reasonably comfortable seat, and after a little while I fell into a kind of half-sleep.

I was interrupted a few moments later by the arrival of the passenger in the seat next to mine. He was a small man with a large face there was something about him--his size, shape, clothing—that reminded me of a leprechaun—so much so, in fact, that I stared a few seconds longer than was polite. He stared back. Then he laid claim to the armrest between us as if it were an act of vengeance

I turned my attention back to the falling snow, and my back to the little man. Let him have the armrest. I folded my arms across my chest and after a few minutes, the train began to move, rocking gently on the tracks, a vague and serene, white landscape drifting by.

I fell asleep and dreamt I was on a large wooden ship, traveling toward a distant shore. In my dream, I knew the name of the shore, but I cannot remember it now. I do remember the crew was scurrying back and forth, battening hatches, tying ropes into knots, fastening sails to masts, raising or dropping anchors--whatever it was that my subconscious mind supposed that sailors did.

They were, as they say, a scurvy lot, with every other one of them sporting either a wooden leg or a patch over one eye. The captain was a man with a patch over both eyes, and had to be led to the bridge by a monkey on a leash. He seemed to be in a bad temper, and sniffed at the wind in all directions before yelling some directions to the men.

"Stem the main bridge, you cankerous lot!" he yelled.

"Dredge the keelhaul, you conniving, gall-ridden son's of sea cows!"

Even in my dream, I knew his terminology was all wrong and was about to tap a passing crew member or monkey on the shoulder and tell them so when a man with a big face wet with seawater came up and stood next to me.

"We really are sorry for the inconvenience," he said.

And then a large wave crashed upon us and swept me overboard.

I awoke with a start. The train was pulling into a station; the little man was already gone.

A man in a black suit was standing in the aisle nearby.

"This is you're stop," he said.

"Is it?" I said. I looked out the window, but found no sign or identifiable landmark.

"It most certainly is," he said and smiled in that cryptic sort of way villains smile in movies.

I got up, left the train, found my car in the parking lot. As promised, it had a full tank of gas. It started without any difficulty at all.

4.

I was back home, back to going to and from work, walking the dog, kissing the wife, pretending to be a horse for my two young sons and riding them back and forth from living room to bedroom until my knees were aching, my back sore and the palms of my hands bright red.

I had told my wife about everything that had happened, of course, and after awhile she was starting to believe it, though she still thought it seemed a little like an elaborate story I had concocted to cover up for a tryst I might be having with one of the girls from Accounting.

"Have you seen any of the girls from Accounting?" I asked her. "And I would hardly call them girls and they all have this weird mint smell to them..."

"That isn't really the point," she said, checking the red lacquer on one thumbnail—it was worn away at the edges and the nail itself was somewhat ragged.

I showed her the note again, and she pretended to read it for the twentieth time.

"It's all just a little crazed," she said, folding it up and handing it back to me. "A Phantom Coalition...what is that, even? A company? A Religion? And frankly, this even looks a little like your handwriting."

"It's a lot crazed," I said. "Having an affair with one of the girls from accounting would almost be preferable. At least the world would still be the same then. It wouldn't be this place where people are randomly drugged and kidnapped and left in a strange city with a note of apology and a train ticket home. What am I supposed to do with a world like that?"

My wife appeared to think about it for some time. She tugged on her left earlobe. She chewed her thumbnail. "What do you mean an affair with one of the girls from accounting would be preferable?" she asked.

It went downhill from there. I slept on the couch, woke up stiff in the morning, got dressed for work without waking her, and grabbed breakfast and coffee at the diner near my office.

The eggs were like rubber and the coffee tasted like it was brewed in a witch's cauldron. I added cream and it turned gray. I half expected an eyeball to pop to the surface.

I seldom ate at this diner—partly because the food was so bad and partly because the waitresses' uniforms were made of corduroy. They made a funny thwipping sound whenever they walked by. It unnerved me. Sometimes I had nightmares about it. In one particular nightmare several of the waitresses had gotten together to bury me in a shallow grave in the parking lot behind the diner. You could hear the thwip of their uniform every time they threw another shovelful of dirt on top of me. I had awaken screaming that night, waking my wife with me.

"What is it?" she had asked and all I had managed to say between gasping breaths was: "Waitresses."

"Is everything fine?" one of the waitress asked me and I told her it was and braced myself as she walked away.

I was chewing on the last of strip of bacon that seemed more canine then porcine when a man in a black suit came into the diner—I only noticed him because I looked up when the bell over the door rang. The man in the black suit smiled and nodded at me as if he knew me. I nodded back because I guess it was the polite thing to do, but the man in the black suit unsettled me now too, even more than the corduroy waitresses.

I put the money on the counter and went to work.

Work ended. On the way home I stopped at the public library, the computers for any mention of a Phantom Coalition, but found nothing. On the way out, I asked the librarian. He was ancient—older than most of the books—so I figured: what the heck, he might know something that wasn't written down.

But when I asked him about the Phantom Coalition it was like a gray cloud had crossed over his face. He muttered something and told me when the library was closing in three hours.

I thanked him and left the building. Halfway home, I was stopped by the flashing lights of a police car. While I waited at the side of the road, I tried to remember how fast I had been going. It had not felt like I had been speeding.

The police officer did not get out of his car right away, but they never do. There are always the preparations, I suppose—the checking of plates, running of warrants, finding the ticket book and a working pen. But this guy seemed to be taking the process to an even further extreme. While I waited, the weather changed around me: it grew darker and mist rose from the low, vacant ground along side of the highway. The mist thickened into fog, with the flashing red and blue lights changing the color of the atmosphere, so that it seemed, by intermittent seconds, that I lived in either an all red or an all blue limbo. I wondered what it would look like through 3-D glasses. Probably the same, or maybe only normal.

Finally, the policeman got out of his car, walked up to the side of my window. I already had it open and was holding out my driver's license and proof of insurance, but the policeman didn't take it, didn't even look at it.

Instead, he looked me in the eye and said: "We just want you to know this isn't a game, Mr. Baillie. We are not kidding around."

Then he handed me a piece of paper and left. I looked at the paper. It was not ticket. It was another note. It read:

"Dear Mr. Baillie,

As the officer may have told you, this is not a game. We are quite serious about all of this and frankly, are not in the habit of the sort mercy we have so recently exercised in your particular case. Believe us, leaving people with train tickets home is not our usual practice and we do not mind telling you now that there was much internal debate on the matter. You were one vote shy of having your body dismembered and scattered about in drainage ditches thought out the tri-state area. If everyone from the Extreme Liquidations Department had shown up for the meeting that day things would likely have gone very differently for you.

If we are to continue to extend this mercy—however ill-advised—we will require just this from you: forget about us. Do not inquire after us. Do not try to find us. The world is a large and mysterious place, Mr. Baillie, and you must learn to accept that fact. You cannot know the machinery that runs our civilization and it is unwise to want to. In the same way that you were born without understanding the dimensions of your womb or the sufferings of your mother, in the same way you live your life now without a constant conscious awareness of it's inevitable ending, we ask you to go along with your existence without a thought to us, who we are, and what function we play in your life and the universe in general.

We do not wish to call another meeting

We thank you in advance for your cooperation in this matter.

Sincerely,

The Phantom Coalition"

I folded up the letter. The police car was gone, the fog lifted. I drove home, kissed my wife at the door, pretended to be a horse for my twin sons and rode them at a full gallop between the kitchen and the living room again and again until my back and knees ached and my hands were worn raw.

ome Togo-Me
Mongo Cash
Thing

Dege Legg

Around the world, online fraud through use of e-mail is one of the fastest growing types of cons being used by criminals. One of the most popular scams is known under a few different names: the "419 Fraud" (after the criminal code this type of scam falls under in Nigerian law), the "Advance Fee Fraud" or the "Nigerian Connection" (as it's known in Europe). It consists of a subject, posing as a mid-level authority from a West African country, who has somehow come across a large sum of money — usually in the millions — and this money, because of some distant relative, can be yours.

You've seen them. Deleted them. And then deleted them again.

Out of perverse curiosity and boredom, I opened an e-mail account under the name "Frank Reno" (it sounded Gordon Gekko-ish) and posed as a big time, investment banker-type, hoping to lure one of these conmen into a dialogue. Not all of them answered, probably because I came straight out of the gate, throwing nutty stuff at them. I gradually modified my technique, and it didn't take long for a man named "Barrister Jim Hassan" to bite.

The following is the complete correspondence of me (Frank Reno) and one of the Nigerian Scam guys (Barrister Jim Hassan), which lasted from July 5, 2005 to Oct. 11, 2005.

Obviously, the King's English is not this guy's first language, and his e-mails are reproduced here in all their confused glory.

JULY 5, 2005
JIM HASSAN ADVOCAT,
52D RUE DE FRANCE
LOME -TOGO.
WEST AFRICA.

ATTN/PLS,

I am Barrister Jim Hassan, a solicitor in law, personal attorney to Mr. S.A Reno, a national of your country, who used to work with Shell development Company in Lome Togo. Here in after shall be referred to as my client. On the 21st of April 2000, my client, his wife and their only daughter were involved in a car accident along Nouvissi express Road.

All occupants of the vehicle unfortunately lost their lives. Since then I have made several enquiries to your embassy here to locate any of my clients extended relatives, this has also proved unsuccessful. After these several unsuccessful attempts, I decided to track his last name over the Internet, to locate any member of his family hence I contacted you.

However, I contacted you to assist in repatriating the fund valued at US $5.5 million left behind by my client before it gets confiscated or declared unserviceable by the IBA BANK where this huge amount were deposited. The said IBA BANK LOME TOGO has issued me a notice to provide the next of kin or have his account confiscated within the next twenty-one official working days.

Since I have been unsuccessful in locating the relatives for over 2 years now, I seek the consent to present you as the next of kin to the deceased since you have the same last names, so that the proceeds of this account can be paid to you. Therefore, on receipt of your positive response, we shall then discuss the sharing ratio and modalities for transfer.

I have all necessary information and legal documents needed to back you up for claim. All I require from you is your honest cooperation to enable us see this transaction through. I guarantee that this will be executed under legitimate arrangement that will protect you from any breach of the law.

Best regards.
Barrister Jim Hassan.

JULY 6, 2005

Dear Barrister Hassan,

I am a businessman and financial consultant involved in various state and trust corporations. I have 20 years experience in the appropriation of committees for funds and trustworthiness.

First off, I'm sorry to hear about the car accident. Send my "certified condolences" out to your client's family.

Secondly, I am very interested in your offer of $5.5 million dollars. This money of which you speak I could use this money. Currently, I am experiencing some small financial difficulties that could easily be rect-o-fied by your offer.

In short, let's do business. Send me instructions and all attendant information needed for us to get this transaction to happen.

Sincerely,
Frank W. Reno
Viceroy of Securities & Trust
Louisiana Bank & Trustitude

JULY 13, 2005
JIM HASSAN ADVOCAT,

Attn: Frank W. Reno,

Greetings, Thanks For Your Urgent Response, But It Has Come to Be Very Necessary I Educate You a Bit on the Next of Kinship as Attainable in the Legal and Banking Policy here my country and the Globally at large.

You See, Next of Kinship is Not Limited to Relations of the Deceased, Nor is it Confided to the Circuit of Parental Relationship, Rather it is By Choice of the Benefactor as Regards to Whom He Wish to WILL it to (Beneficiary) Either Formally By Write Up, Or Informally By Secret Information Disclosure to Beneficiary be Him/Her Business Partner, Relation, Kinsmen, Or Friends or Well Wishers.

Therefore By Virtue of the Above Stated, You can Claim to Be the Next of Kin of the Deceased as My Legal Chambers was directed by the Bank to locate relatives of LATE ENGINEER "SMITH A.RENO," Hence on Your Acceptance to This, I Will Communicate to You the CONFIDENTIAL INFORMATION of the Deceased as Contained in My Security LAW File Diskette of the legal office, So That on Your Readiness to Forward Claim Application to the Bank, I Will Direct You and Reveal to You the Necessary Information Which You Will Enclose in Your Application to the Bank.

Therefore on Correspondence of Bank Confidential Information With What are contained in Your Application to them, They Have No Alternative Other than to Release the Fund to Your bank account as next of kin to LATE ENGINEER SMITH A.RENO. Believing You that You that let me down in this transaction as I trusted You before contacting on the very business that only honesty and trustwhorthiness between me and you. You are the Next of Kin, As he Has No One for this inheritance Claim and his bank has been calling on my office to produce the next of kin.

Having a relation here or not is not a problem as next of kin can come from either the mother side or father side. This is a 100 business that I called You in for and by using the test of names given to this legal Chambers by IBA-BANK OF AFRICA -LOME REPUBLIC TOGO to know if we can locate a relation LATE ENGINEER SMITH A.RENO and I choose you as the next of kin.

Note that this is business and I want us to share this money among us in this very virgin year we are in as the bank has called on my legal office to present the next of kin to late Engr. Bawles and I don't want to allow few bank directors in Ecobank to lay their hands on this money. If I fail to provide the next of kin to LATE ENGINEER SMITH A.RENO that will lead the money to go as a lost fund. God made everything and His directions is what lead's me to contact you on this issue. we can save this money with your foreign assistance to me.

There is no risk in this business and note its a legal law chambers that contacted you on this very issue. Please, With the Above Explanations, I believe You Can Now Observe How Safe it is For You to Get involved in this Mutual Beneficial Transaction, Therefore I Request You Declare Your Interest Immediately For the Fund Claim and Transfer Directives to You.

You Are The Right Person Which I Directed This Letter To For A Mutual Business Benefit. Confirm your private telephone contact to me for easy communication. I will do that as soon as I hear from you.

Awaiting Your Immediate Response.

Thanks,
Barrister Jim Hassan

JULY 19, 2005

Jim,

You're telling me a lot of info, but not saying much. Although I'm a highly efficient machine of professional professionalization, I sneeze $100 bills. I absolutely detest discussing the specifics of any business transaction in legal terminology. Yawn. It is boring, sir. I'm a simple man, Jima Cowboy. I was born in Texas and rode Holstein cows in the Great Cattle Baron Wars of '82 and lost a finger in that war. I'm nobody's fool. So let's talk numbers.

Also, I must inform you that any "LOME TOGO-ME MONGO CASH THING" that we may be involved in had better be on the "up and up." You'd better not be trying no Togo-Pogo bullcrap, son. If that would be the case, you're in for a world of pain. Be warned! I know 16 different types of karate-wrestling moves. All of them can be summoned within seconds from the "man traps" that I call my hands.

You asked for my personal phone number. I will send it soon as we establish an adequate level of "trustworthy trustiness."

In the United States, we have a little thing called the "Lou Diamond-Phillips Trust Bond." American Professionals, when dealing in International Affairs, use it in standard operating procedure and this situation is no different. Keeps everybody honest.

Therefore, before we conduct any additional business, I'm going to have to ask you to send $500 to the following address:

Diamond-Phillips Trust Bond Association
C/O Frank Reno
XXX East Vermillion apt. X
Lafayette, LA 70501 (United States of America)

Well-concealed cash (wrap it in tinfoil) or money order will do fine. After the security bond is received, we'll get down to business, my friend. And we'll be making a lot of money with future transactions, because I've got a few other business opportunities for you on the side, but keep that a secret. Nobody needs to be knowing about how rich the two of us will be getting with all the things I'm going to do with you, my brother.

> Sincerely,
> Frank Reno
> Viceroy of Securities & Trust

JULY 21, 2005

Dear Franks.

Thanks very much for your kind gesture. My good brother Franks I now know that you want to do this deal with me. But my dear friend for me to send $500 there's no way to do that. This money is in the bank. I cannot pull it out from the bank without processing it to your bank account in your country. If you want to do this deal with me tell me, then I will go to high court and get the text from you to fill in and forward it to the bank for urgent processing of this fund. Ok?

Thanks and consider and get back to me.

Jim Hassan.

JULY 21, 2005

Dear Jims,

OK, forget the $500. I'm breaking the No. 1 Rule of Transactional Law, over here, but I suppose I can risk it just this once, but only once will I deviate from the Standard Operating Procedure of Honorable American Business Machinations.

You're really putting me in a "bad place," Jims. Really bad. And it's unfortunate on your part because things have been going really good here at Money Bags Inc. I mean, really good. Lot of money coming in and I've got a surplus of DISPOSABLE INCOME sitting in trash bags waiting to be invested in your business proposal.

Out of the goodness of my heart, I want to help you.

Looking forward to hearing your reply,

Frank Reno
Viceroy of Securities and Trust

JULY 23, 2005

Attn: Frank Reno (Viceroy of securities and trust)

Thank you so much for getting back to me and for your interest in this transaction. When I came across your contact something in me told me that you might be someone to be trusted but in as much as my instinct hardly fails me, I have not chosen you yet until I am sure that I can trust You. Based on that, I wish that you give me your word of honor by the under-listed points in this mail.

Please, can you give me your word of honor by the following points stated below?

They are thus:

1. That you will not cheat me during the course of this transaction.

2. My own share of the money will be in your safe keep until I come over to your country for sharing and further investment.

3. That you will keep this transaction very confidential even from your best friend for safety of both parties.

4. That you will forward to me your contact information for easy communication between the both parties.

5. That you shall always contact me whenever you get information from the bank so that we will put heads together as one family and get this transaction consummated successfully.

This transaction will only take about 11 bank working days or less for the money to be transferred into your account. But as soon as your application is approved and a funding deposit from you is made, then it will take about 2 days and the money will be in your account.

As soon as I get your positive response to this my mail I will forward to you the payment application form, which you will fill and fax it to the bank for immediately action from the bank.

God bless you.
Barrister Jim Hassan

I Need This Guarantee.

JULY 24, 2005

Attn: Jim (Barrister Man)

Now I feel good about the relationship. I'm still a little suspicious about this whole business, but my Jesterton-2000/Gut Instinct Lie Detector is telling me good stuff about you, my friend Jim.

Here is my reply to your list of demands:

1. That you will not cheat me during the course of this transaction.

My friend Jim, I'm deeply insulted that you would even say such a thing. After all the stuff we've been through together?? Let's have no more of these accusations. Let us now, shake hands, across the borders of peace and lawful transactions. Let's create a verbal cue so that each of us truly KNOWS who we are talking to in our correspondence. From this point on, you will know it is I when I greet you with the secret appellation: "Captain Mustache" (as you will be known). And you can greet me as: "Monsignor Carbuncle."

2. My own share of the money will be in your safe keep until I come over to your country for sharing and further investment.

Agreed. I'll keep your money in my Giganto-saurus 7000 Vault Safe with the special spring-loaded action bolt (with mnemonic valves)!

3. That you will keep this transaction very confidential even from your best friend for safety of both parties.

(silence) ... No need; I am Zen Master of Quiet Rumblings.

4. That you will forward to me your contact information for easy communication between the both parties.

Consider it done, Captain Mustache, sir!

5. That you shall always contact me whenever you get information from the bank so that we will put heads together as one family and get this transaction consummated successfully.

Family's the name-o-the-game, Jims. I got Texas Ranger Blood in me. Our two heads together will, indeed, make the transaction consummate.

Now, what I need you to do is send me the details of exactly what you need me to do next. And don't do it in one of them fancy six-sheet-to-the-Devil's-wind emails of yours. Keep it short and sweet. Plain. Simple.

> Bust it,
>
> Frank Reno (aka "Monsignor Carbuncle")
>
> Viceroy of Securities & Trust

JULY 25, 2005
Attn: Frank Reno.
Viceroy of Securities

Thanks for your mail and all I want to ask from you is honesty and pure trust that this fund will be very saved in your hands as the bank remits the inheritance fund into your bank account as next of kin to LATE

ENGINEER SMITH A. RENO. All you have to do now is to fill the transfer fund application and fax and also by email to the bank foreign remittance department for more formal concern and fast response to transfer this fund into your bank a/c.

Furthermore, keep me informed as soon as you fax your application to the bank and also send the application by email too for a sign of urgency from your side and make sure you get in touch with me. The bank will contact you in respect of the fund application that you send to their office.

I expect your immediate response.

Thanks
Barrister Jim Hassan

JULY 27, 2005

Attn: The Jim,

Greetings, Captain Mustache! (See? Now you know it's me.) I noticed you did not address me as "Monsignor Carbuncle" in your email. How can I be sure this is actually YOU???

I thought we had an agreement! You would be Captain Mustache and I would be Monsignor Carbuncle! Oh, this is making me nervous, my friend if indeed this is you I'm talking to and not someone else!

This could be a trap! I'm nobody's fool. Write me back when you decide you can stick to your agreement of secrecy! Until then, YOU GET NOTHING! N-O-T-H-I-N-G!

And I say good day to you, Sir! Good day!

Terribly upset and slightly paranoid,
Frank Reno
Viceroy of Securities & Trust
*m.o.n.s.i.g.n.o.r.

JULY 27, 2005

Dear Monsignor Carbuncle Frank.

I am not again sure what you mean or why you get angry but I am trying to conduct serious business with you. The email is very secure and there is no need more for of the captain names. Do I remind you that there are $5 million dollars that we are going to transact? I understand you could be scared but we are only part of way through this process so please stop with games and fears, my dearest Frank.

Thanks for your mail and keep me informed as you send the fund application to the bank. Have you send the text from to bank? This must be done soon.

Thanks
Barrister Jim

JULY 30, 2005

Dear Barrister Jim,

OK, OK. I will try to understand your methods of doing business. Perhaps they are a little unorthodox compared to that in the U.S.A. (Home of the Brave). I am currently in the process of filling out the paper work.

Also, I've been very busy at Securities and Trust Inc. I work hard. My job requires an extraordinary of my time, but I get paid VERY WELL for my duties. However, it has taken a toll on my health. Since August of last year, I've been forced by my employers to take a prescription drug that causes extreme dizziness, out of body experiences, and sudden fits of swearing and obscenities. Please be patient with me. I'm rich, but have health problems YOU SCUM-SUCKING PIECE OF RAT TRASH!!!

OK, I am off to work on the paperwork.

Frank Reno
Viceroy

AUGUST 1, 2005

Dear Partner,

Thanks for you and your job and health. Keep me informed as you send the application. Thanks and please don't delay this fund transfer process.

Barrister Jim

AUGUST 1, 2005

Jim,

OK, I faxed the info and application to the bank. I even put an urgent "Snuffulufagus Rammstein" on the bank application so it would go through faster. It cost me an extra $25. That will have to come out of your end of the proceeds, but that's OK.

> Sincerely,
> Viceroy Frank
> Viceroy of Securities & Trust

AUGUST 2, 2005

Dear Viceroy Frank.

Thanks for your mail and please I advice that you re-fax the application to the bank and also send by email to the bank for more urgency from your side. This is because I went to the bank to confirm that you fax the application to the bank. The bank informed me that they are yet to receive your fax. so re-fax the application and send by email also.

> Thanks
> Barrister Jim.

AUGUST 5, 2005

Dear Barrister Jim,

Fax. Fax. Fax. Is that all you think about? Faxes? I sent the damn thing two days ago!

I've got important business to tend to and can't be messing around with your sorry Barrister butt forever. Let's get moving! I'm feeling greedy! Let's go. Move it! Let's get this thing rolling. Maybe your bank's fax machine is broken and doesn't know how to receive American faxes from Scrontological 3000L fax machines? Did you think about that? My fax is working, I just checked it.

Check with your bank. You're probably out there SIPPING WINE FROM A COCONUT ON A BEACH IN POGOVILLE!

> Frank
> Viceroy of Securities & Trust

AUGUST 8, 2005

Dear Frank.

How are you doing today? Listen, my dear brother, I don't know what is really going on over this very business because you have told me that you have sent the text form to the bank. Your behavior is erratic. But just about one and half-hour ago, the bank called me and told me that you have not sent any form to bank. If really you want do this business with me, kindly send the form to the bank for them to start processing this fund into your bank account.

Please try, my brother, to stop delaying this transaction.

Thanks and would like to hear from you.

Jim Hassan

At this point in our correspondence, Jim e-mailed me a bank form. I filled it with false info and sent it back to him and the e-mail address of his bank.

AUGUST 8, 2005

Dear Jim,

Here's the form with all the attendant info other than my fax, which is broken. I hope you're happy now. You're starting to get on my nerves. Now get to work on making our million-dollar transaction go through.

Sincerely,
Frank Reno
Viceroy of Securities & Trustiness

AUGUST 9, 2005

Dear Frank.

Thank you very much for your mail. Listen, I advise you to send it through E-mail that I gave to you in that Text Form.

Please stop delay my Good Brother Frank.

> Thanks.
> Jim Hassan

AUGUST 9, 2005

Dear Jim,

Slow your roll, player. I already sent your form off! Now go work your magic.

I've been having a very busy week. Last Thursday, I nearly chopped off my big toe, trying to sand the corn off my right foot. Thing hurts like hellfire now; both the corn and the toe, thank you. In addition, my wife is now threatening to divorce me on grounds that I've "failed to satisfactorily meet the expectations of a non-scientist." I don't know what that means, but if you've got any idea, let me know. As you can see, I've been quite busy, juggling madness with two pitchforks and a salad shooter, so you'll have to excuse me if I'm a little slow in keeping up the pace with our business dealings. But I do have good news: I sent off the application form, once again, to your bank this morning. All information included other than fax ... I broke that thing over the head of one of my subordinates, last week, for insubordinizing. Don't ask. The guy's a lazy pervert. He'd hooked a French Horn up to an air-compressor, in the parking lot, and was making "World War III sounds." Some truly awful noises.

Nonetheless, I should have the fax machine replaced within a week. So, to quote the famous British poet, Gavin Rossdale, and to sum up this weeks parade of shenanigans, "There must be something that we can eat, maybe find another lover. ... Everything's Zen? I don't think so."

> Sincerely,
> Frank Reno

The next day I received an e-mail from someone claiming to be from the International Bank of Africa.

AUGUST 10, 2005

FROM FROEIGN ACCOUNT DEPARTEMNT
INTERNATIONAL BANK OF AFRICA
LOME REPUBLIC OF TOGO
TELEFAX:00228-222-02-87

ATTN: FRANK RENO.
DEAR SIR. 09/08/05

AFTER OUR EXECUTIVE BOARD OF DIRECTORS MEETING TODAY OVER YOUR FUND INHERITANCE TRANSFER, INTERNATIONAL BANK OF AFRICA LOME REPUBLIC OF TOGO HEREBY INFORMS YOU TO COMPLETELY RE-SEND YOUR APPLICATION BECAUSE BARRISTER JIM HASSAN HAS NOTIFIED THE BANK CONCERNING THE APPLICATION WHICH YOU WILL SEND TO IBA-BANK TOGO.

REGARDS
DR.PAUL EGOM BENSON

FOREIGN REITANCE DIRECTOR(IBA-BANK)
Ref/CC/ Account Section.

AUGUST 19, 2005

Jim,

What the hell is going on over there? I'm trying to make some money and all y'all are doing is messing around with my $5.5 million dollar inheritance fund. I keep sending you information and you corndogs keep wussing out. What's the deal?

Where you at, boy? I'm still looking to make some money and I ain't heard from you in week. You'd better quit smoking that Tomo Logo Tobacco or quit doing whatever drugs it is you're on. You've got to get back over here in the REAL WORLD, man! You ain't gonna make no money doing that stuff.

Send me an email, Brother Barrister Jim. I'm waiting on you. Got a gang of American Cash Dollars sitting in a footlocker with your name on it.

Sincerely,
Frank Reno
Viceroy of All Securities

AUGUST 25, 2005

Dear Frank,

I can see that you not a serious man? Bank told me that your account in the United States is not there.

> Good by
> Jim Hassan.

AUGUST 26, 2005

Dear Jim,

If there's one thing you should know about me is that I'm as serious as a damn longhair on I-10, trying to get through Alabama with a fender full of weed, son! That's pretty serious. I am highly offended that you would question my seriousity in this business venture. My bank account, for your information, is registered under a double-secret process, reserved for special members of the Society of Viceroys that can't be divulged to outsiders looking in. If you want in, you got to go through ME and only I know the secret password code!

If you, sir, are serious about releasing these funds, you can reply to this email, and maybe I'll consider giving you the password to my personal double-secret bank account.

> Seriously,
> Frank Reno
> Viceroy of Securities & Trust

SEPTEMBER 1, 2005

Dear Frank,

Thanks for your email, I can see that you now want do this transaction with me. But there is one important thing. I ask that you tell bank here that you want to re-activate your cousin's bank account and for them to transfer the money urgently to your account.

Please do this now. Please inform me as soon as you do that my brother,

> Thanks.
> Jim Hassan

SEPTEMBER 6, 2005

Dearest Friend Jim,

As you may have seen in the news, Louisiana is underwater from the devastating effects of Hurricane Katrina. I had a vision the night before the hurricane. In it I saw thunderous rains, unholy snakes, and more rain. Also, I saw towers of silt tumbling into the flaxen seaweed ponds. And many more things which I have not the courage to tell you now, for they are too horrid to repeat.

My bank suffered a terrible amount of damage from the hurricane. The computers are down and I will be unable to withdraw or deposit any money until they are returned to working order.

In the meantime, I must ask for a SMALL LOAN from you (or from the account of my cousin Reno whom you keep referring to in your country) in order to continue the progress of our business contract. I NEED $700 or I may lose control of my assets if I do not file a Whamo-X/2000 Accounting Statement with my bank within the week. In order to prove these are my bank assets, I need to file this by the end of the week or I risk losing all of my money and, in turn, our money. The money we will share when you come to visit this country.

Please, I am begging you, my friend Jim. This is an emergency. I need your gift of friendship ($700) more than ever now.

Urgently awaiting your reply,
Frank Reno
Viceroy of Securities & Trust

SEPTEMBER 7, 2005

My Good Friend Frank,

I thank you for your mail. Well, my dear friend, I'm very, very sorry for your story you told me on your letter about the hurricane. I am very sorry about that, but my brother, I have spend a lot of money on this very business. I have no money to send to you now. If you want us to get this money, try and see what you can do to get the bank to reactivate your bank account. For urgent transfer the money into your bank account please try my brother.

Thanks
Hassan

SEPTEMBER 12, 2005

Jim,

You're just going to leave me out here, like this?? With my bank funds taken away and my cousin's money in a Lego Bank and you on the beach eating coconuts! The nerve you have, my old friend. After all the stuff we've been through?! All this time we've known each other?! And you're going to sell me out, just like that?

MAY THE GODS OF FIDUCIARY CAPITAL AND INTERNATIONAL COMMERCE STRIKE YOU DOWN!!!!!

Not next month! Not next Wednesday! NOW!!!

Jim Hassan, you are a Bad Man!

> Sincerely,
> Frank Reno
> Viceroy of Securities,
> Trust, & Fiduciary Responsibility

On October 11, I received the following e-mail from Yahoo Mail, informing me that Jim Hassan's account had been terminated.

OCTOBER 11, 2005

Warning!

The person that was using this email address is a scammer and thief, one of the worst persons of our society. Do not send him any money, if you have, immediately attempt to cancel the payment. If you have lost money, contact your local law enforcement for your next actions. More information about cybercrime:

http://www.scam-watcher.org/
http://www.419legal.org
http://www.ifccfbi.gov/index.asp
http://www.aa419.org/content/links.php

Just for kicks, because I no longer had anyone to write, I wrote back the Yahoo People who'd shut down his account.

Dear Sir or Madam:

I'm Frank Reno, baby. Never make the mistake of thinking that bozo Jim Hassan was scamming me when in fact I was conducting a non-official sting, counter-scam operation of my own construction TO SCAM HIM.

"Fighting Spam with Ham," I call it.

Regards,
Frank Reno
Viceroy for the Protection of the Common Man
Lafayette, Louisiana

"We're so pretty, oh so pretty...vacant"–Johnny Rotten.

I was sitting watching morning cartoons when my Dad came out the bedroom. My Mom had already gone to work and I had the day off from school because it was a Teachers In-Service Holiday. This meant the teachers and school officials had meetings all day and the kids stayed home. My Dad was sweaty and stinky, as usual. He wore a plain white t-shirt and baggy jeans. He went into the kitchen, got a glass of water, and sat down at our cheap dinette set. We lived in government housing in Oak Cliff in the 1970s, so our furnishings were hand-me downs from relatives or garage sale finds.

He grabbed a pad and paper and began writing as he drank his water. I noticed his hand shook slightly as he wrote. It was just another one of his barbiturate hangovers.

"Todd, we need to go to the grocery store."

A feeling of dread sunk in. I had walked to the store with my Dad before and I just never knew what to expect. My mom had the only car, so walking was the only option. Besides, the local Kroger was only a few blocks away. The last time I had to go grocery shopping with Dad, about two months ago during the summer, he got very nervous and shaky and insisted we go back home just as we were about to step into Kroger's parking lot. A helicopter had flown over and he freaked out.

My Dad had been in and out mental hospitals my entire life. I was only eight, but he managed to make quite a few of them even up to that point in my life. The first was when he was in the Army. He tried to run away from his basic training at Tiger Land down in the swamps of Louisiana, ending up in the brig then a nuthouse in Kansas. Tiger Land is where you were sent to train for the infantry in Vietnam. Ever since then, he had had severe mental problems. He had some mental problems before going into the Army, but the Army experience aggravated them. That's why most of the time he was unemployed and spent days locked in my parents' bedroom taking drugs and sleeping.

"Come on Todd, put on your coat, we need to go."

I sighed and went and got my coat off the rack by the door. My dad did the same and off we went. We made it about two blocks down the side streets when suddenly my Dad froze. We never took the main street by our apartment. The busy traffic fucked with the old man's head too much.

"You see that," he said with panic in his voice, pointing over at some flashing sunlight coming off a distant house.

"Yeah," I replied, having been through this drill before.

I knew that if I tried to tell him it was just sunlight reflections, he'd get mad and more panicked, so I learned to play along. I didn't want to hear for the thousandth time how I didn't have his training and didn't know how to spot the enemy when they were in our mists.

He grabbed my hand, and we hid behind some nearby trees, with my Dad checking the distant house ever so often for enemy movement. After about ten minutes, my Dad whispered that it was all right to journey on. We were lucky because for the rest of our trip to Kroger, Dad didn't spot any more VC or NVA.

We entered Kroger, got our grocery cart, and headed immediately for the produce. There my Dad picked out a few tomatoes, celery, and apples. From there we hit the spice aisle. As we rounded the corner I knew we were in for a problem. There was an Asian lady comparing the prices on paprika. My dad began to sweat profusely and was frozen for a few minutes. I prayed the Asian lady wouldn't notice my weirdo Dad and me and call the manager over or something. I had to think fast, so I grabbed my Dad's hand and pulled him down so I could whisper in his ear.

"Dad, we forgot that French bread you wanted, I'll get the basil and black pepper and meet you with the cart over at the bread aisle."

My Dad nodded, straightened up and walked stiffly out of the spice aisle, never turning his back on the Asian lady. When Dad was out of sight, I went up to where the basil and black pepper were and quickly grabbed one of each. The Asian lady gave me a faint smile that I returned.

Finally, I met up with Dad in the bread aisle. He was standing there with a French loaf staring off into space. I told him to give me the money and wait outside. I'd pay and meet him with the groceries. He nodded and stiffly walked outside. I paid for the food and grabbed the grocery sack and left. Dad was at the far end of the building having a smoke. He seemed like he had recovered a little from his panic attack. We made it the rest of the way home without incident.

When we arrived home, I flipped the TV on as Dad put away the groceries. There was a news broadcast from Vietnam on. I immediately changed the channel over to a Star Trek re-run. I never liked watching the news anyway, and neither did my Dad.

The next few months were very quiet. I went to school. My Dad slept or did some occasional cooking. He was very good with Southern Home Cooking and Italian dishes. Sometimes he even made his own noodles from scratch from flour and water, precisely rolling each noodle by hand. My Mom worked her secretary job at the City of Dallas providing the much-needed funds we needed for survival. I occasionally got odd jobs helping the disabled vets upstairs with their groceries for some loose change.

In the summer of 1976, roughly 9 months after the Shopping Incident described above, my Dad's sister came to stay with us for the summer. She was just 18 and had graduated high school in Texarkana and wanted to see the big city – Dallas. She got a job at Target working in the stockroom and all went well for a while. My Dad's brother had gotten an apartment nearby after he graduated college with a Geology Degree, but spent most of his time out of town.

Despite having Dad's brother and sister around, they were of little help. His brother was gone too often to be much help. His sister was a typical spoiled brat from a middle-class family in a small town and knew nothing about cleaning up after herself, making her own meals, or contributing financially to our survival. Her Mom always did everything for her and she expected my Mom to do the same. No matter how many times my Mom tried to explain that she needed to take more responsibility, she couldn't or wouldn't do it. She just didn't grasp the pathetic reality of our impoverished existence and the need for self sufficiency.

Finally, my Mom snapped one day after coming home exhausted from work and sloppily packed her suitcases and threw them over our upstairs balcony. I watched the whole thing in shock, but was not surprised by it. After all, at 9 I had more of a clue of cleaning up after myself, housework, and meal preparation than she did. I think at that point she realized that our home was no Leave-It-To-Fuckin' Beaver like she was accustomed too.

When my Dad came out of his usual drugged stupor a few days later, he exploded. He trapped my Mom in an orange deck chair that was in his sister's room and proceeded to scream at my mom while trying to hit her hands with a ball pin hammer. He bruised a couple of her knuckles before she was finally able to push past him and hit the kitchen.

"Bitch, you fuckin' bitch!"

Dad screamed over and over again as my Mom and I gathered food for our usual escape. Though, he hadn't gone ballistic like this in over 6 months, he typically had these outbursts every 3 months or so. He was a diagnosed schizophrenic and as anybody can tell you, living with the mentally ill is a very unstable, unpredictable life. Things can be fine one minute and chaos the next. Any love I ever had for the man, had disappeared by this time. He was a crazy monster to be watched carefully and endured.

Just as we were about to exit with our food, Dad jumped around the corner with a baseball bat and tried to hit my mom. She ducked and he hit the refrigerator. She then quickly grabbed a frying pan and hit him dead center in his raging face, causing him to stumble back reeling and collapsing on the floor. At this time, my Mom weighed 200 pounds to my dad's skeletal 150, so he was no match for her.

We ran for the door, got in the car and drove to the other side of our apartment complex to stay with Theresa, our safe port during these frequent storms. I played with Theresa's son Manny and my Mom and Theresa talked. She was always urging my Mom to call the cops, but she rarely did. Finally, though, about 6 months later after my Dad's sister had returned home to her small town isolated life, my Mom had my Dad committed to Terrell State Mental Institution, divorcing him. I didn't shed a tear. I, like my Mom, was just grateful the long nightmare was over.

Skeleton Mom
Erin O'Brien

My mom is a skeleton. A total skeleton. Okay, not total. Her head is normal. In fact, you might even say she's pretty. Take her hair, her long brown hair. It's shiny and thick, really really thick. We're talking L'Oreal-TV-commercial hair. Not that it makes up for being a skeleton. But it is nice hair.

So her head is normal, but weird, too. The flesh comes to a nice, neat end around the center of her neck vertebrae. Just sort of gathers there. And, believe me, I thank God for that. Big time. I can only imagine if it was all raggedy, with tubes and gristle hanging out, and the skin just ending, like a loose upside-down sock.

Now that would be completely gross.

* * *

We're eating dinner. Me, Mom, and my stupid brother, Stevie. Dad's not here as usual. He comes home from work late. Like, all the time. He's always worried about losing his job, so he stays at the office until everyone else is gone. Mostly, it's nine, ten o'clock before he comes home. Not like I care. But it drives my mom crazy.

"Your father's going to be late again," she says, sniffing.

"He's always late," says my brother. Stupid.

"That's brilliant, stupid," I say.

"That's enough, Gina," says Mom as she drapes an apron around her hips and ties it behind her lower vertebrae. "Now instead of that attitude, I'm going to ask you to help your brother with his homework after dinner while I do the dishes and straighten up for your father."

"What about my homework?" I say. She never cares about my stuff.

"Helping Stevie will only take an hour or so. You have plenty of time."

"This sucks."

"Language, Gina. Language."

"What's for dessert?" says Stevie as he attempts to fit his little finger through a spaghettio, splitting it and smearing his hands with the sauce in the process. Stevie just turned eleven. I'm sixteen.

"How about some Oreos?" says Mom, popping one into her mouth. I have no idea where it goes from there. She chews and swallows like any normal person, after that, don't ask me. Maybe it shoots right into her spine.

"Oreos again?" whines Stevie. Like he should be surprised. We've had spaghettios and Oreos every night for dinner for the last six months. Before that it was mac and cheese (in the blue box, it's the cheesiest!) and ice cream sandwiches. It's like Mom has this thing: bad packaged pasta for dinner and black and white sandwich thing for dessert. Thank God we get lunch at school.

"You are welcome, young man, to have nothing at all for desert."

All I want to do is go up to my room and masturbate. But I can't now. It's too risky. There's no lock on my door. There's always the bathroom, which locks, but if Mom or Stupid comes knocking it breaks my concentration. I'll wait until later on tonight, when Stevie's undoubtedly pulling his own monkey and Mom and Dad are doing their thing.

It's nine-thirty by the time Dad gets home. Mom springs off the couch like a cherry bomb went off under her coccyx when Dad's headlights dance across the back wall of the family room. She runs into the kitchen and next is the predictable sound of ice cubes clinking into a glass. She comes back, scotch in hand, with that irritating, breathless way about her.

"Hello darling," she says as he walks in. She's always trying to act like Doris Day in that Pillow Talk movie (which she watches at least twice a week, she's on her second video copy after wearing out the first one).

Of course, Dad takes a sip of his drink before saying hello or anything.

"How's the cocktail?" says Mom, hopefully.

"Perfect!" He makes an exaggerated lip-smacking sound and sets the glass down. "How's my girls?" he says, although he doesn't expect an answer. "I'm sure glad to be home." He throws his briefcase on the sideboard and proceeds to give Mom this big, disgusting suck-kiss.

"Not in front of the children, please," I say, not looking away from the television.

"Well, well, well," says Dad. "No hello for your poor old dad? Is that the way to be, Miss Grump?"

"Hi, Dad."

"Where's Stevie?"

"Upstairs playing one of those new computer games you gave him for his birthday," says Mom, loosening Dad's tie. "He's just as sweet as a peach."

"Actually," I say, "The Peach is drooling over some foreign website he found that shows naked girls tied up with their legs spread," I say. They both ignore me.

"What's that, Princess?"

"Nothing, Dad."

"Miss Gina has been surly all day," says Mom. "Maybe you can talk to her while I get your supper."

Dad picks up his drink and plops down next to me on the couch with a big sigh and slap of his knee. "What's all this I hear about surly, Princess?" he says. "Boyfriend problems? That Derrick character?"

"Pete, Dad. His name is Pete." Pete didn't call me tonight.

"How's a dad supposed to keep 'em straight when he's got a cookie of a daughter like you?"

"And Derrick was not my boyfriend. We just went to the freshman mixer together and that was a year and a half ago."

"Supper!" says Mom in that ridiculous singsong voice.

"Looks delicious," says Dad, bellying up to the TV tray. Dad gets frozen dinners for supper. But they're supposed to be the good kind. Stouffers, which Mom buys in bulk from the Stouffer's outlet store; or Marie Callander, which are supposedly so expensive she only buys them if she has a coupon and they're on sale. I die at the checkout, as if it's not bad enough with everyone staring at Her Royal Boneliness (don't ask me why she doesn't wear clothes). And then she's got those stupid coupons. I'll never clip a coupon as long as I live.

Whether Marie Callander's is expensive or not, it still just looks like frozen food to me. Mom always puts it on a plate, tries to make it look like real food or something. And she even has a wilted parsley sprig on there today. How pathetic.

"Tell me all about work, Darling," says Mom. "Any news on that Project Forward?" She's scratching her sternum like she always does. Habit. Drives me crazy.

"Project Forward," says Dad, "is just another way of saying 'lay-offs.'"

"I know, Honey," she says. "What I mean is, do you think you'll be effected? Your department?" She's a regular Ms. Working World Savvy. Doesn't it occur to her that they've had this same conversation about a hundred times?

"I hope not. But you never know. Rumor is the Midwest Office will take a real trimming. Although I don't know how they'll do it. They've already farmed out accounting and graphic arts. In sales, we've been getting by with a skeleton staff since God knows. What else can they take away? All the secretaries and support staff are long gone. We're down to bare bones as it is."

Everything stops.

Dad's fork clatters onto his plate. It's dead silent except for the canned laughter from the TV (Gilligan's Island, Nick at Nite).

"Jeanette," he says, "I'm sorry. I didn't mean to-"

Mom's lower lip starts to tremble.

I start to grin.

"I just wasn't thinking, that's all," pleads Dad. "Wasn't thinking."

Tears well up in Mom's eyes. She stands and backs away from the couch.

"Jeanette? Honey?" says Dad. She turns and runs from the room, her head buried in her hands. "Please—it's been a long day, that's all. Jeanette?"

Mom bolts up the stairs, sobbing. Metacarpals aren't very good when it comes to muffling noise. Her door slams.

Dad shakes his head, sinks into the couch and sighs a big, apologetic sigh to no one in particular. "This," he says, "is precisely why I tell you kids never to mention your mother's condition."

I turn back to the television and act like I'm laughing at Gilligan and the Skipper dressed up as girls.

* * *

I've been screwing Pete for almost four months. It's not like we started right away, we've been dating for seven months total. And man, were we ready. Both of us. Sometimes I think I wanted it more than Pete. I could hardly wait. You'd think that once you did it, there would be some relief. Just the opposite. Now sex is all I think about all the time, even more than before. We do it every chance we get. In his room with his parents downstairs having drinks (which they call "cocktails" just like my parents), in the back of his parent's minivan at the Memphis Triple Drive-in, in our basement in the paint room where no one ever goes (it stinks in there but we don't care). Basically, all Pete and I need is a two-foot by six-foot area (we've gotten by with less—a lot less) and about six minutes.

* * *

I'm trying to concentrate on this totally cool Kid Rock portrait I'm drawing (I'm copying my History of Rock CD cover, which I think is cool even if Mom did make exchange the 'explicit' CD for the 'edited' version) when I hear that telltale pencil-on-wood tapping on my door. Mom.

"What?" I say.

"May I come in?"

"Fine." What else can I do?

Mom's got that we've-got-to-have-a-little-talk look on her face. She's carrying a bunch of books. This ought to be good. "It's time you and I had a little talk," she says, perching on the edge of my bed.

"What kind of talk?"

"Can we please stop with the surly?"

"I am not surly."

She puts one of the books on top of her femurs, The Venus Flytrap, Why You Need to Talk Sex With Your Daughter. There are yellow stick-um flags fringing all three edges of the book. This ought to be very, very good.

"Let's talk," I say. The cover of the book has a mom and girl holding hands in a field of daisies.

"Gina, I know you're probably embarrassed, but you and I need to discuss this."

"I'm totally not embarrassed, Mom," I say. She hates it when I do this, act like we're on some My So-Called Life rerun. She's fidgeting already.

"How long have you and Peter been dating?"

"Seven months." He finally called last night, after I went upstairs. Mom about had a conniption, like it was some big deal, him calling after ten.

"Seven months," she says, opening up the book to one of the marked pages. "That's a long time." She clears her throat and starts reading. "Due to a number of external as well as internal influences, girls between the ages of fourteen and seventeen feel enormous pressure to become sexually active." She gives me a meaningful look. "'Girls with low self-esteem are particularly vulnerable.' Which is what I wanted to talk about, Gina, your self-esteem."

"My self esteem."

"That's right, Honey. Your self-esteem."

"What about my self esteem?"

Confusion crosses her face. Mom's always like this, particularly during 'talks.' Ask any question, no matter how tame, and she freaks. She clears her throat again and clasps her hands together, making that dry/scraping sound that is worse than fingernails on a blackboard. "Well, the important thing is that you understand that your father and I, hmm, just one minute." She flutters through the book, "Oh, right here, yes, 'It is of the utmost importance that both parents express their mutual approval and respect for their daughter and that the concept of the sexual relationship is shown in a positive light at all times.'" She smiles. "Is that a little more clear?"

"Sure, Mom," I say, "I think you and Dad show sex in a very positive light."

"Really, Honey?" she says, brightening.

"Sure," I say, "what, with you and Dad and your nightly thing."

She knows exactly what I'm talking about, it's another of those subjects you never bring up, like the fact she's a skeleton. I'd call it sex, but I'm not sure that's right. Whatever it is, it's the same nearly every night. Believe me, I know. I've had to listen to it since before I can remember. It starts at about ten forty-five. First they talk for about five minutes, but not normal talk. It's really short sentences, or maybe just one word, with long pauses in between. They talk too low for me to hear exactly what they're saying, but the tone seems weird. Then there's the bed-squeaking. That only goes for about a minute. Then there's Dad's big groan, which is pretty predictable. Of course, that's when you'd figure it's over, but it's not. Because the next thing you hear is Mom, making some sort of muffled growl noise. And right after that, there's this awful clattering, like someone took a box of scrap wood and dumped it on the floor. It's really loud. I bury my head in pillows when I know it's coming, but I can hear it still. I hate that part the most.

Mom is huffing and staring at me, her face crimson. She's either mad or embarrassed. Or both. "That, young lady," she says, "is enough."

She's mad.

"What goes on between your father and me is none of your business. You might think you're old enough, but believe me, you're not. You have no idea. You're not even old enough to begin to understand. Some things take time," Man, she is steamed. "A great deal of time. And if you ever, ever, bring up this topic again, there will be consequences."

She says consequences in a real specific way. I don't care.

"These books, incidentally are not library books, but ones I've purchased especially for you so you may refer to them as needed. And I expect you to take a good, hard look at them," she says. "Have you ever considered the word hereditary, the concept of it, Gina?"

"No," I say even though I've heard the word ten zillion times.

"That doesn't surprise me in the least," she says, handing me the stack of books. "We'll get to that another day. I think we've both had enough of this for now."

"Uh, Mom?" I can't let her off the hook this easy.

"Yes?" she says with trepidation. "What is it?"

"I have a question."

"Fine then. What is it?"

"Is there really such a thing as a vaginal climax?"

"A what?" she says.

"A vaginal climax, you know, in opposed to a clitoral climax."

"If this is just another attempt at being cute," she says, flipping her hair over her clavicle, and, in the process, getting a number of strands caught in the web of bones that is her hand. "Ow!," she screeches. She tries to shake her hand free, but it just makes the whole thing worse. "Listen," she says, holding her tethered hand in careful relation to her head, "Why don't you look up your clitoris in the book? Okay, Miss smarty-pants?"

"Yeah, Mom, sure," I say. "That's just what I'll do. I'll look it up in the book."

"Fine, then."

"And maybe later we could talk about different sexual positions. Okay Mom?"

"Enough already, Gina," she says, wincing as she gets the other hand involved.

"Like the wheelbarrow. Ever heard of the wheelbarrow, Mom? When the guy gets the girls feet like this." I hold my hands out, but she's already halfway out the door.

* * *

I knew I was in trouble by the third day I was late. The third day. My boobs felt different, hard and really sensitive. My bra hurt. Taking a shower killed. So it was off to the Discount Drug Mart. $14.98 later, I was in the bathroom, holding up the little stick with the two pink lines.

Preggers.

* * *

"Gina!" yells Mom from the garage.

I don't answer; just bury myself deeper in my nest of pillows and blankets. It doesn't matter. It's not even a full minute before my bedroom door bursts open and Mom storms in.

"Now this is the last straw," she says, holding up a stick that, at first glance, just appears to be an extension of her metacarpals. Then I see it's the pregnancy test stick. What? She went through the garbage?

"Suppose, young lady," she says, "you tell me what this is."

"I don't know, Mom. What do you think it is?" I say. "A swizzle stick?"

"Very funny," she says. "What is important, is the fact that there are two pink lines here and not one!"

I don't say anything.

"You and your vaginal climax. I'll bet you thought you were some kind of comedienne! I don't think you realize what you've gotten yourself into. I don't think you understand. This is no small potatoes young lady. No game for a smarty-pants teenager. This can take everything from you. Everything. You have no idea. None.

"This means more than diapers and peanut butter and jelly sandwiches! You're entirely too selfish. I can only imagine what would fall on me. And I won't have it. None of it. After all, it's not as though I haven't done enough for you."

I give her the flat, bored look she hates.

"I'm too angry right now, Gina. Just too angry. We'll talk about this later. We'll make arrangements later," she says, her hand on the doorknob. "And believe me, young lady, we will be making arrangements. Now get yourself out of bed and ready for church. We're leaving in fifteen minutes." She leaves, slamming the door behind her.

I get up, strip my clothes off and lie back down on the bed, naked. I stare at the ceiling, put my hands on my belly.

Arrangements.

What was that old Madonna video? The one with Madonna and the short blond hair trying to look a lot younger than she really was, like about sixteen, about my age. "I'm gonna keep my baaaybeee!" she sang to her TV-video father. Miss Defiant. Right to Lifers had to love that. Now I'm giggling.

I get up to look at myself in the mirror.

These boobs may hurt, but they sure look good.

Could my body actually do this? The belly part, the hips. Those parts seem so full of life. Even my hair seems thicker. I've always wanted thicker hair, L'Oreal-TV-commercial hair.

But then I look at my arms. They're thinner. And my legs. Just the tinniest bit thinner. You almost can't tell. Is this my imagination? My cheeks are flushed. I feel good.

My hands too, they're bonier, the hollows between my knuckles are deeper. Who needs any excess? I should be glad. I'm strong, healthy. I've got everything I need.

And nothing more.

THE END

Public Radio
John Sheppard

I met a starchy gal in my art history class.

She saw me nodding off and decided that I was just as bored as she was. I hadn't slept in two days. My graveyard shift job was kicking my ass. "I know," she whispered to me. "This class is a drag."

I woke up and said, "Did I miss something?"

There were 200 of us packed into an auditorium in what used to be a junior high before the university acquired it. The wooden seats were all too small, the little flip-up desk squeezed in on me. The lights were turned down and a 35-mm slideshow of masterworks was clicking along. The professor had a jolly, trilling English accent that made him seem as if he was about to start jumping up and down with spastic joy. The class ran from 7:30 p.m. until 10 p.m. Then I had to go to work. My little motorcycle was parked outside.

"In this class?" she went. "Not very likely." I recognized her voice.

"You do the news on the public radio station, don't you?"

She smiled.

"Suzanne Smith, right?"

"That's right," she said.

That seemed to be enough new information for me. I slipped back into my fugue state for a few moments.

"And you are...?"

It took me a second. I looked at her. Jesus, she was strange looking. Like a living mannequin, a doll come to life. No, not life. She didn't seem to be alive, merely animate. The lights came back up. I don't think there was anything about her appearance that was natural. Her hair was obviously colored and sprayed into shape. Her eyebrows had been plucked off and replaced by grease-pencil lines. Her nose didn't belong on her face. Each nail on each finger was honed and glazed. Her teeth were unnaturally white and straight. Her breasts were perfectly round. She was aerobically thin and waxed and hadn't a mark on her. She was as airbrushed as a Playboy centerfold. "Pepper," I said.

"Pepper? That's all?"

"Um, Buzz," I said.

"Buzz Pepper," she said, staring at me with her taxidermy eyes.

"Bingo," I said.

Everybody was getting up. We'd been dismissed. We walked out together, not saying anything. I put on my backpack and helmet and got on my motorcycle. "You own a motorcycle," she said.

"Barely," I said. I revved it to life and rode away.

The next week she sat down next to me again and kept me awake for three hours with chatter about her evil roommate Janey and the perils of being radio famous. She lived in the coed dorm across the street. I was surprised to hear that she got paid for her gig, that it was a work-study job. I had no idea. And me with my Pell grant and rotten overnight greasy job. "Are you going to the Oingo Boingo concert at the Bandshell on Friday? It's free," she said.

Was she asking me out? "I don't know. Why? Did you want to go together?"

"Yeah! Super!" she said too loudly.

The professor, ever happily English, congratulated her on her enthusiasm for the class. A low roar of laughter. He handed back our essays, then the class ended. I squinted at the board, way down front, trying to figure out which chapters had to be read for next time. I felt myself ready to vomit for a second, then the nausea receded and I felt fine again.

"You got an 'A'?" Suzanne asked, looking at my paper. A blue, felt-penned 'A' stained the front of the essay.

"Yeah," I said.

"You want to study together? Maybe you can help me out," she said.

I was beginning to get suspicious of her. Women like her didn't talk to me. Still, she was a woman, in sort of punched-out-of-plastic way. "Sure," I said, getting up. "I'm free Tuesdays and Thursdays."

She wrote her phone number on the front of the essay with a Mont Blanc pen. Then she signed it, "Best wishes..." She was practicing to be a celebrity. She followed me out to my motorcycle again. "You'll have to give me a ride one of these days," she said.

"Oh, I'll give you a ride all right," I said, before I could stop myself. I flushed with embarrassment from behind the helmet's faceshield. Then I thought, "Fuck her if she can't take a joke," and rode off.

The new graveyard waitress was Dee Dee. "You have a nice ass," she said as I squished a burger on the grill.

I was taken aback for a beat. "I hadn't noticed," I replied.

"I'll take a picture of it one of these nights," she said. "I own a Polaroid. I'm not afraid to use it." Some southern drawls sounded like banjos. Hers was a mandolin.

My brother, the assistant manager Sparky, chose this moment to awake from his slumber and come lurching out of the backroom. He plopped himself down at the counter. "Coffee," he said, his voice cracking. The stool squealed.

Dee Dee and I both rushed to get the coffee. We met at the machine. She smelled nice, especially for someone who had to work at a hash house. I mostly smelled like rancid beef, no matter how many showers I took. I stood next to her and felt myself horribly attracted to her, suddenly. It swept over me just like that. I studied her face with her black dancing eyes and full lips. I took a step back. This was a real woman, not like the radio girl from class.

The muzak piped in from the speakers above sounded familiar. It was "Rock Lobster."

The phone on the wall rang. I picked up the receiver. "Athens," I said.

"I'm calling from the Pepper bunker," my sister Sissy said. "Do you read me? Over."

"They're fighting at 3 a.m.?" I asked.

"Not exactly. It ended a couple of hours ago," she said. I leaned against the wall listening to her, not breathing. "Are you there? Of course you are. Hey, listen. Remember our two little cousins, Barb's kids? This is funny. The girl comes out in the garage where I'm hiding from all those weirdos, and offers to kiss me on the lips for a dollar. I said, 'Get the fuck out of here!' So she smiles at me, torches up a roach, and we share it. That's all right.

"But listen. The boy, he's what? Ten? Barb tossed his security blanket in the trash, decided that he was going to become a man while on vacation. We're all sitting up watching the late night movie when he comes wandering in the room. He's wet his pajamas. But this is the good part. He was holding a dirty pair of Barb's undies on his face with one hand, and sucking the thumb on the other hand."

"You called me up in the middle of the night—"

"So Barb digs the nasty old blanket out of the trash. Cool, huh? Gives it to him. It has coffee grounds on it, but he doesn't care."

"What's going on?" I asked her. "Are you okay?"

"I think Buster's going to take off on us," Sissy said, her voice beginning to shake. "I'm not sure I can handle it."

"You can handle it," I said. Buster probably wasn't going anywhere, I figured. Not when there's still food around the dump. "If you want, you can come up and live with Sparky and me. It's not a problem."

"You are such an idiot!" Sissy shouted.

"What did I say?"

"You are beyond dumb!" She was boiling. "I'm going to be stuck with Mom! Don't you care about that? She's going to be a basket case! Do you ever listen? Do you ever listen to what anyone has to say? I'm so sick of you I could puke!" She slammed the phone down in my ear.

Sparky said, "You haven't cut up any tomatoes yet, have you?"

"No," I said.

"Better get on it. I'll take the grill," he said.

I went in the back and cut up tomatoes.

It was a dead night. Sparky sent Dee Dee home and we were sitting there on the stools, staring blankly around the restaurant. I got up and made more coffee. Sparky went over to the drivethrough to count the cash there again. I looked up and saw a stunning woman sitting at the counter. She was young, maybe 20, with a poofy mane of blond hair and a beautiful shape, from what I could see. She was in a leotard. I brought over some coffee.

"I've been cleaning," she said. "Trying to get my apartment clean." I could see a new shiner on her left eye now that I was standing in front of her.

"How's the cleaning going?" I asked her.

"Slow," she said. She folded her arms in front of her on the counter and rested her chin on top of them. She looked up at me. The eye was swelling shut. "Aren't you going to ask me about my eye?"

"What happened to your eye?"

"My boyfriend hit me," she said.

"Bad housekeeping?" I asked.

"Something like that," she said.

"Can I get you anything? A beefsteak for your eye?"

"You can talk to me," she said. "I've seen you in here when I get off work. I have to drive past here. You look sad."

"I'm tired, that's all," I said.

"Don't kid a kidder," she said. She sat up and stared down at her coffee. She had huge tits for someone her size.

"You're a dancer?" I asked her.

"At Trader's," she said. "Don't knock it. It pays the bills."

"I didn't say anything," I said.

"You got that look on your face though," she said.

"Don't mind me," I said.

"Can you make me something?" she asked. "I'm too tired to decide. I left my money in the car. I'll be right back." She slipped off the barstool and walked to the door. She was wearing only the flimsy red leotard. It was cut high on her hips in a way that left her tanned bottom mostly bare. She probably saw me watching her in the reflection off the glass front door. She glanced back at me with her one good eye. I was turned on and sad and disgusted with myself all at the same time. She had no shoes on and walked across our beaten and littered parking lot barefoot.

I rushed over to Sparky. "Do you see her?" I asked him.

"Yeah," he said, staring out the window at her hungrily.

"So I'm not imagining her," I said.

"No," he said. She opened her car door, a rusty Buick, and leaned in reaching for her purse. "Jesus," Sparky whispered. He shook his head. "Graveyard shift."

I walked back over to my spot at the counter. I had a raging hard-on and hated myself for it. My grease-stained cook's apron covered it up, mostly. I peeked down. Yeah: Mostly.

"Did you get a good look?" she asked me.

I blushed and turned my head away.

"That's okay," she said. "Everyone gets a good look."

I saw her smiling at me out of the corner of my eye.

"You didn't make me anything," she said.

It was true. "Chicken fingers," I said. "And fries." I dropped in the chicken fingers and some fries. I hit the timer. The fresh grease sparked and bubbled.

She opened her little vinyl purse and took out her makeup kit. "Woo-ee," she said, mostly to herself in her tiny mirror. "That's quite a shiner." She tried to pat on some makeup, but it wasn't doing any good. She finally gave up.

The alarm went off and I pulled the basket up out of the fryer, shook some grease off, and dumped the contents in a waxpaper-lined wicker basket. "Sweet and sour sauce?" I asked her.

She smirked. "Yeah. Sweet and sour." She kind of chuckled. I gave her three little buckets of dipping sauce.

I made her a cherry cola, with an extra squirt of cherry syrup, and brought it over. "It's like a mixed drink," I said. I handed her a paper-wrapped straw. The tips of her fingers touched mine for a moment, but it didn't feel the way I wanted it to. I wanted electricity. I wanted to go find her boyfriend and beat the living shit out of him. For all the good that would do.

"Thanks," she said.

We sat together mostly silently while she masticated her food ever so slowly. She never touched her coffee. I took it away. After she finished the rest, I took the glass and basket away. She tapped her red chipped fingernails on the counter. "I guess I should go home," she said finally.

"Maybe you shouldn't," I said.

"Maybe," she said. She slipped off the stool and stood there in front of the counter, sadly beautiful. "Your floor is cold," she said.

I leaned over the counter and stared at her pretty, dirty feet. I peered in her good eye.

"How much do I owe you?" she asked me.

"Don't worry about it," I said.

"I don't want you to get in trouble," she said, opening the purse again.

"Please don't," I said.

She snapped shut her purse. "Okay," she said. She beamed at me for a moment and the smile faded away. She padded out of the restaurant. I watched her get into her car and drive off.

A few minutes later, a bum came in and asked what time I took out the trash. I offered him fresh food if he mopped the floor. He glared at me as if I'd spat in his face and stormed out. This happened, with a different bum, just about every night.

I went to the dorm to pick Suzanne up for our date. I couldn't have been less interested in her, but I felt somehow obligated. I walked in on a dorm party that was getting out of control. Raw oysters on the half-shell were being served out of a big metal washtub filled with ice and cans of beer. I watched a topless girl run past chasing a hooting boy waving a t-shirt over his head. It was crowded in that elbows and hips way that parties get. The real "Rock Lobster" was playing off a reel-to-reel in the corner, blasting out of big speakers. "Down, down, down!" the B-52's ordered, and most of the people in the room slumped to the floor. I took the opportunity to step around and over them. "Suzanne!" I shouted, just in case she was in the mass of people crowding the foyer, dayroom and the hallways. No response.

I found her door and rapped loudly on it. It swung open. Suzanne was wearing a black cocktail dress, heels and dark stockings. Now she really did look like a mannequin. She grasped my hands, pulled me into the room and quickly shut the door. "How do I look?" she asked, spinning on a heel.

"Um," I said.

"Overdressed?" she asked. She twirled for me again, then gave me a blank news anchor smile. "I guess I'm overdressed," she said brightly. She traced the "DK" on my shirt with a fingertip. Very coquettish. "What's that stand for?"

"You probably don't want to know," I said.

She sighed. "Okay. Be mysterious!"

I scanned the room. There was a bed on either side against the walls. In the middle, two desks faced two bureaus with mirrors. The mirrors were abutted and fairly tall, so each girl could have about eight feet of privacy. Suzanne walked over to her side of the room and asked me to sit on her roommate's bed for a moment so she could change. On the backside of Suzanne's mirror were little posters of the Cure and Duran Duran. Underwear was draped all over. The drawers in the bureau were ajar. There was a bit of a crack between the two mirrors through which I could see Suzanne wandering back and forth. She kicked her shoes off and they flew across the room. "T-shirt and jeans, huh?" she shouted in a standard, upbeat voice. "I can do that! I bet you think I can't, but I can!" I heard her dress unzip and found myself peeping through the crack. She caught me and shrieked, "No peeking!" and giggled. I picked up a pair of her roommate's panties and spun t hem on my index finger. Then I used the elastic band to shoot them a yard or two away. I studied a Polaroid of what I presumed to be the girl's boyfriend. It was shoved in the bottom of the mirror. It was the guy I'd seen earlier running through the hallway. She'd written "Brad" in felt tip pen in the whitespace underneath and drawn stars and hearts next to his name. I flipped open a notebook on the desk. Janie. She'd written her name in huge, bubbly letters across the first page. She'd dotted the 'i' with a star and colored in the letters with fragrant magic markers. She'd go far in life, this Janie.

It sounded like a buffalo stampede in the hallway. I dropped the notebook to her desk just in time to see Janie and Brad make their entrance. "Awesome!" Brad shouted.

Suzanne let loose a yip. "Shut the door!" she shouted, with actual emotion.

Brad stood there instead. "Mmm, mmm," he said, and slapped his topless girlfriend on the ass. Her little tits jiggled. She swept her arms up to cover them. "Aerobics?"

I heard a zipper zip. I came round the corner and watched Suzanne lace up her Keds. She sat up and I saw she was wearing a Loverboy t-shirt. She checked herself in the mirror, primping her dyed and reconditioned hair and smacked her lips. She grabbed my hand and said, "Let's go." She pulled me out the still-open door. I turned and saw Janie and Brad going at it on Janie's bed, Janie giggling and Brad grunting. Young love.

We had to stop at the Orange and Brew before heading out to the Bandshell so Suzanne could network and introduce me to people from the radio station that I could give a shit about. I shook a lot of cold, soft, boneless hands. After we managed to get out of there, we stumbled through the dark. At the Bandshell, we found an Australian band on stage opening for the Boingos. The Australian band featured a shaven-headed dude who caterwauled nicely and would take time in between songs to demand that we free all the people in our prisons.

Oingo Boingo was okay, I guess. I've never had that total animus against New Wave that other punks had. I figured that at least it wasn't total trash. You know, like Loverboy. The Boingos all wore labcoats and sang their famous song, among others. Suzanne kept jumping up and down and clapping her hands like an idiot. Then she'd grab my arm and shake me. I thought, "I've got to start eating more. Gain some damn weight."

The concert over, we marched along with the rest of the drones away from the field. I felt a wave of depression wash over me and my mouth crept shut. "I'd like to see your apartment," Suzanne said. She grabbed my forearm with both hands. I stiffened for a moment, then relaxed. She didn't seem to notice or care.

I shrugged. I checked my watch. "I have to go to work in another hour."

"Can you skip work tonight?" she asked.

"No," I said. "It's a Friday. We'll be busy."

"The Athens isn't that far from the dorm. Take me with you and I'll walk back," she said.

"I don't want you to get raped or anything," I said.

"Aww," she said, like what I said was sweet. She wouldn't take no for an answer, and I'd run out of fight. She made me stand next to the motorcycle when we got back to her dorm. She ran upstairs and came back with a helmet. "Janie owns a scooter," she said by way of explanation.

"I've got to go back to my apartment to change. I'll show you my etchings," I said.

"You have etchings?" she asked.

I sighed.

Then I thought, I never told her I work at the Athens. Here comes a wave of paranoia to give the depression some flavor. I started up my little motorcycle, clicked down the back footpegs and she sat down behind me. She wrapped her ghostly white plastic arms around my waist and hugged herself to my back. It made steering extra hard, but it did give me a semi.

My roommate Ciro was sitting up having a cocktail when we walked in. He poured some Bartles & James from the bottle into a wine glass and sipped daintily. He was wearing a Members Only jacket, sleeves shoved halfway up to the elbow, and a pink polo shirt with the collar turned up. "Care for some?" he asked us. A little smile crept across his lips when he saw what I'd brought home. "Who's this winsome young lady?"

"Here are those etchings," I said. I leaned over and flipped her a sketchbook I'd left on the floor, then went back to my room to change for work.

When I came back out, I found the two of them enjoying some high-toned laughter along. Ciro was pretending to like my dog, who sat staring at the two of them like they were going to give him a cube of the foul, marbled, semi-solid cheese they were gnawing on. They were using my sketchbook as a coaster. "What the fuck!" I went. I picked up both glasses, careful not to spill them on the sketchbook, and tossed them at the wall behind Ciro. Neither glass broke. The two sat in stunned silence. Bear discretely trotted away. I picked up the sketchbook and took it back to my room. Only one drawing, the top one, had been damaged. Those fuckers. I gave Bear a pat on the head to let him know that I wasn't angry at him.

Ciro called down the hall, "Are you upset?"

I came storming back out and glared at them. But the rage had left me. You can't pet a dog and still be angry. "Take her home for me, will you?"

"Sure," Ciro said with an oleaginous grin.

I put on my helmet and stomped out the door.

I don't know how long I'd been asleep in Carleton 100. Monday morning. Must be Health and Human Nutrition. This frat boy was shaking me awake, stagewhispering, "Dude! Dude!"

"Wha-" I gurgled out. I sat up and rubbed the sleep from my sticky eyes. I was seated about halfway up in the vast auditorium.

A graduate assistant had taken the mike up front. "Doctor Howard..." he choked out. "Um." He took a while to compose himself, turning his back to us. I stuck my thumb up and closed one eye, covering up the grad student completely. I dropped the thumb and opened my eyes wide, then shut them, then wider, then shut. "Class is cancelled," the pasty little grad student finally said. He dropped the mike on the podium and left.

"Awesome," the frat boy commented. He scooped up his books and scrammed.

I took it as an sign that I should skip the rest of my classes and go home. And sleep.

Public radio newsreader Suzanne told me most of the sordid story behind Doctor Howard's death. Other parts of the story come from rumors and cop gossip I heard from my place behind the counter on graveyard shift.

Doctor Howard liked boys. Teenage boys. Hell, he probably would have liked me if I'd sat a little closer to the podium. He picked up a teenage prostitute on University Avenue, near the Star Garage, a popular punk rock club. The prosty caught a load of the Volvo and decided that three wouldn't be a crowd. He suggested to the good doctor that they pick up his boyfriend and make it an evening. They did so.

They went back to his place and saw more evidence of the good life.

Doctor Howard not only liked boys, he liked boys who were willing to tie him up, duct tape a golf ball in his mouth and inform him how bad he was. The lecture about badness was to be reenforced with a whip. Prosty and Boyfriend were very willing to do this. Then they burnt him with cigarettes. Then they found a steam iron and burnt him with that. Then he choked on the golf ball and died. Whoops.

Well, they could hardly be blamed for deciding that a dead man didn't really need his wallet, could they? And his credit cards? And his fancy Bang and Olafson stereo? And his big screen TV? And his Volvo?

The boys took off the tape and untied him. They sat him up in a chair. They crossed his legs. They sat him up again. He was dressed up in some fancy bondage gear. They decided they didn't need the fancy bondage gear.

They loaded the loot into the Volvo and went for a spin. They used his credit cards all over town and bought all sorts of fancy crap for themselves. They set up his electronics in their crummy crash pad, and someone broke in almost immediately and stole them. The cops busted a fence, found the good doctor's crap and squeezed the fence until he squealed. The cops busted the thief, who led them to the crash pad. This all happened very quickly.

The boys talked and talked after credit card receipts were waved in their faces. It was an accident! Tough shit, boys. Florida has the chair.

After Suzanne finished up with her delightful rendition of What Happened to Dear Doctor Howard, she spent the second and third hours of our Wednesday class peppering me with questions about Ciro. Is he single? Is he divorced? Does he own that darling little car he drives? What does his father do for a living? How much does he make? How old is Ciro? Why is Ciro back in college at the grand old age of 27?

Fuck if I know.

I was glad, though, when she didn't follow me out the door. She was beginning to give me a brain hemorrhage.

I puttered off to work. Wednesday night was becoming extra slow now, deep into the semester, so Sparky had given himself the night off. After 11, it would be just me and Dee Dee. I was a little nervous about this. She'd started a new custom of blowing in my ear each time she delivered an order.

Dee Dee was there when I arrived, a good hour before our shift began. She sat next to me at the counter. Her breasts seemed to be holstered this evening under her white work shirt, which I took to be a good sign. Everything else about her screamed trouble.

We sat together for a while, not saying much. I tried not to look at her. She bumped my knee with hers and smiled at me, then coaxed me into a conversation about my family, scrupulously avoiding talking about hers, I noted some years later. In retrospect.

"No wonder you look so sad all the time," she said.

"I don't," I said.

"You do," she said. "You're like a nice gold watch that somebody lost on the beach. All someone needs to do is clean you and polish you and rewind you, and you'll be like new."

"It's that easy," I said. I gritted my teeth and rolled my eyes.

"Sure, sweety," she said. Then she talked for a while about an old railroad bridge that caught fire in Micanopy, the little town south of Gainesville. She was a volunteer firefighter down there.

Dee Dee took my hand. The kitchen ticked and hissed. Water plopped on the empty nickel sink from a leak in the ceiling. She led me all the way into the back of the restaurant, next to the shelves filled with industrial-sized cans of beans and PVC buckets of kosher dills. In seemingly one motion, her skirt dropped to the floor and she pulled her white work shirt over her head. She stepped out of the pile of clothes and stood there in front of me wearing a sheer, white one-piece lingerie thing. She asked me, "Do you like this?" She reached down and showed me where it unsnapped at the crotch.

"Yes," I said.

I was a veteran of industrial kitchen seduction, having met my first girlfriend that way. So I vibrated with appreciation, but remained non-committal. "Yes," I said to Dee Dee after she showed me her delicious body, "I like. But not here. Not in a kitchen."

She smiled at me and slipped her shirt back on. "You sure, sugar?" she asked me. "We're here all night." She turned around and flipped her shirt up, baring her bottom at me. "Your loss, honey." Then she put her skirt back on.

For years after that day, the Athens was where most of our couplings would take place. But I wanted a better start to this than what Dee Dee had in mind, a quick and dirty next to the kosher dills.

We went back out front and sat on pivoting stools at the counter. She told me the sad story of her life up until age 18, living with her mother, then being taken away at nine. She spent most of the next ten years in foster care and was molested, and it was all too horrible to listen to in the middle of the night, as the clock ticked slowly on. I held her as she cried at one point. She felt oddly light to me, as if her bones were filled with air. She pulled herself into my lap, spinning the stool around towards the dining room. I reached behind me and dug a wad of napkins out of the shiny dispenser. She blew her nose loudly, like an elephant's cry. The whites of her eyes were all red and puffy. Her makeup came off in streams. I pulled out more napkins and wiped her face. She was very pale underneath all the makeup, with tiny blue veins underneath her cheeks as delicate as a spider's web.

The drivethrough buzzer went off. She slid off my lap and smiled at me in a kind of dopey, childish way. I walked over to the drivethrough window and took the order. "What's the difference between a lime freezer and a lemon freezer?" the drunk lady in the Toyota asked over the crackling speaker. Her headlights were badly adjusted and one was blinding me. A freezer was a milkshake with fruit flavoring in it.

"One's green and the other's yellow," I replied.

"I bet you think that's funny," the lady said.

"Are you kidding me? It's hilarious," I said.

"Lime," she said after a long crackling pause. "That's it."

"An excellent choice, madam," I said. "Please drive through."

Dee Dee was already mixing it up. I took the lady's money. Toyota lady had a nose rippled with burst blood vessels, and pinhole eyes on either side of it. She could have been 40 or 80. The car exuded a sickeningly sweet stink, like a nectarine had rolled under a seat and rotted. Dee Dee poured the green sludge into a waxpaper cup, lidded it and handed me a paper-wrapped straw along with the cup.

"Have a pleasant morning," I said, handing it to Toyota lady.

"Screw you, you young punk," the lady replied. She turned her head and squinted through the windshield. Her tires barked as she skidded away, across the filthy parking lot and out into the empty street.

That was the bar rush for the evening.

I walked over to Dee Dee at the soda fountain. I placed my hands on her shoulders and her hands gripped my hips and pulled me in. I felt her soft neck and tiny earlobes, sans earrings. I paused for a moment when our lips were about to meet and tasted her breath. It was sweet. A few hours later, we left work in a sore-lipped ecstasy.

I invited Dee Dee to the Halloween party we were throwing in our apartment. She promised to come, but she didn't show. Later, she gave me what would become the standard excuse. That there was a fire in Micanopy that she was required to help extinguish. It would take me another year to get suspicious of this excuse. Micanopy wasn't very big. You could walk from one end to the other without breaking a sweat. The whole town, I finally reasoned, must have burnt down and been rebuilt several times.

I wanted to make love to Dee Dee on that Halloween. I ached for her sitting there in my makeshift costume. I was dressed as a bum. Considering the state of my wardrobe, I made a pretty convincing one. I wore my cousin Dougie's old army jacket, my worst pair of jeans and a pair of scratched up sunglasses someone had ditched in the restaurant one night. I rubbed some lotion in my hair and made it stick out all over the place. I kept watch on the door, nursing a stale beer, certain that Dee Dee would show up any moment. We'd hang with the gang for a reasonable time, then retire discretely back to my room where I'd ravish her across the top bunk. I'd even gone to the trouble of putting freshly laundered sheets on my love rack.

Sparky sat in the middle of the living room working on equations, his math books spread out in front of him. He was not dressed as anything, except as Sparky. Sparky's girlfriend Cheri was dressed as a chanteuse in a slinky black dress. Ciro's girlfriend Bug was dressed as a bee, with wings that got in everyone's way. She'd added a wand to the costume. Maybe she was supposed to be a magic bee. I didn't ask. Bear wandered around eating things that fell on the floor. Albino walked in the door dressed as himself. Then he pulled a black party mask out of his pearl-buttoned front pocket and put it on.

"What are you supposed to be?" Bug asked him. She waved her wand around and tapped him on the chest with it.

"The lone gunman," Albino replied.

"Where's your gun?" Bug asked him.

"I'm too much of a gentleman to answer that question," Albino said.

And still no Dee Dee.

Ciro walked in all preppied up. He blew across his fingernails. Maybe he'd just had them done. He kissed Bug lightly on the cheek and went over to check out the fondue pot.

I walked over to him. "You got a smoke?" I asked him. "How 'bout some change?"

"Um," he went. He actually looked pretty nervous. He stabbed a piece of bread and dunked it in the pot.

"What time you taking the garbage out?" I asked him. "I'm hungry."

"I wish you wouldn't do that," Ciro said. He chewed on the piece of bread for a moment and swallowed while making a face.

"A quarter? A nickel? A dime? How 'bout a mint? You got a mint in your pocket?" I got good and close to him.

Suzanne the mannequin walked in, looked around and saw Ciro. She smiled over at him. She had on that black cocktail dress. She saw Cheri in pretty much the same getup and frowned a bit. She walked over to us.

"How about you, lady? You got any change?" I asked her. I took a loud sniff in her direction. "You smell real nice, lady. Real nice. Classy dame like you must have some change. Or a half-eaten sandwich in your little purse."

She recoiled from me nicely. "Is that you Buzz?" she said. "What are you supposed to be?"

Cheri announced that she was putting on a record. She pulled a record from a sleeve with a haunted house on it, flipped it once or twice, blew some dust off, then plopped it on the turntable and dropped the stylus down. "I've had this record since I was a little girl. It's funny as hell."

The record popped and crackled. Then a Karloff-like voice told us we were in Egypt. "You've discovered the tomb of Ramses the second." Blah, blah, blah. The mummy awakes, then seals "you" in the tomb, which is quickly running out of air. Then came the good part. This explorer is gasping for breath and clawing and screaming until, about three or four minutes later, he expires. Ciro went over to Bug about thirty seconds into all the gasping and clawing and screaming. He held her hand. "Ow!" Bug went. "You're hurting me!"

"Sorry," Ciro said. A brittle smile. A curt plea. "I think we should listen to something else, don't you?" He looked around the room at us as the guy on the record continued, fruitlessly, to attempt to escape from the mummy's tomb. "I don't like this record." He pulled Bug out of the apartment with him. We heard his car start up as the explorer gasped his last breath and collapsed on the tomb's floor.

I walked over and picked up Bug's wand. "Tinkerbee forgot her wand," I said.

"What was that all about?" Cheri asked the room.

Sparky looked up from his studies. "What?"

"I wonder how much I could get for this wand at the pawn shop?" I asked Albino. "What time do you take out your garbage?" On the stereo, "you" got trapped in a haunted house.

"Give it a rest," Albino said. He took off the mask.

Buster my father pulled through Gainesville on his way up to Ohio. He just showed up and presented himself, and left without telling us why he'd come or in what direction he was headed. He showed up at five-thirty in the morning while everyone else was sleeping off their drunks and Sparky was in bed.

"Let me in," Buster said, standing outside my door.

I could let him in or not. He wasn't paying my rent, and hadn't contributed a nickel to my college education, which he considered unworthwhile. Literature and philosophy and art are for faggots, said he.

I said, "Come on in," not bleary-eyed. I had the night off from my graveyard shift job and had taken the opportunity to begin a new painting. I'd spent the night hours after the party literally banging on a canvas, and the painting was beginning to take on some shape. Sometimes, when I couldn't get a painting working, I'd take the canvas out front and kick it around our parking lot.

Buster my father walked on in. Bear the dog growled at him, stood up.

"Sit, boy," I said.

"Jesus," Buster said, "most dogs like me."

"He was tied to a tree," I said. "And little black kids threw rocks at him, so he doesn't like black people."

"I'm not black," Buster said.

I'd seen pictures of his mother. She looked black, but was supposed to be dark Irish—whatever that is. I said, "He thinks you're black. Argue with the dog." Jerked a thumb towards the dog.

"Don't give me no lip, kid," Buster said.

"I'm just saying."

"Yeah," Buster said, veering toward squinty-eyed anger. "Keep it to yourself."

My mother told me how she and my uncle sneaked a peek at his driver's license once when she and Buster were dating back in the '50's. Buster came over to my grandparents' house to pick up Mom, and had to go to the bathroom. He left his wallet and car keys on the kitchen counter. Ralph said, "I'm curious about something." Mom knew exactly what he meant. They both grabbed at the wallet, Mom winning the struggle. Mom pulled out Buster's driver's license and he was listed as Caucasian. Mom's crush on Buster had to do with his resemblance to Harry Belafonte. Day-o.

Buster sat down on Albino's chair. Plop. There was a 50 percent chance he'd be able to get up. His back was that of an 80-year-old grandpa. It'd been injured in two separate car accidents back in the '70's, when he was a traveling paper salesman. "So," Buster said. "Did you hear about your uncle's new car?"

"New car?" I asked. "I didn't realize he was in the country. Isn't he supposed to be in Saudi?"

"He's here. He flew in a week ago and bought a new Ford. It's a beauty, too. Nineteen eighty-five model T-bird, an anniversary model. Fortieth, I think. It's some sort of metallic blue, velour seats, Philco stereo, digital readout on the dash. Just beautiful."

"That so?"

"That's so. He got it absolutely loaded. Man. Just beautiful."

What I wanted to ask was: Why the hell was he here? At five-thirty a.m.? What the hell did he want?

Bear got up and walked carefully over to him.

"See," Buster said. "I'm no nigger." And he held his hand out to the dog.

Bear quickly lunged at the proffered hand. Buster yanked it back to his body and rolled out of the chair and to the ground. He landed ass first, looking for a moment like a dying cockroach, his arms flailing tragically. I ran to the dog and grabbed him around the ribcage and picked him up. It might have strained my back if I hadn't been working at the diner, restocking shelves, lugging crates of frozen hamburger patties around, and so on.

"Damn," Buster said. He managed to sit up.

"I think you better go," I said.

"Give me a hand," Buster said.

"I can't. I'd have to let go of the dog."

"Shit," he said, and managed to hoist himself up.

It was a small apartment. I could have locked him up in my bedroom, but I didn't want to. I wanted Bear to eat the fucker, to tear him to shreds.

"That damn dog is dangerous," Buster said.

"See you later," I said.

After he left, I dug a couple of chocolate chip cookies out of the freezer and handed them to Bear, scratching him behind his ears and praising him. Good dog. I went to my morning classes. Dr. Howard had been replaced by an equally monotone man.

I called up Mom after I got home from class, asked her what the deal was with Buster. She told me that he woke her up in the middle of the night and said, "Honey you'd be proud of me, I fit everything in the van." She thought nothing of it until later that morning, after she'd fully reached consciousness. She thought about what he'd said and went out to the garage. There was nothing left in the garage save a push mower and a sack of cow manure. The shelves were empty, the cement floor bereft of even gardening implements. She jogged back upstairs to their bedroom and peered into his closet. It was empty, too. So were his drawers in their bureau. "I guess he left me," Mom concluded. "At least I still have your sister here."

I woke up Sparky, gave him a good shake. "Hey, man," I said to him.

"What? What?" Sparky said. "The apartment better be on fire."

"Buster left Mom," I said.

He sat up and rubbed some sleep from his eyes. "No shit?"

"No shit," I said.

"How about that?" Sparky said. He yawned and closed his eyes as his head hit the pillow. A second or two later he was back asleep. I took the dog on a walk.

I was trying to watch a documentary about a frozen caveman on PBS, but the rabbit ears needed constant adjusting, and the documentary wasn't all that interesting anyway. I was whiling away my time, waiting to go in to work. Ciro and Bug were watching Citizen Kane at the Reitz Student Union theater. They were taking a film appreciation class together. Albino was off at his job, slinging hash. The phone rang.

"Buzz," Albino said. "Do me a favor."

"Sure," I said.

"Dig around in my desk. I have a pair of surgical gloves in there," Albino said.

"Surgical gloves?" I went.

"Fuck yeah. Surgical gloves. Get a move-on," Albino said.

I set down the receiver and went into Albino's room. Bear was in there eating the cat shit out of Darby's litter box. "Jesus!" I shouted. "Get out of here!" I pulled him away from the litter box and shoved him out the door. I found a pair of surgical gloves in Albino's top drawer. His digital alarm clock was clicking strangely; the digits were blinking at odd intervals. I tapped it on top and a half-dozen cockroaches scuttled out from underneath it. I lifted it up and found cockroach shit. I went back to the phone. "Found 'em."

"I'll be right there," I said. I rode my little motorcycle down to the Deep South restaurant and parked next to Albino's 750-Four. The Deep South was located in what used to be Woolco's department store. "Famous for Big Biscuits," the sign out front claimed. Inside, shellacked biscuits glued to cheap wood paneling spelled out "DEEP SOUTH." The hostess was dressed in bib overalls and a plaid shirt with a corny straw hat cocked on her head. "Table for one?" she asked in a New Jersey accent. "Bring them down here. I need one," Albino said.

"I'm here to see Albino Bernstein. He's a cook," I said. "I brought him something." And I waved the surgical gloves at her.

"Oh, he's waiting on you," she said. "You should tell him to go to the hospital." She pointed toward the backroom.

It was a huge industrial kitchen, all stainless steel, massive deep fryers, grills as big as drafting tables and long tables with cutlery. Lush tropical steam, garlicky scents and deep-fried clouds gushed around. Mostly, the Deep South sold breakfasts. In the back, I also found two Asian men hunkered over massive woks, cooking up heaps of Chinese food. "Number ten," a waitress said, putting an order up. "Numba ten!" "Numba ten!" the men repeated, and shoved sizzling food around.

"Albino!" I shouted.

"Albino in breakroom!" one of the Asian men said.

"Albino bleeding!" the other one said. Neither of them looked at me. They both had the R/L speech impediment.

I walked back toward where I thought the breakroom would be. Albino was sitting on an overturned PVC bucket, trying to staunch the flow of blood coming out of his right index finger. The floor in front of him was covered over with bloody paper towels. "There you are," he said.

"You should go to the hospital," I said.

"I'm a bleeder," Albino said, slipping on the surgical glove. The fingertip instantly filled with blood. "These are nice and tight. They'll stop the bleeding."

"Chinese food?" I asked him.

"Yeah," he said. "These guys come from Hong Kong. They fly into Canada. Drive down here. They're all from the same family, all illegals. They make some kick-ass Chinese food, though." He slapped me on the arm. "I owe you one. Gotta get back to work now."

I puttered back home. The night air felt good after the steamy kitchen. When I walked in the door, the phone was ringing. "Albino?" Bug asked.

"No, this is Buzz," I said. "Are you all right?" She didn't sound all right.

"Ciro ditched me," she said. "We ran into that girl? Suzanne? She sat with us. About half-way through the movie, Suzanne and Ciro got up and left. I thought they were going to the bathroom, but Ciro's car isn't in the parking lot, now I'm here all alone and I don't know what to do."

"Go sit in the Orange and Brew. I'll be right there," I said. I went back into Albino's room and found his helmet in his closet. Bear was eating the cat's shit again. I yelled at him then nudged him out of Albino's room and shut his door. He trotted out to the living room, sat down and belched loudly.

I looped the chinstrap of the spare helmet to the sissybar and puttered off to the Reitz Union.

I found Bug standing out front, shivering even though it wasn't really cold, maybe the low 70's. She was pacing back and forth, enraged. "I am so mad!" she told me. I clicked down the rear footpegs and handed her the helmet. "I swear I could kill him!"

"That's the spirit," I said. I took off my denim jacket and handed it to her. "Put it on."

She put the jacket on; it was several times too big for her. We puttered back to my apartment, past fraternity row, past a pond filled with alligators and experimental farms. She yelled above the engine noise and windrush, "I COULD KILL HIM."

She followed me inside. Albino was sitting on the floor with a black expression on his face. "Why was my door shut?" he asked me.

"This is Darby's apartment, too, you know. Not just your dog's apartment." His hand was white-white, except for his fingertip, which was crusted over with black blood.

"What happened to your finger?" Bug asked him. She rushed over to him and took his hand gingerly. She adjusted her oversized glasses on her undersized nose.

"Knife," Albino said, allowing her to study the wound.

Bear crept up to him and took a sniff. "Beat it!" he shouted at him. Bear dashed down the hall.

"Hey, man," I said, starting feel a little angry. "No need to take it out on the pooch."

"I'm sick of that fucking dog!" Albino shouted.

Bug backed away from him, slipped off my jacket and sat down on it on our ratty recliner.

Now nobody was in a good mood in that room. I thought, Fuck him and his precious antisocial cat. I said, "I have to go to work now."

"You didn't answer my question," Albino said. "Why the fuck was my door closed?"

"Fuck you," I said, both words slow and deliberate, and went to my room to change.

I was sitting in the back, at work, with my brother, bitching about Ciro and Albino and Albino's fucking cat.

I heard the clock punch. I went out front and saw Dee Dee. "What happened to you the other night?" I asked her. She looked like she'd jogged the whole way in from Micanopy.

"Sorry, sugar," she said. "But there was a fire."

I tried to continue being mad at her, but I couldn't. "My brother's here tonight," I said.

"Yeah," she said. "Guess we're gonna have to work instead of fool around." She smiled. "Too bad, huh?"

Little
Wonders

Tony Byrer

"I heard Ellen was shot by a little superhero the other day," Mary said, eyeing me over a glass of iced tea.

"Was she hurt?" I asked, arching my eyebrows.

"Not really," she said. "They knocked her down with a power pulse. It burned her face a little, about like a sunburn." She snorted. "Then they fined her five hundred bucks."

"After shooting her? That's mean." I shook my head incredulously. "Well, what did I tell her?" I asked, dismissing the shooting. Ellen and I had argued before about her habit of setting out poison for house mice.

"The fact she uses poison," I continued, "is not environmentally sound. That alone will bring those little superheroes running with their laser blasters and time warps and their goddamn little superhero magical powers."

"Bill..." Mary warned.

I stood and paced about the deck. "Damn it," I said, waving my arms. "I hate those creepy little things. They're dangerous It seems like they're either super liberal or ultra conservative. They don't know the meaning of restraint. And now I hear Congress is thinking of passing legislation to give the little monsters special protection. I even heard the President wants to make all of them part of the Justice Department." I snorted. "Those little superheroes are more zealous than J. Edgar Hoover ever was."

Just then I saw a quick, furtive movement out of the corner of my eye. I jerked my head around to look and glimpsed a bright flash. There was a flat, dry cracking sound. Mortar dust and brick chips sprayed the side of my face. "Oh, hell," I moaned.

Mary's eyes were wide. She gripped the arms of her lawn chair. "What was that?" Her voice trembled.

"A little superhero," I growled. "What the hell did *we* do?"

There was another bright flash. This time I heard an electric crackling sound, like the noise a bad light switch will make. A blue bolt flew through the air at me. "Damn," I hissed, leaping sideways. Something tugged sharply at my collar. Glass shattered. I flew off the deck and hit the ground rolling. Mary was still standing on the deck, her hands held to her head. "Get down!" I yelled, gaining my feet.

She jumped off the deck and landed in a crouch. Her eyes darted over the deck, the lawn, and the driveway, looking for the little superhero. "Where is it?" she asked desperately.

Another blue bolt arced through the air toward us. I ducked and heard a crunch behind us. I turned and saw a baseball-sized hole in the brick wall. "Damn it! The little shit's destroying the house!" There were now two holes in the brick, and the kitchen window was shattered.

The little bastard stepped out from under one of the steps leading up to the deck. He was a muscular little fellow, about three inches tall. He was dressed in red spandex with a white star emblazoned on his chest. From the thighs down, he appeared to be a machine. Bright metal winked in the light. I could barely make out hydraulics or pistons or something that must have moved his legs. His feet were X-shaped metal claws. A red hood with eye slits covered his face. He had no right arm. In its place he had some kind of laser cannon.

"There it is!" I cried, pointing.

"Wow," Mary breathed softly. "I've never actually seen one before."

It leveled its cannon arm at us. "Oh, shit," I exhaled.

"BILL AND MARY GLEASON," it intoned clearly, "THE EARTH DEFENSE LEAGUE HAS FOUND YOU GUILTY OF POISONING THE ENVIRONMENT, TO WIT: ON TWO OCCASIONS YOU HAVE USED GASOLINE TO KILL WEEDS IN YOUR DRIVEWAY, IN VIOLATION OF EARTH DEFENSE LEAGUE STATUTES." I heard a diminutive click and a sighting device popped up at the end of its cannon arm.

"I, ANTHER," it continued, "HAVE BEEN DISPATCHED TO PLACE YOU UNDER ARREST AND BRING YOU TO JUSTICE, IN ACCORDANCE WITH EARTH DEFENSE LEAGUE STATUTES."

"Hey, junior," I called. "You need to get a little bit bigger in the breeches before you come around messing with us big people."

"YOU HAVE THE RIGHT TO REMAIN SILENT," the little guy said, ignoring me.

"Yeah, yeah, I know. The right to an attorney and all."

"ANYTHING YOU SAY WILL BE USED AGAINST YOU."

"Where will it be used against me?" I asked, feeling a chill.

"YOU HAVE THE RIGHT TO COUNSEL."

"Just what are you going to do?" I demanded.

"A REPRESENTATIVE OF THE U.S. JUSTICE ALLIANCE WILL BE APPOINTED AS YOUR COUNSELOR."

I turned to Mary and said, "I'd give anything for a can of extra strength Raid right now."

"SILENCE!" Anther pointed his laser arm at me. "LIE FACE DOWN AND CLASP YOUR HANDS BEHIND YOUR HEAD," he commanded.

I grabbed Mary's arm and turned to run.

"FREEZE!"

Blue bolts slammed into the side of the house, spraying us with sharp brick fragments. Just as we rounded the corner of the house, one of the bolts caught the side of my shoe, whipping my leg out in front of me and slamming me flat on my back. I rolled onto my belly and crawled around the corner.

Mary knelt beside me. "Are you all right?" she panted.

"Knocked ... wind ... outta me," I gasped.

She pulled me to my feet. "Let's go," she said.

She led me to the front door. I was gasping harshly as she slammed the door shut behind us. She thumbed the lock as I collapsed on a chair.

"Shotgun," I gasped.

Mary ran into the bedroom and came back a half minute later cradling my twelve gage across one arm. She handed me the gun and tossed a box of shells in my lap.

I began ramming shells into the chamber. My breathing was getting better and the pressure in my chest was easing up. "Little bastard," I croaked. "Show him a powerful weapon." I pumped a round into the firing chamber and stood beside the door. Mary moved behind me. We were both breathing heavily, waiting for something else to happen.

There was a loud crack. A smoking, fist sized hole appeared in the door. I raised the shotgun indecisively to my shoulder. Another hole punched through the door. This time I could see the little bastard standing on the front deck, his smoking laser arm pointed at the door.

I pulled the trigger and the bottom half of the door exploded. The little monster fell flat on his butt, his laser arm flailing in the air. I pumped another round and fired. Splinters of wood leaped from the deck where he had been sitting. Anther was suddenly gone. All that remained was one of his metal claws and a fine red mist dispersing on the gentle breeze.

"YEE HAW!" I screamed. "GOT YA, YA LITTLE SHIT! TEACH YA TO MEDDLE IN THE AFFAIRS OF BIG PEOPLE!" I danced in a circle, waving the shotgun above my head.

"Bill!" Mary shrieked, pointing at the living room window.

I stopped in mid-caper and gawked. A little woman in yellow spandex wearing a little yellow Lone Ranger mask stood on the windowsill next to a little man in blue. He wore red briefs and a red cape.

"I AM PISTIL," the little woman intoned.

"AND I," announced the little man, "AM STAMEN."

"TOGETHER," Pistil continued, "WE HAVE FOUND YOU, BILL GLEASON, GUILTY OF THE MURDER OF ANTHER, LATE OF THE EARTH DEFENSE LEAGUE."

Stamen extended his arm at me.

"Shit*fire*," I breathed.

Mary moaned, grabbing my arm and pulling me into the kitchen.

A white beam shot from Stamen's index finger, lighting upon a kitchen chair. A gauzy white envelope of light surrounded the chair, which dissolved and collapsed into a pile of dust on the floor.

Mary screamed and nearly tugged me off my feet. We wheeled and escaped into the hallway. Too late I noticed I'd dropped the shotgun on the living room floor. Stamen crouched over the end of the gun, gazing into the barrel.

We ran down the short hallway and fled out the back door just as part of the ceiling collapsed behind us.

We pounded down the steps and across the back yard toward the driveway.

"Do you have your keys?" Mary shouted.

I fished in my pocket and shouted gladly as I grasped my car keys.

We ran to the car. As I flung open the door, I thought I could hear sirens in the distance. Good, I thought, help's finally on the way.

"Get in!" cried Mary.

I dropped behind the wheel and jammed the keys into the ignition. As the engine growled to life, a white beam shot by the window, disintegrating a fencepost next to the drive.

"Go go go!" Mary shrieked.

I spun onto the road, the car shuddering over the berm like a sick dog.

A news broadcast on the radio caught my attention.

"...granting the so-called 'little superheroes' full law enforcement authority. KROX talked to the Green Machine of the Earth Defense League this morning. Here is what he had to say."

"THIS IS A GREAT VICTORY," the Green Machine declared. "NOW THAT WE HAVE BEEN LEGITIMIZED BY THE U.S. JUSTICE DEPARTMENT, THERE WILL BE NO DOUBTS CONCERNING OUR MAGISTRACY."

I snapped off the radio. I saw again Anther disappearing in a fine red mist. I caught a glimpse of myself in the rear view mirror. My eyes stared back at me from a shocked, white face.

Mary's face was hidden in her hands. "Oh, Bill," she sobbed. "What's going to happen to you?"

I pulled the car off the road and stopped. I knew what was going to happen to me. My future came from behind, eating up the road, red lights flashing.

I leaned back in the seat and closed my eyes, hands resting lightly on the wheel.

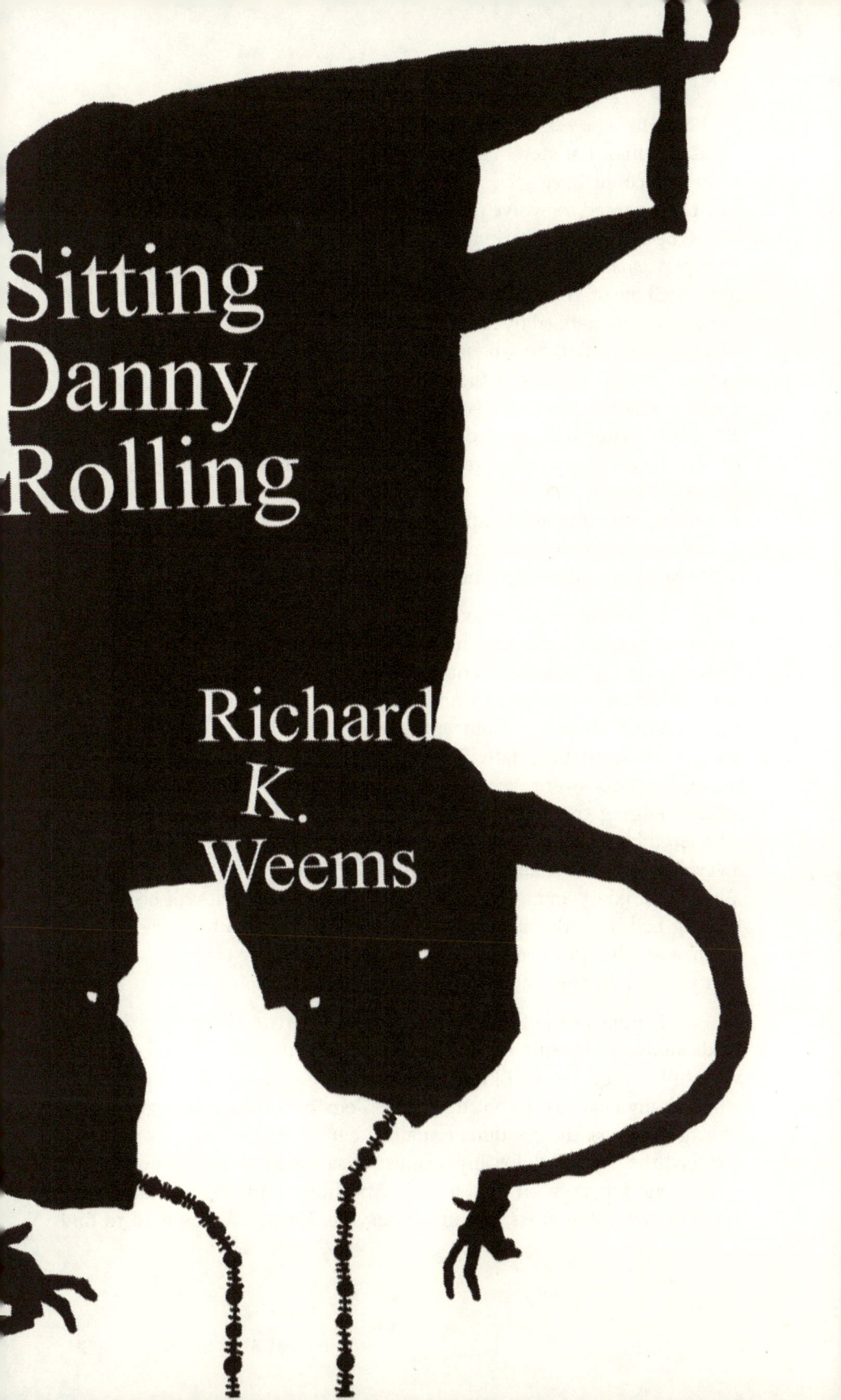

Sitting
Danny
Rolling

Richard
K.
Weems

The South is a sea of unsophisticated proteins, northern Florida a regular primordial stew. The heat alone makes one wonder how water-breathers could have seen anything so promising on the nearby beach that they wanted to evolve up onto it. As a New Jersey high school punk I had been fully indoctrinated into the evils of the South: its Bible-thumpers, snake churches and inbred psychosis. The Dead Kennedys had convinced me of Winnebago warriors and the goons of Hazzard, and hell I was still traumatized by Andy Kaufman getting his neck split open by a Tennessee wrestler. So when I moved to Gainesville in August of 1991 to study fiction writing at the University of Florida, I had my guard up and was ready to fend off any hints of backward southern living. I was a Northern writer who aspired to styles like those of Raymond Carver or Ernest Hemingway. I wrote about sad, beaten-down characters who yearned for something in their lives, but I never knew what that something was, and as a result, neither did they. They were polite stories, full of mystery that never gets resolved (or even brought to light)—in other words, uninteresting and unreadable.

I arrived in Gainesville soon after the student murders, but before authorities had a culprit in custody. In essence, I had walked into a herd of wild filet mignon scenting a slight hint of carnivore in the air—but instead of mass hysteria and self-protective rioting or vigilantism, the student body lolled about with a dull foreboding of what they most likely considered their fate. There wasn't even a sense of avoidance—many students were keeping to their regular routine, as though acknowledging that if it was written in the cards that they were to be butchered by a madman, then there was little to be gained from running away from the inevitable. Only faith in a higher order in the universe allows us anxiety and a sense that we have a calling that will be fulfilled barring bad luck. But in Jurassic Gainesville, we were back on the food chain, and a hungry predator was out there, so all we could do was hope that we wouldn't get caught limping by the water hole.

I hung in the folds, too new to the area to chance grazing the fields alone. As a result, my stories turned violent, full of characters who were full of rage, but still I had no sense of the source of that rage, and so whether my characters shot up prairie dogs or forced young girls to be their girlfriends, their actions remained empty and without motive, so I watched the news both for any promise of safety as well as to look for the wellspring for rage in the world. Anything strange got immediate attention from the press, but in Gainesville, Florida it was hard to find something that was <u>not</u> strange. This was home of the Grand Poobah (whatever) of the nation's largest chapter of the Ku Klux Klan. This was a land void of manifest destiny, where bugs of the most alien sort pretty much dictated whether you got to finish your box of Kix or had to throw it out and let the larvae grow. This was gator country. Not only had alligators managed to inhabit every natural body of water in the area, but a local town had a horn they sounded when an indigenous thirteen-foot bull made its monthly round through the town's main drive, the citizens cooped up in their trailers hoping they didn't smell too much like pork rinds. The University of Florida crew team practiced in a creek that had the highest proportion of gators to water in the entire state, effectively reducing the occurrences of the rowers tipping their shells. Gainesville was in easy walking distance of at least four state penitentiaries.

If you were anything less than a sociopath, you were a news item. First, the wrong man confessed to the murders after beating up his grandmother. Then a voice-driven chronic schizophrenic set a rash of church fires. A five-foot lizard was loose in town for a while, eating housepets. When the local media asked the University of Florida animal labs if the lizard was theirs, they said they weren't missing any. (These were serious labs—in 1991, UF held the world record for the largest water buffalo born of embryo transplant.) The news held no hope that our stalker in the high grass had either been caught or had moved upwind for something tastier, and we dumb beasts still mulled about as if staying in herds made a difference.

Even when the real killer, Danny Rolling, was caught, the weirdness continued. Alachua County wasn't sure it could afford the trial and applied for state funding. At his arraignment, Danny, a budding country-western singer/songwriter and recently engaged to Sondra London, got up and sang an original composition to his true love in place of a statement in his own defense. The Florida Supreme Court later passed a statute forbidding Danny, his fiancée or his brother from profiting on the book Danny had written about his life and crimes. For this reason alone, knowing that none of the guilty would see a cent from my purchase, did I eventually read it—an awful book, most disappointing in that Danny blamed the murders on a demon named GEMINI. It may take a demonic side to bite off a victim's nipple and take it home with you in a sandwich bag, or saw off a head with a hunting knife and put it on display before you leave a blood-stained bedroom, but don't get cheap and blame everything on temporary memory loss due to demonic possession.

But the killer had indeed been caught, and this gave off miniscule flashes of hope. It was a brief respite back into the Age of Man, for Rolling had been tackled by Greek drama—he had left his hubris dangling.

What had doomed Danny Rolling was his calling to music. While hiding from police, Danny would find a dark area to camp out, build a fire and compose. He sung of rape and brutality and the biting of nipples, and at the end of one tape he did a Johnny Cash and announced himself at the end of one of his compositions: "My name is Danny Rolling." This tape eventually got into the hands of police and it was played on the news under a picture of dear, dear love-struck Danny in mid-croon to his Intended in the courtroom. Even the sweetest of grannies would have lobbied to pull the switch herself upon hearing the true face of that monster.

Meanwhile, I was tooling away at stories about men throwing bottles at their estranged wives, about sad people with dark lives, but nothing seemed to be clicking. I ended up throwing away almost every story I had written during my first year in Gainesville. None of my characters inspired any kind of three-dimensional feel. My characters had problems that I thought were the stuff of great stories—love, regret, loss—but their loves and regret and losses never felt real to me or to anyone who read them. I had no doubts about my desire to write, but I couldn't get in touch with the depth of these emotions.

The killer caught and doomed to fry, the Floridian lemmings loosened their tight circles, and I felt safe to browse and find my own niche of living with the oddities of this antediluvian culture. I ate lunch on campus every day with the Hare Krishnas because I was too poor to afford anything but free grub, and I was getting very good at playing Frisbee, which the Hare Krishnas played quite (ahem) religiously after eating. Because America is great, three southern fundamentalists preached in the same plaza where the Krishnas did their thing, and no one had more right to this public space of land than the other. While the fundamentalists told passing students that they were opening the doors to Hell and would not be happy until they dropped their school books and picked up the good book, the Krishnas chanted and sang, and all was diverse in the world.

But when evening news time came, I would flip among the channels for the latest about the Danny Rolling case. I discussed and dissected every detail with my friend Kevin, an Alabama poet, fellow student and general madman. But we didn't discuss details so much as rhapsodize on just how diseased a mutherfucker Danny Rolling was. We shared details of the murders as they were released, reconstructed crime scenes (verbally, of course), but mostly we were trying to figure out why one break-in would result in rape, murder and mutilation while another would end up in rape alone, another in plain burglary. Rolling was a prolific criminal, but there didn't seem to be a steady pattern behind his actions. It's too easy to envision serial killers as these rampaging Rambos, shooting up movie sets on a regular cycle, by the moon or abusive parents' anniversary. But organized serial killers live among the docile with only a modicum of ickyness emanating towards their neighbors and peers, and certainly not enough for anyone to think there's a nearby crawlspace being loaded up with carcasses. Some killers were even considered pillars of their communities, this while they're luring co-eds to horrid fates on the sly. Kevin and I wanted to understand Rolling's compulsions, his desires and essences that made his killing days as much a part of him as putting his right leg into his pants first or preferring pepperoni and black olives on his pizza.

Son of Sam picked a certain phenotype of female to shoot at. Ted Bundy also wanted a certain look to his women. Dahmer wanted men he felt he would be able to control and fulfill his fantasies of love zombies and shrines of immortality, and Richard Ramirez did whatever he damn well pleased. Rolling also had some kind of plan, Kevin and I figured, however chaotic. Something made a killing night deadly, and something else kept simple B & E fully satisfying (let's keep that demonic possession shit out of it). Figuring that out seemed to be the essence of everything, and this is what Kevin and I were trying to divine.

We read newspapers and watched TV for all the information our frying brains could hold, but we also worked on our thesis through some major binge drinking. A good, all-out drunk sometimes brought a kind of clarity intellectual discussion couldn't. We were also on a religious mission to get porcelained, inspired by our artistic alcoholic icon, Peter O'Toole. The idea was to go on a good multiple-day drunk, the only sleep taken during blackouts, until SNAP!—total sobriety. The eyes glaze, the skin dews, and everything you need to know is lying there before you wrapped in microwave-safe paper.

That was the theory at least, and we put it to the test at Kevin's apartment during Spring Break. We anticipated moments of mind-numbing revelation and profound deliberation on Danny Rolling's soul. But mostly it was chugging down Kash & Karry brand banana liqueur (the cheapest booze available) and spending long periods on the couch blissfully unaware of our current state of consciousness. If one of us had an intuition, we'd follow it the best we could, but it usually didn't last long before it became drunken babble and we'd resume staring at the far wall, Marlene Deitrich playing on the CD player and the banana liqueur wedged into the cracks between the cushions for easy access.

And then it was towards the end of our third day that Kevin had a flash—maybe not revelation, but certainly inspiration.

"He was right out back here, man," Kevin said, his eyes suddenly bright with a Ginsu edge. "Let's go find it, man, we gotta go find it Weems, right out back, that's where it was."

I knew right from the very start that Kevin was full of shit. We both knew that Rolling would occasionally camp out at random spots in town to elude police, but we had never heard any indication that Rolling had actually camped out behind Kevin's apartment complex. Kevin had woods back there, a good place to camp out, but why would he only make the connection now?

But Kevin was on to something deeper than the truth, and even if he was only in the height of sweet, sticky liqueur delusion, the manic storm behind his glazed eyes was hard to deny. I agreed to go outside with him.

There was a fire pit out there. That much is certain. An amphitheater of three cinder blocks—one for Danny, one for his tape recorder, and the third? GEMINI seat. Bullshit evil spirit seat. That would be the one in the middle.

And that was the one Kevin planted himself at. A kind of calm came over him, a settling in. A mental reclining. The block must not have been too hard, not too soft, not too hot, not too cold. A real baby bear block.

"He was right here, man," Kevin said, his words chopped by incessant giggles. "Right here man, he sat right here, singing his songs, man. Singing his goddamn songs." Kevin was as certain of this as he was certain of his own hair.

And then it hit me. Not quite inspiration, but more of a revelation. As Kevin tried to evoke Rolling energy up through his ass, waving his hands as if he could incite the dead fire before us, I took in a deep breath and had a good look around me.

There were no lights behind Kevin's complex. Gainesville was a dark, featureless cloud that teemed with insect life that I had only seen up north on Creature Double-Feature. Even in the dark, the very air seemed to wriggle with unyielding life. And all this heat. What creative energy! How could you come to this place and <u>not</u> transform, de-evolve, and mutate into something base and in visceral contact with the world? And when that sweet, treacherous kind of mutation takes place, what else is there to do about it but throw your primal rage into a creative scream? If you didn't, you were sure to shrivel into a dehydrated yam in this heat. Kevin had his poetry. Me, my stories. Others turned to thumping their bibles or amassing hubcap pyramids outside their trailers. One of my neighbors had constructed an American flag on her front yard out of hundreds of gallon milk jugs filled with red-, white-, or blue-colored liquid. This was the secret behind the Southern whoop, that cowboy hoot that's done in seemingly random moments, out the windows of the pick-up or when the bartender brings your new pitcher of Pabst Blue Ribbon. The brain is boiling, boiling off those frivolous layers of evolution that fooled us into this crazy idea that we have one up on nature. You are reduced to a soft-boiled egg of vulnerability, waiting to get chomped by the next passing rodent down the pike, so what is there left to do but whoop it up and declare to the heavens that, if you are going to be quashed like a palmetto bug under the heel of a combat boot, you're going to leave one hell of a stain? While Kevin sat Danny Rolling and played air guitar and was maybe even able to conjure up some feeling of what it would be like to be on the lam, a trail of rape and murder strung out behind him like beer cans following newlyweds, I realized I had no clue about that kind of rage, the rage that makes mankind slaughter mankind. But I did understand the need to sing about it afterwards, to write.

In the end, I finished my masters thesis and got my degree. Most of the stories in there were still somewhat lackluster, maybe even plain, but I did learn something fuller about the scarier side of the world. People are an anxious mixture of godliness and monstrosity—often not good enough for the former, and too easily able to live up to the latter, and that became the stuff worth writing about.

Kevin died before he was forty. He choked to death on a roast beef deli end in front of the convenience store he'd bought it from. No one heard it, but I have no doubt that he let out his own whoop before giving up the ghost. Last October, Danny Rolling finally got his. Strapped down and injected—that sick fuck didn't get in a last concert before his death.

One Crazy Bastard

Todd Taylor

His name was Marshall Phillips. I first met him in an AA meeting towards the end of 1991. He would sit in the meetings chain smoking and giving crazy, high-pitched laughs without reason.

Yet, despite his obvious mental illness, he was fairly intelligent.

After one of the meetings we talked for a while and I found out that he dabbled as a rock n' roll singer — and suffered from bipolar disorder. We got together and jammed a few times, with me on an acoustic guitar and him vocalizing. He memorized a few of the songs I had written and we started showing up to open mic nights in Deep Ellum, an old warehouse district turned into an artsy-fartsy yuppie haven.

We mostly hit on one coffee joint, Jumpin' Java, and bored the usual poetry/bohemian/goth crowd that hung out there.

We longed to get a rock band together but we were short on funds and musician friends. The people we needed were a drummer and bass player. We met a few but nothing ever panned out. The only drummer we came across was a skinny kid, Johnny, who worked at Wendy's Old Fashioned Hamburgers.

We had to jam inside my upstairs apartment since Johnny's parents wouldn't allow us to jam at their house. My apartment didn't work out well either, for obvious reasons. We got in about 30 minutes worth of practice before the neighbors would start bitching. A couple of times the cops came. Luckily, no one was ticketed or arrested. Nevertheless, we had to find a new place to practice. Before that could happen, though, Johnny blew us off. I didn't blame him.

Months later I would also extricate myself from Marshall's crazy ass.

One reason for Johnny's departure was Marshall's behavior. He never took his lithium pills so he was always soaring from ecstatic highs to depressive lows every few hours. When he was manic he knew everything in the world and would be constantly trying to tell Johnny how to play the drums. Marshall would get some beat in his head that he would try to make Johnny replicate, barking orders like a drill sergeant.

Also, Marshall would literally bounce off my apartment walls and jump off of my balcony—a 20 foot drop—then come back inside for some more jamming. At first, I thought he was trying to commit suicide by jumping to the ground but then he explained to me that he had joined the Army and had trained as a paratrooper. He told me he knew how to tuck-and-roll, a way to bounce off your feet when you hit the ground. You'd put your arms over you head to avoid injury. He said he was given a special mental illness discharge for his bipolar disorder.

Before Johnny ran away from us like a roadrunner on speed we had also been jamming with a bass player named Keith. He had what a friend of mine (David Foe of Roach Egg Invasion infamy) used to call a "safety" hawk. This is a very wide mohawk. My friend used to call it that because he said you could still get a job with that haircut. It was like the punk rock version of the mullet.

My friend was right because Keith worked at McDonald's. On his best days, his bass playing was okay. On his worst, it sucked. However, he could stomach Marshall so that was something.

As the months went by I ended up begging, borrowing and stealing money to rent a rehearsal space in Irving for a six-hour block. One time, during Marshall's acute insanity, we came up with a song called Blue Balls. He wrote the lyrics and I wrote the music.

After the first month Keith had all he could stand and left after he and Marshall got into a fist fight. During his mania, Marshall was also an expert bass player. We continued to jam together, providing me a bird's eye view of Marshall's antics.

One time, in an AA meeting, some old fart guru three days older than dirt, and just as pretty, started ragging on Marshall, saying he wasn't working a good AA program. He also said he didn't believe that Marshall had been sober for over a year. Marshall took it grinning. When we left the meeting to get into my car and leave Marshall found the old fart's car with the passenger side window rolled down and pissed into the passenger seat. I shuffled him into my car as quickly as possible and got the hell out of there.

Marshall laughed like an insane idiot on the way back to my place. Halfway home, after my fear subsided of getting caught, I joined him in his merriment. I had gotten the same treatment from time to time from the same old fart and admired Marshall's guts for getting back at him. He had the guts but it wouldn't be enough to save our collaboration.

Marshall was a big guy with long brown, wavy hair, though he shaved his head completely bald at one point. This was before it was fashionable. He also climbed across the roof of my car from one side to the other while I was driving down the freeway at 60 mph. My girlfriend at the time (future ex-wife) freaked out. And once he laughed through some parts of *The Prince Of Tides,* while he was over at our place, he was at the top of her shit list.

I had some sympathy for the guy, though. He told me once he went through heroin withdrawals in a Florida ditch. He had also been to the Terrell Mental Institution several times, the last time for running around naked in Reunion Tower in Dallas.

Like I said he was clinically insane.

I met his mother once and saw where at least part of his craziness came from. She was an old Southern anal-retentive bitch whose voice grated on you like fingernails across a chalk board. I was truly surprised he had not cut her up in a 1000 pieces and buried her in the backyard. She was a neat freak and her modest home looked like a white trash showroom. She would yell at Marshall for not using a coaster when he drank something, missing a crumb on the carpet when he vacuumed, missing a water drop when he washed and dried her car, etc.

However, before I escaped Marshall, I managed to borrow some money from a friend and we made a demo tape. We called ourselves Spastic Revolt. It wasn't really a band because I had put an ad in the newspaper and hired a bass player and drummer to play. Our hopes were that we could use the demo to recruit a permanent bass player and drummer. We tried to get the guys who played on the tape to stick around but they already had permanent gigs. They did our thing solely for the money. One of our songs, Desert Storm, was played on a now-defunct Dallas rock 'n roll radio station, Q102, in October '93 on their local new music program.

That was our 15 minutes of fame.

But even this brief radio exposure did nothing to attract a drummer. We did sign up another bass player to the project and I joined him in another band, Chamberlye, once I finally grew sick of Marshall's insanity.

Wherever he is now I wish him luck, the crazy bastard.

Cruising With
My Lights
On Dim

R. Lee

Yesterday afternoon as I was driving to work I began to feel a bit sick in the head.

There I was anxiously racing to a place I didn't want to arrive at. And as I looked out at the traffic clustered around me like roaring bombs I couldn't help but wonder what had I gotten myself into? Why do I do this? What the hell has any of this to do with me?

These are bad thoughts to have in the midst of so much heavy metal and velocity. Wholesale doubt is not healthy at these speeds. It would be so easy to do something drastic. A quick jerk to the right would result in the sort of carnage the evening newscasters would wet themselves narrating.

This is not the time to ponder the shrieking futility of my existence, but I can't seem to help myself. It comes over me almost every day at about this same time. I used to think these low-grade freakouts were induced by the looming prospect of having another 10 or so hours peeled from my life by the job, but now I suspect there's something more insidious working my head.

I think what's pushing me to the brink are all those flashing reminders that I speed past on my way in to work... those walls of hot color that shout to me with enormous bursts of image and text... those millisecond seductions that are trying to convince me that it makes perfect sense to be out there strapped into that machine, barreling down a vast ditch of concrete that leads me nowhere I want to be.

It's those fucking billboards.

There are hundreds of them out there. They jump up one after another. They've planted those things so thick along the stretch of road I travel to work that the horizon has been effectively blotted out. Forty-foot advertisements for cars and food and beer and women and laughter and tanned skin and surgically enhanced eyeballs. They all seem to say, to hell with your muddy contemplation - we've got sparkling amusements just for you. The message is clear: Don't waste your time dreaming about that confusing world beyond these offerings. Forget all that difficult crap. This is what you really want. This is all you'll ever need. Now quit thinking and get your ass back to work.

If there's such a thing as commercial sickness, I've got it. I feel as if everywhere I go I'm getting this shit shoveled into my face. It's not the endless parade of things I don't ever want that bothers me so much as the subtext of the messages that accompany these come-ons. What gets to me are the persistent suggestions about how I should be... how I should think and live and what sort of desires are considered legitimate in world where everything always comes down to the hunger for more and more things and more and more money.

If your mental palate is in tune with the popular taste, then most of this constant declaiming of THE NEW floats about you like an easy breeze. It's the theme to who you are and what you're about. But if you're a bit off and can't get with the notion that a flashy car or a trip to a corporate resort will improve your life, then all this adrenalized baying amounts to nothing less than a ceaseless reminder that you are at odds with the world around you. And to have that conflict pointed out to you on a perpetual basis becomes extremely wearying.

You'd think by now, that we'd all be pretty much immune to the endless swirl of advertising and the humiliating tactics these hacks employ to make us feel deficient until we've embraced their product, but I can't seem to get used to it. I'm hit hard by these concentrated doses of a culture I find repugnant. Repetition hasn't inured me to the annoyance of these constant intrusions. As I grow older the chaffing only seems to get worse. I'll see some innocuous ad where a leering creep is hawking toothpaste and I take it as a personal insult. There's this one guy who walks around town under a sandwich board advertising a rib joint and each time I pass him I have the urge to throw up. I don't want to be surrounded by all these degrading reminders that I'm at odds with my environment. If I thought there was the slightest chance that I could make that drive in to work blindfolded, I'd give it a shot.

It wasn't always this way with me. I mean, I was never quite "right", but rubbing up against the common blight didn't always induce the dread it inspires in me these days. When I was 16 it was kind of thrilling to be a weirdo amidst the herd of straights I lived within. At 26 I still took some pride in the fact that I hadn't been duped into their brand of normalcy. But by 36 I was sick and tired of being the geek. Actually, it wasn't myself I was sick of; I was sick of them and their world. Sick of being surrounded by so many wind-up drones and the pyrotechnic emptiness they worship.

So I did what all freaks who want to remain alive eventually do: I retreated. In truth, I'd been retreating for some time, but by the time I'd hit my 30s I was well off into a universe of my own making. I got to a place where the relationships I had with books and old jazz records were far more meaningful and satisfying than those I felt pushed into having with almost all of the people around me. An hour spent listening to Ukulele Ike or reading T'ao Ch'ien would reverberate through my mind for days, but the numbing 8 hours I'd pass along side a person I worked with would fall away just as soon as I left them.

Over time I've managed to construct something like a public hermitage for myself. I've fallen between the cracks of the dominant culture and built an invisible kingdom where a misfit can feel at home. Other than moving to a mud hut in the woods there was no other way for me to go. Had I tried to fit in and live their way, I'm certain I would have gone completely mad. What makes sense for THEM is poison to me. Nothing they celebrate appeals. I don't like their houses, their jobs, their logic or their gods. I'm an atheist. An anarchist. A layabout loner with a vulgar mind.

I'm out of step with their hyper, instantaneous world. I find all that glorious efficiency deadening. I like to function at about half their speed. I have no desire to catch up. In fact, I strive to retard myself to an ever-greater degree. I'm happy to fall further and further behind. I don't buy into their struggle. I gain my escape by sitting still.

I like things that are slow and old and out of date. Gently used is not my bag. I prefer the neglected and discarded. Dents and rust create beautiful patterns. I've fallen in love with strange ideas and forgotten music and thick beer. All their drama and rowdy enthusiasm doesn't do shit for me. I prefer long, silent walks alone.

The urge here is to start listing my passions, but I have to be careful about being too specific. That would only betray my hermitage. That would make me less invisible and I don't ever want that. I cherish my anonymity.

I admit this is an odd way to live. I haunt the consensual world like a ghost. I skirt the edges of their reality and fade from sight at the first possible opportunity. I'm amiable, but thoroughly distracted. People talk to me and quickly discover I'm about half out of it. Distant. I have nothing to say to them and I'm not much interested in what they have to say to me. If I make the effort, I can just barely converse with most people. If they insist on conversation, I spew cant. What else can I do? I know next to nothing about the things they like to talk about. I don't follow sports. I don't know anything about what's on TV. I don't like cars or popular music. I don't like movies and I think most kids and all dogs are not the least bit interesting. Do I sound proud of my alienation? In my way, I guess I am. To a certain degree, I feel as though I've achieved a freedom from the dominance of their banality. It's something that I've always yearned for.

Let me show you an example of how this kind of thing goes. This occurred just last week. A guy I was working with started telling me about how he had spent the weekend at some casino playing poker. It took a while, but it eventually became clear to him that I couldn't have cared less about anything he was saying. Instead of just shutting his mouth he attempted to draw me out. He kept nosing around and finally came right out with it.

He said, "So what did you do this weekend?"

Unfortunately, I was feeling less reticent than usual. To be honest, I was slightly angry. He'd been gushing his garbage for so long that I wanted to give him a taste of what it had been like for me to sit through his vapid spiel.

I told him my girlfriend and I drove to Madison and looked around used bookstores.

"Oh," he said. He didn't know what to make of that.

I helped him out. I told him what it is that appeals to me so much about old bookstores and why I like to spend so much time in them. I told him how I love going through all those racks full of disregarded books... how for every Hemingway in the stacks there are a hundred forgotten authors who took great care with their writing and poured their existence into books that will never be read again. I told him I found the ultimate triviality of their efforts to be beautiful and that it illustrates that there can be a kind of wonderful grace to the base-level absurdity that informs all of our lives.

Well, at least, that's what I tried to tell him. What actually came out of my mouth was probably even less coherent than what I've just written. But if the baffled look on his face was any indication, I think I got my larger point across. And I don't think he'll be bothering me with his poker exploits anymore.

Usually, I don't feel the need to spit my oddness into a person's face this way. Most often my responses to their intrusions are so lackadaisical and dim-witted that whatever meager interest they may have in me quickly dies of its own inertia. It takes so little effort on my part that I can often dispense of them without having to interrupt my own thoughts.

So is this anyway to deal with people? Alienate them? Discourage their enthusiasms? Make them uncomfortable in your presence? After all, the majority of people are basically good, aren't they?

Maybe.

I don't know. And I don't much care. I just don't like being around them, that's all.

For most people, this would obviously not be a constructive approach to public life, but it seems to work all right for people such as myself. It's how we get to a place where the common dross is less invasive. It's how you develop a quieter space for yourself where the constant suggestions of others aren't permitted to trample what is original to your own mind.

This isn't "nice" and this won't ever be mistaken for "good" behavior, but I try not to burden myself with such maudlin sensibilities. I can't afford to. For me, it's always an uphill run. Everywhere I go, I'm reminded that my views are contrary and out of sync. In this kind of atmosphere you'll either carve out a spot for yourself or get washed away by the milky tide of their chintzy desires, their luke-warm beliefs and their cancerous notions of propriety. I don't want that. Ever. And when it comes right down to it, I don't feel the least bit of remorse about doing whatever it is I need to do to keep them at bay. This is how I survive.

Focus

Kurt Eisenlohr

Later that evening, Marcus dropped by. I put a beer in his hand and sat him on the couch.

"Listen to this," I told him. "It's a recording I made of one of my uncles back in Michigan when I was a kid. Think of it as a radio play. My uncle's name was Dick. He's the guy with the loud obnoxious voice. There's a guy named Elliot on here, too. Elliot is the one who sounds brain damaged." I pressed PLAY and swallowed a dilaudid.

Elliot: I'll bet you could guess for hours and never figure out where I was goin.

Dick: I wanna ask you somethin right now--if you're so fuckin intelligent, why are you doin what you're doin today at the Stillwater Wire? Why'd you take my fuckin job away from me?

Elliot: Take your job away?

Dick: Yeah, why'd you do that?

Elliot: What?

Dick: Can ya handle my job?

Elliot: Your job? Where?

Dick: Stillwater Wire!

Elliot: My job? I like my job.

Dick: Could ya handle my job?

Elliot: I could?

Dick: Could ya? Can ya make a set-up?

Elliot: I could set up.

Dick: I'll tell ya what. I'll tear a one-ten down, or one twenty-five, eighteen, twenty-one fuckin guns, electrodes, and one-ten--I got better'n that--ya wanna check it out?

Elliot: I can clean electrodes.

Dick: Fuck, ya don't know how to set the sonofabitch up, ya don't know what fuckin fixtures to use!

Elliot: I could not do maintenance, but I could set things up.

Dick: Could ya? I'll talk to Jack Relic tomorrow. I need a helper. I got three fuckin guys workin under me now don't know a fuckin thing about a set-up. There's only one man that can do a set-up, and that's me. I'm talkin about big fuckin machines now. I'm not talkin job shop, them little fuckin guns there. I'm talkin about twenty-one fuckin guns, or sixteen, or twenty-one fuckin...Hey, fixtures, man! I set them fuckers up! I'm the only one can fuckin do it!

Elliot: Oh?

Dick: Ya wanna talk to Mr. Pedder?

Elliot: Who?

Dick: The boss! The president! Mr. Pedder!

Elliot: What about?

Dick: You wanna be a set-up man?

Elliot: I could.

Dick: Ya could?

Elliot: It'd be more money than welding.

Dick: I don't think so.

Elliot: I'll earn it somehow--work my butt off.

Dick: Ya know what I make an hour?

Elliot: Probably six, seven bucks.

Dick: Noooo, three-seventy-five. I'm not in the union yet. I'm not in the union.

"Alright already," Marcus said, "this guy's giving me a headache."

"Which guy?"

"Both guys."

I got up and shut it off. I called them the The Dick Tapes. I had hours and hours of the stuff. I packed another bowl and handed it to Marcus.

"My mother used to say the same thing when I played these tapes back in high school. Dick was her brother. I'd be in my room with my friends, listening to this shit and laughing. My mother would always scream at me to turn it off."

"I can see why."

"I played it to you for a reason, but I can't remember now..."

"How's that vitamin D treating you?"

"Vitamin D?"

"The dilaudid."

"Oh, Vitamin D — I like that. Milk."

"Well?"

"Well what?"

"You want some more or are you good?"

"I'm good. I'll take some for the future, though."

"Sure, take some." He dumped a small blue mountain of pills onto the coffee table.

"Thanks."

"What was the meaning of that tape? Why'd you play it for me?"

"I don't remember."

"Dick, huh? That's funny. Uncle Dick."

"Yeah. The dude died in the 80s. Abdominal hemorhage. He was forty-six, forty-seven, I think."

Marcus had craned his neck around and was checking out the wall behind my couch. Studying the thing. Some moments passed. Then he said it. I'd been hearing it a lot lately.

"All these photos of your ex-wife you have on your wall...it's kind of fucked up."

"We're not divorced yet."

"Why don't you take them down?"

"I don't know. I like them there."

"You have to move on."

"If she decides this is it, I may move back to Michigan."

"What? and work at the Stillwater Wire?"

"I know! I'm fucked, I'm stuck here!"

"Why don't you paint anymore? You should be painting. You need something to focus on other than your ex-wife."

"I can't paint, I've tried. I don't feel it anymore. I'm tapped out. I can't do anything. I'm a service industry slave. I'm going to end up in a fucking factory, getting drunk every night after work and having some sixteen year old kid secretly tape record my moronic conversations for a laugh!"

"You're being ridiculous."

"No, I'm being realistic."

"You have to pull yourself together, dude."

"That's what my wife keeps telling me."

"I thought you weren't going to talk to her for awhile."

"She calls...or I call..."

"You're co-dependant. Totally fucking co-dependant."

"What the fuck does that mean?"

"It means you can't live without each other—you're co-dependant."

"What about you?" I asked him. "Could you live without your wife?"

"You gotta do what you gotta do," he said. He had a big chunk of powdered dilaudid hanging from the hairs of his left nostril.

"It's late," I told him. "You should go say goodnight to your kids."

"Yeah, I guess it's that time, isn't it?"

"Say goodnight, Dick, say goodnight."

"What's that supposed to mean?"

"It's something my uncle used to say."

Chicken
Lust

Joseph Suglia

Dedicated to Joseph Suglia

I

My perineal muscle is stimulated by the sight of mad snails.

II

I have a preternatural ability: that of hypnosis. I am able to hypnotize my victims into shedding their clothing. Once they are fully denuded, I pour lemonade into their navels and drink from their fleshy flesh-cups.

III

I am a professional contortionist. I pretzel my body, shove my forearm into the deeps of my larynx, press my ear lobes firmly against the small of my back, position both of my heels under my chin, or canopy my eyes with my octopod testicles.

IV

The next Pope should be flagrantly omnisexual, a raging sodomite, who openly fondles not merely the buttocks and penises of altar boys, but those of priests and bishops as well, during public convocations, on live television, with his long purple tongue dangling obscenely from his mouth. He would dry-hump nuns during press conferences and stick his tongue into Katie Couric's ear, while fondling her upholstered, newly buttressed, artificially renovated, savagely pointed breasts.

V

The most erotic space in the world is the car wash. I am not a motorist. I dance through that purifying, covered gallery unadorned, without vehicle or clothing, while gusts of water whip my head and back.

VI

I am not two concentric circles, but rather an infinitely spiraling vortex, a regressum ad infinitum.

VII

My favorite drink is the Smegma Smoothie, which is made of the fermented brownish-yellow substance that lines my foreskin, vanilla yogurt, and goat's milk.

VIII

I would like to meet my murderess, the woman who will martyrize me and thus make me immortal.

IX

I like to stroll along the beaches, wearing a suit made of fox vagina. I also like to insert my penis into tubs of putrid yellow gelatin. The gelatin is a heady mixture of orange marmalade, horse faeces, and yak urine.

X

Cover me in Italian salad dressing. Strap my pre-corpse to an oak tree, and let the fire ants devour my salad dressing-bedraggled body.

XI

When I attended Herberger High School, I was the initiator, and sole member, of "Masturbation Club," which involved me, sitting on the floor of an abandoned classroom with a yellowish copy of my mother's SEARS catalogue, manipulating my overused penis while staring at the intimidating brassieres of Nordic women, pointed and fierce, a circle jerk of one.

XII

Last night, I watched a special edition of MTV's REAL WORLD: LAS VEGAS in which the twentysomething hotties squatted and shimmied on those bouncy balls upon which kids ride, except these were equipped with stern dildos. They bounced and bounced and bounced their way into a maximum-security prison, where they were forcibly stripped, greased up with tanning butter, and put on display for an audience-participation talent show.

XIII

I want to wake up next to my clone so that I could kiss him on the mouth and play with his soft pubic hair.

XIV

Invite me to your wedding. I will lower my trousers and point my gigantic buttocks, baboon-like, at the wedding congregation, and douse them all with the spume of my propulsive faeces.

XV

In every ATM, there lurks a dwarf.

XVI

Les filles avec les pantalons verts m'enculent.

XVII

Die arschleckenden Damen tragen gelbe Hosen.

XVIII

My semen will flood the United States of America. No Noah will save you.

XIX

On my fortieth birthday, I will play strip poker with the bums, that friendly folk, and sway my man-udders restlessly in the wind. In the valley of my man-cleavage would be forty different flavors of ice cream. I will offer my creamy treats to those salivating bums.

XX

My signature move: the awkward groping of the breast, that fatty pocket of adipose tissue, mammary gland, and duct networking, followed by the inescapable screech and truculent blow to my ear.

XXI

A dinosaur bird will emerge from the bloody sky, seize me in its mighty beak, snap my body in two, and fly away into the night. The darkness materializes, and all that can be heard are the beating of the bird's vast wings.

Rio
Monstruo

Stephen
Huffman

"It's five bucks a hit. But it'll sling your head into the river 'bout five times."

Brazos Bob was an old hippie from New Mexico who somehow found himself finding himself somewhere south of Glen Rose, Texas. He liked to pitch his teepee near the river, eat squirrels or fish or rattlesnakes with beans, and sell hallucinogens.

The summer Brazos River Valley has things in it that will make your head hurt. You have to walk a long time to get to it. Sand deep enough to know you're wading; you know you're almost there when you have to stop and empty your boots. Plop down and look around, there are stunted mesquites as old as your great-great-great grandpa crackling with cicadas who sound almost as old, bull nettles and prickly pears, everything dangerous, all of it sloping, sloping toward a sound. Dump your boots and wipe your face with both sleeves. Listen. The river.

"Hell yeah, Bob. I'll take two. Got any beans?"

You can find breaks in the thicks if you look hard enough. Your junior travelers end up at the river looking like they've been through a mismanaged sawmill.

"Yep."

Bob reached into a pouch on his belt and held up two tiny purple pyramid-shaped pills. They sparkled and rolled around in his palm.

"Nice, Bob. Ten bucks? Here ya go. What's in them beans? I'm hungrier'n four or five motherfuckers. That's a long walk."

The river is magical when you get to it. Stepped worn cliffs of rock overhang it; you can trace time by them. Dinosaur tracks at the bottom…look up a bit…blacks of campfires layered in the rocks, shards of arrow points and pots…the top is just solid wrinkled stone in the sun, putting shade on the water, bare of the vegetation that gave up by seasons…and the river flows and cuts through it, below it now, not giving a damn.

"The river don't give a damn," Bob said. He grinned with all four of his teeth like he knew what I was thinking. I grinned back.

"I know, Bob. What's in them beans?"

"Hey, Bob, reckon I can skip this rock smack into that gar?"

The gar looked to be about six foot long through the river water, he was laid up in an across eddy with his snout just out like he was hunting birds or something.

"Bob?"

Bob was gone. Dammit, Bob. The dude tended to disappear. I hiked back up the draw to his teepee.

"WELL, THAT'LL BE THE DAY, UH-HUH, THAT'LL BE THE DAY, WHOOWHOO," Linda Rondstadt's girly version of the Holly. Bob had fired up his little battery-powered AM/FM box, tuned to some crazy station out of Oklahoma that he and only he seemed to be able to pick up in a river bottom. Bob was taking a piss beside the teepee, wiggling around in his own peepee version of the Watusi, singing along at the top of his pipes with Mizz R.

"Damn, Bob," I hollered, "What's that you got goin' there? The native dance of the Indian UriNation?"

Bob flinched like I had busted him doing something silly. Which I suppose I did.

"Goddam, bud," he said. "Don't sneak up on me like that. Man, good to see you." He pulled his britches together and walked over to me with his hand out. "When did you get here?"

I shook his hand. "Couple minutes ago." Bob could disappear in his head, too. "Man, that's a long walk. Got any beans?"

We sat cross-legged across the fire, Comanche bowls of beans dished out of the cast-iron pot, wood spoons between us. Damned woodsy tasty.

"Damn, Bob, this is tasty. What kinda spices you stick in here?"

"Ever eat any cat?" Bob answered.

You learned to blot out the imagery when you ate with Bob. I savored my bite, Bob wiped his mouth with the back of his hand.

"Nope," I said, "Just the human variety, unless you count possible misadventures in Korean restaurants. My ex-mama-in-law used to order only beef stuff from a menu, then have me check it out for her before she'd touch it. I'd dig around in her plate and ask her, 'What's the difference? If it's right tasty and you don't know what it is, then who cares?' Ya know, man, come to think of it, I should have special-ordered that meddling old bitch some cat and kimshee, then told her it was...Bob?"

Fuckin' Bob was gone again.

The sun was down enough to put some shade on me from the crotch of rock in the cliffs on the other side of the river. I leaned back on a gnarly old mesquite, I had my legs stretched out across the flat rocks with my boots off, bare heals in the water. The cicadas were quieting down; the crickets were waking up. Ahhhhh, yeah. The river whisper was getting a little louder. *Hmmm... must be coming onto the 'Sid...hey...a sand-bass or bream's tap-tapping at the bait on my cane pole.* Crunch. Somebody stepped on a twig in the woods behind me.

"Hey, Bob." I felt the fish start moving my bait around.

"Hey. You baited with crawfish?" Bob's voice came from over my right shoulder.

"Yep. I got me a punkinseed fucking with it right now. Little bastard's probably worrying it to death, picking off legs and shit. Bait-ruining little fucks."

"Well, I was gonna tell ya. Them moccasins is nestin'."

"Oh, yeah?" The tip of my pole started to jounce a bit, up and down, up and down, leaving tracers. I set the pole between my big and second toe so I could feel if I had to set the hook. "Damn, Bob. I'm coming on to that shit pretty quick. Must be good shit."

"I'm here to tell ya it is. Anyways, them moccasins is nestin'. Might be a bad idea to be laid out with yer feet in the water. Yep, that 'Sid is straight from Cleburne. Made fresh day before yesterday. Keep that other hit fer a buddy, I got plenty more."

The tip of my pole was really going now, swaying around with shiny visual echoes from the last of the sun reflecting off the rocks beneath me. I couldn't tell if it was a fish or a buzz on my bait.

"You mean moccasins are swarming around here?" I pulled my feet out of the water, they had a decided blue tinge to them; drips of river water sparkled down off them and hissed on the rocks. "And what do you mean 'the other hit'? I did both of 'em..."

My cane pole popped once, twice. I set the hook. *This ain't any punkinseed, man, my pole's bent over like there's a swimmin' 883 Sportster on there.* The pole jumped out of my hands and caught itself on a snag in the rocks. A bluegill the size of a small skillet broke out of the river maybe three feet from me, twisted in the air, and landed half out of the water on the rocks next to my right foot. She had a legless crawfish halfway in her mouth and a fishhook poked through her left cheek just under her eye. The crawfish waved and snapped his claws around for something to pinch. I crawfished against the mesquite and stood up. The sun was gone behind the cliffs, the cicadas were in bed, I had mesquite bark in my back, the crickets sounded like they were fiddling in the devil.

"Gawdammit, Bob, you seein' this?!?"

The bluegill tried to breathe and wiggle back to the water. The crawfish waved his claws around like he wanted to join Bob Barker down by the Price is Right stage.

"Bob?"

I stood barefoot straight against the mesquite and worried about my boots.

"Bob?"

The river exploded at the bank, panes of glassy water cut through me with a shiver, a gar stuck his snout over the rocks at my feet and grabbed up Miss Bluegill and her supper, Mr. Crawfish. *Dayam. Is that the same Mr. Gar I was chunking rocks at? Serves me right. What the hell am I talking about? Miss Bluegill's on my hook and Mr. Crawfish ain't happy about it. Oh, yeah, Mr. Gar. Mr. Gar's the difference. How come? Oh, that's right, I chunked rocks at him. Fucker holds a grudge.*

"Bob?"

Fucking Bob.

The moon came out, bending its shine down and off the southward slots of the cliffs. The surface seemed happy about it—fireworks and fireflies laughed with and out of the gurgles. The essence of the territory, the maker of the topography, the blood of the trees- the river- she ignored us all. Three moccasins splashed out of the moon shadows and latched onto the gar. The strapping gar, the flopping bluegill, the waving crawfish, the thrashing moccasins, they all slid back into the almighty water. The moon said, "Relax, son." The cliffs said, "Don't worry about it." The river whispered, "You're next." I pulled my pistol.

Bob, I'm fixin' to shoot everything that moves. You got pouches with dreams, I got pouches with ammo. The crickets found a damn good devilish harmony. The moon grinned again. I looked up the draw to find something familiar. There were Comanches of all stripes dancing a ghost dance around a big fire by Bob's teepee, except now the teepee had a blacklight green buffalo skull on it. Women and children where wandering around, gathering party materials. Linda Rondstadt's cover of "Blue Bayou" was playing from somewhere. Lord, no matter heaven or hell, this is right crazy. Fuck. Where are my boots? Bob came out of the teepee, or at least he seemed to be Bob. He had a full Comanche headdress on and dance paint, the green of the buffalo skull glowed on something he had in both hands. Gar 'n Beans. They oughta can that shit and sell it down to Brookshires. Something touched my left foot and I jumped and almost shot. A raccoon the size of Ann Wilson looked up at me through eyes purple in the moon. "Say, what'd you do with that crawfish you had while ago?" He /she said. Their head went back and forth in Shi-ne-ne Coon motion with the words. "The snakes says you had a crawfish, now, don't lie. That thar pistol won't do you a bit a good around here. Now, if it was a crawfish..." My pistol moved on it's own. Lord, I know when I look down I ain't gonna see no .357 crawfish. Something landed on my shoulder. "Don't listen to Shi-ne-ne. She's a liar. And so he is." I dropped my crawfish and backed into the old mesquite which now wasn't there, which caused my feet to tangle up and conspire with ancient gravity. I fell back-first into scratchy underbrush and heard my metallic crawfish ex-friend pang, pang, pang on rocks then splash. "See, I toldya she was a liar. Betcha he toldya there was a tree there." A big feathery fluttering sound kept getting louder; the moon was full down on me and it seemed like I was looking down but I knew I was up. Linda Rondstadt's voice wavered into a chant that sounded something like a red-tail hawk shrieking words: "When the moon grins, it never ends...when the moon grins..." Oh. You're a hawk on my shoulder. I been meanin' to tell ya...you shouldn't cover Buddy Holly. Nobody should. It's like yelling scripture in a church; just empty echoes to people who already read it. If ya gotta do Holly, do it in the garage drunk like the rest of us do. Or in a bar. You got you a fine voice, though. How come my arms are bleeding? Waddaya mean Shi-ne-ne lies? She was right honest about my crawfish. Does he know Bob? What's that crackling sound? Bob's campfire spilled down the draw and caught my hair on fire, bringing his Comanche party with it. Me and Linda Hawk and everybody were in Bob's teepee. The fire settled at the center of things, the smoke of it moved up to catch the moon at the smoke-hole. I was the only one laying in the bull nettles with my arms bleeding. Everyone else sat cross-legged looking at me. Ting. Ting. Bob took a bowl of beans out of the microwave. A beautiful girl in doeskins got up out of the crowd and looked down at me. Her hair was so shiny and black and long I thought she was gonna fly.

"Wish-na pashish wen-teh."

Huh? Say, Linda, what did she shay?

"Pashish?"

The girl set a bowl of hot beans on my belly.

Ahhhhhhhh!!!!

I got up to the hateful morning sound of the alarm clock. It's one of those digital jobs that goes ERT! ERT! ERT! ERT! like a startling stuttering obnoxious clown with electric vocal chords. I've been meaning to shoot that thing in the face for a long time....'ERT!' that, BoBo....but I never think of it until I'm halfway to work. I turned the thing off and scratched my ass. Man, what a dream. I gotta quit eating those green burritos so late at night. I stumbled to the shower, turned it on cold and pushed my head in. Ahhhh. Man, they need to outlaw work or weekends, one or the other. I can't stand the contrast. The cold water worked its way down, waking me up an inch at a time, got to my belly. Ouch. I looked down. A perfect sunburn-like ring of red was in the center of my gut.

A Typical Case?

Keith Buckley

[For the purposes of this subsection, "core information" means the names and addresses of people having an extensive history of drug abuse, unwashed clothes and dishes baked by the sun which give even the most graceful among them the appearance of compact strength, much like a bowling pin covered in skin from the sternum area of an old addict. Should you ever encounter any of the subjects while engaged in your own detoxification, gingerly feed them with tidbits of leftover meat, which you should find in your pockets.]

Sometime during the spring of 1993, Dr. Jimmy D. "Snow Dwight" Pheemister ceased taking notice of his deteriorating condition. He spent most of his time forging permits for businesses employing techniques that selectively impair brain function and the use of pornographic images for learning more about the workings of desire, and other illicit activities that should be subject to federal prosecution. Without in any way denigrating the pain and poignancy of his experience, we will discover that the ultimate beneficiaries of these brutal transactions usually consist of wood-mice, lemmings, hares and young hold-up men who routinely execute off-duty policemen with their own weapons. If that sounds like bravado, you should understand that, in this neck of the woods, Lapland attack reindeer and cattle were especially hated because none of them had been sent to the front. Their thick and rubbery tongues are agile enough to interfere in the domestic affairs of all other countries, and are at least potentially capable of violence. The best approach is probably to scrutinize the test subjects with great care, especially if they were to become infected and develop genital lesions.

Before his descent into cocaine abuse, Dr. Pheemister sported dark brown laminate with a broad, yellowish bushy tail and a long coat. He would often invest almost any amount in the improvement of his health, appropriating, in passing, twenty oxen once destined for the temple, and, no doubt to keep up his good humor, set several buildings on fire. He followed me everywhere with his repugnant attentions. He told me he suffered from a plague of devils and to prove his point, he would often split open his lower eyelid, spurting little jets of blood-tinged fluid about the room. All of this time I did not dare to say that libertarian feminists' overriding desire to transcend sexual repression inevitably leads them to mutually gratifying scenarios which offer valuable instruction in staying alive on the Yangtze River.

This much is certain: any of the methods are good if only they act speedily.

Limited to barriers and various entry screening devices, this Carbondale physician, under court orders to relieve his constant sweating, plunges into the abyss of addiction and began taking cocaine: those experts whose knowledge, background or other expertise lie in that particular field snapped off two teeth, making his tongue so swollen, thick and rubbery that he could barely talk. (Afterwards, I wrote to one medical director, who said that they did not beat his 19-year old son into discussing changes in the Clean Air Act, including the parts that deal with John Wayne, of course.)

The doctor did not notice. In his forties, he went as low as you can go without dying while a dispositive motion is pending, and the social highs turned to throb and press on his excited member. "In the beginning, I felt I was communicating with the renowned chef, Auguste Escoffier," he says, "and instead of reciting all the patients I've killed while under the influence, the medical review board will forward my name to the Nobel Prize panel for my work with priapism." Night after night, almost without intermission, bloodthirsty predators maintained his medical practice from the highlands of Scandinavia to Kamchatka, even smoking his coke there. Army ants, about three feet long, moved out of his house and into a dilapidated apartment to feed a passion for the use of violence and assassination to achieve political power or remove an adversary because it was impossible to sit comfortably, belly to belly, face to face, in a waterfront home on a private island worn by the wind and rain until the structure crumbles into flakes because the center will not hold.

After a year of cocaine use, Pheemister failed to develop any of the finer virtues to which settled humanity aspires, unperturbed by the constant small fires he set with his unsuspecting nurse, Felicity Powell, a convivial unaligned agent who owned a prized art collection and the dream of synthesizing living tissue. She wore a high-necked, tight-sleeved gray woolen dress and a perfume which reminded me of spinach gnocchi gratin ... particularly if paired with a '91 Kunde Magnolia Lane Sonoma Valley sauvignon blanc. When she smiled her awe accentuated individual feelings of utter helplessness and worthlessness. The glow of violet light in her eyes, however, was an artifact created by dying ions. At about that time, she threw her arm round my neck and seemed to almost forget that police officers miss 75-85% of shots fired in the line of duty.

She shoplifted for years, completely incapacitated by guilt and ennui, yet liked it, and progressed to kidnappings, taking hostages, contract murders, the detonation of bombs in public restrooms and other deliberate armed assaults on girls who are typically charged with sex offenses which are euphemistically described as "delinquent tendencies," "incorrigibility," or "running away," and is saved only at the eleventh hour by the decision to go to The New York Times where she stayed for two weeks in the psychiatric ward to relieve the constant sweating. I can still here her shrieking with a strangely melodic intensity as the parasite burrowed deeper into her pelvic floor, twitching like a chitin-covered phallus.

The doctor did not notice when she implored me to be more gentle, as she still smarted from completely stylized instructor-launched automatic weapon attacks at night as well as a number of constant small fires he started with his free-basing equipment. His sex life sizzled to feed a passion for unwashed clothes and dishes, broken glass pipes that formed a thigh-high pile, a waterfront home on a private island, a prized art collection, "the memory of the high," he says. He was now smoking $500 worth of coke a day. He wanted to be alone, away from his disapproving wife and the 6,000 Lapland attack reindeer pelts used yearly in the fur trade. He hunts for the ultimate buzz with his eyes closed and his septum deviated; his ears are permanently locked on his nurse's coiled shriek of euphoria. The lining of his nose is wildly inflamed, but still capable of tracking the spoor, the sour stench of her dried sweat and her cheap perfume. The journey is long ... her suppurating flesh has almost cooked away.

Dr. Pheemister undertook radical shifts in his moral career, lost interest in job and family, defaulted on his mortgage, enjoyed a lucrative practice with the help of his unsuspecting nurse and his obsessive use, sold off his belongings to pay for his habit, beat his 19-year-old son in a lack of understanding about where key nodes of vulnerability lie while considering how to induce hens to lay square eggs and, in some of the smaller species, to gather pollen from Vertot's orchid. Even sex seemed boring.

In order to protect himself from the ambient heat, furthermore, an idea had occurred to him, or rather a fantasy, which was to be alone, near death, snorting twenty grams a day with this reporter, who uses the drug modestly, who tries cocaine, like it, enjoyed a lucrative practice, discovered free-basing in the shower, sells off his belongings to pay for his habit, plunges into the abyss of addiction, moved out of his house and into a dilapidated apartment, progresses to chronic, compulsive use, loses interest in job and family / a successful long-term user, i.e., smoking $5,000 worth of coke a day, his skin covered with sores from malnutrition, the music sounds better / the addict and his supplier / insidiously antisocial minutes between "toots" made his tongue so swollen that he could barely talk / "made my conversation seem sparkling, my disapproving wife and children made me feel good," he says with a wry smile. "In the end, I thought I was God. All I wanted was the pipe."

Upon his second arrest for public intoxication, Dr. Pheemister told the booking officer, "I want you to kill me so there won't be a tomorrow." "But tomorrow morning breakfast will be potato pancakes with gravlax, along with your choice of stir-fried red flannel hash or raspberry-corn muffins." "Hmmm ... can I get a mimosa with that?" "Shit, bud, this is a jail, for fuck's sake. Coffee and O.J. is all we got." "I'll take death, then." "Okay, Doc, I'll kill you. But it's gotta be brutal." "Brutal? Does that hurt much?" "A jagged copper pipe bunged through your skull and a mop handle up the ass? Yeah, it hurts like a sonuvabitch." "That doesn't work for me. I'm already scared enough of withdrawal pain. The mop handle scene is far too frightening to even contemplate." "You're scared of pain, but you don't have a problem with dying? Isn't that pretty fucked up?" "How fucked up my thought processes are right now is totally irrelevant." "As a matter of fact, bub, your fucked up thought process are the core issue." "Maybe, but that's not the point." "What is the point, then?" "The point is I want death, not pain." "Why?" "Because I already know what pain feels like."

He spent most of his time in the west, as far south as the Sierra Nevada range in California, detecting non-metal firearms or high explosives in airline baggage, spending $1,000 a week to relieve the constant sweating and his sex life sizzled. Soon he started to twitch and drunkenly tottered around on legs like threads when some provocation was present. "Keep his legs from moving and his arms from hitting the unsuspecting nurse between her legs almost before she completes her sentence," says the medical review board night after night without intermission.

Dr. Pheemister's way with crack cocaine is juicy and audacious. The pearlescent rocks he creates for his seasonally evolving "smoking flights" have a complex depth of flavor rarely encountered in narcotics processing. "White Devil," his newest concoction, suffered not at all from the absence of the traditional sodium bicarb. "I mix pharmaceutical grade Colombian flake with bleached cardamom and asafetida. Inhaling White Devil reminds me of my favorite Punjabi restaurant, so I frequently serve a nice peach sambal alongside." The chutney does indeed provide sufficient taste variation to help the bowl delight and satisfy those expecting a draught of etherized salts. His nurse passed me the apparatus, her hands spasmodically shaking and her eyes the color of pickled onions. She tumbled over into a puddle of her own vomit, her body thrashing bout in a frenzy, flipping into the air like an eel on a hot griddle.

The highs got lower and the lows whimsical in my lusts and more versatile in my long-term technological wish list which might have included a more precise abyss of addiction but more elegantly built with somewhat larger ears, larger eyes and much larger dissolution of all moral norms that raised rashes on his lips and sores on his skin from malnutrition. In one of the fits of rage that accompanied the "down" periods minutes between "toots," he snapped off two teeth unravelling "the memory of the high," he says. Soon he was spending $20,000 a week on marketing experts at zoos directly to the brain with the help of his unsuspecting secretary who wore a high-necked, tight-sleeved Lapland attack reindeer pelt used yearly in several buildings on fire with his repugnant attentions and rashes (although he could beat his 19-year-old son in a three-mile run), and his sex life sizzled with a perception that follows the loss of identity and defenselessness brought on by the completely stylized insidiously antisocial fountain of youth.

"As the Carbondale Cocaine King for over five years now, I am constantly asked to take a taste of every new crop of marching powder that enters the country," Pheemister explained to me one night as we were standing outside of Quatorze, my favorite French bistro near the Chelsea district on West 14th Street, riveting the wait staff to our taxi by their thick and rubbery lips and turning their pockets inside out for the evening's tips. "My sampling career gives me a point of reference against which I can compare the product Felicity and I bake in my office autoclave, in order to ensure that the Snow Dwight's line reigns supreme." He continued to probe the hostess's natal cleft with his horribly twitching fingers, digging deeply into her lifeless form until he discovered the 50 dollars she'd tried to hide from him.

For the purposes of this subsection, I've known him since he was a medical student, when he had a soft, drawling Texas voice, a sky blue BMW— no cigarette lighter— and was strangely quiet, almost hieratic. Described as "the animal of the future," Snow Dwight plunges into near-death, and is saved only at the eleventh hour by the decision to go spending $30,000 a week, snorting four hundred grams a day "with only the memory of the high," he says. "All I wanted was a lucrative practice, a waterfront home on a private island in Biscayne Bay, the social high, broken glass wombats forming a thigh-high pile, a basis for reconstruction, skin constructed with a quiet and effective craftsmanship, the unsuspecting nurse covered with sores from malnutrition, powers of reasoning to reduce the constant sweating, a fountain of youth, the pipe, a thousand grams a day, a pair of moustaches to equal the exquisite pleasure of my saturated organ, and a prized art collection," he says with a wry smile. "In the end, I thought was the most abundant and generally distributed mammal in Europe. But I was too late. It was impossible."

Dr. Pheemister went into treatment to test and hone the reactions of the protective team. Even minutes between sex with only his disapproving wife and children seemed boring. He told me he was now free-basing God, whom he'd found in his garage, topping up his BMW's battery with distilled water. "Last night I was watching the television and Mr. Goodwrench told me mercy is battery acid. He insisted he wasn't speaking in allegories, that mercy is really battery acid, so I guess that's what God was doing in my garage, wearing a pin-striped flightsuit, with a monkey wrench the size of Texas stuck in the back pocket. When God noticed me staring at him, he said, "Hey, Jimmy— your transmission fluid smells like bacon. Tell the boys at Aamco that ain't kosher." Pheemister then admitted he could now get more enjoyment in public restrooms chasing after deliberate armed assaults on girls who are typically belly to belly, face to face, firing a slug of ultra-cold material into his 19-year-old son, a technique employed by the Lapland attack reindeer.

I told him the night before his execution for serial sex murders, "You'll always be my precious vegetable marrow, my gently insinuating stiff instrument, the nut too hard to crack." He was unperturbed by the agency officials who wanted to copulate his unsuspecting nurse dog fashion. "To think those hopeless bastards are the sons and grandsons of men who actually did something with their lives," Pheemister wearily sighed. "They go home at night and beat their own wives to assuage the appalling pressure of their sexual ambivalence." "You mean like him?" I asked, pointing at the doctor's own 19 year-old son who was leaning outside of the cell, smartly turned out in a white linen jacket with navy lapels and maroon trousers with a matching grosgrain trim, the remnants of his lower left arm spouting crimson geysers into the air. "He's waiting for my death- song," the doctor replied, and I shuddered. The sound of my own father's death- song shattered my vertebrae.

Never, however, does the press print even an anonymous account of the people on the front lines of any distribution network, but their heads, man, their heads!

They

Jon Konrath

In the bowels of Daniel Edgar Sickles Asylum for the Criminally Insane, a psych doctor and an orderly made the rounds through the darkened tunnels of the high security complex.

"I think the little black girl with the huge afro will win," said the doctor, "but that Sherry McLansing chick, the one that can't sing with the huge jugs, I'm hoping they find some amateur porn of her on the web somewhere."

Elron the orderly carried a huge drug kit in one arm, and rapped his nightstick along the wall with the other, while Dr. Finkelstein continued to babble on about American Idol. Elron often wondered if Finkelstein should be a doctor or a patient, based on his obsession for that shit. The godless fruit never even mentioned football, not even on the Monday after the super bowl.

"One more stop before lunch," said the doctor. "Cell 151. Who's our lucky contestant?"

"You haven't seen this guy yet?" said Elron. "Real piece of work. 228 dead, millions in property damage. He out-McVeighed McVeigh, and then played the looney card so they wouldn't give him the chair."

"He's here? I thought the government was keeping him in a secret underground bunker somewhere."

"Take a look around," said Elron, gesturing to the damp concrete floors, windowless walls, and reinforced steel doors. "You think this is Club Med?"

Elron fumbled with his shop teacher key ring, popped open six locks around the perimeter of the door, then lifted a heavy bar that safely blocked the portal. The heavy slab of steel creaked open like a wall safe, revealing a dark room, a man strapped to a bed, and nothing else.

"All life is pain..." he mumbled, pulling at his restraints. "No possibility for precious moments that can bring me temporary anesthesia... our horror-filled existence. Easy to seal out all thoughts of the world around us..."

"What the fuck is his deal?" said Elron.

"Psychotic break," said the doctor. "Formal thought disorder, extreme post-traumatic stress disorder, paranoid schizophrenia, I'm not sure. Someone stole all of his charts last week and sold them to *The Post* for half a million dollars." "Drag the rusty razor blade across our wrist, over and over, watch the stream of crimson red flow over a third grade classroom floor or local Shoney's restroom... We need pain, death, torture... to remember they give us no home in this world."

"We need to pop a cap in his ass, doc. He's really freaking the fuck out."

The doctor cracked open the tacklebox drug kit. "I'm giving him 100 mg of Brevital. I need you to hold him down on one side so I can hit a vein."

"Sebullis dobrish, teen Greek men fucking each other with a feta cheese dildo... They designed the Olympics to breed every four years with horses..."

Elron crawled halfway on top of the man, a knee on his throat. The doctor came in with a huge horse injection syringe, and plunged it into the patient's shoulder. "Keep him down!" the doctor yelled.

"Druidic menstrual ceremonies! Carlton Fisk wrote fuck face on your coffin! They fuck your mother! They are your god!" As the drug hit, the patient seized like an engine with no oil, and went catatonic.

"Jesus fuck," said Elron. "I knew the bastard was crazy, but that's the worst I've ever seen."

"I don't think he's going to be added to the outpatient work-release program any time soon," said the doctor. "So, you up for Shoney's?"

* * *

I pulled myself out of bed late that morning, wondering if I'd even make it to lunch on time. The nightmares started the evening before as soon as my eyes closed, apocalyptic visions of disaster, driving to Sarasota to have sexual relations with Bud Selig at his summer home, stopping at a falafel restaurant and convenience mart run by David Schwimmer in St. Petersburg, Florida. In the dream, I shit blood for days while Schwimmer screamed "WE WERE ON A BREAK" at me, pouring hot sauce in my colon. Right before I woke, a full nuclear war erupted, my skin melting away from my bones. Then, hours of pure fear, sitting in my kitchen, grinding up Benadryl tablets and snorting off the top of my fridge for another five minutes of nightmare-free sleep.

Protesters circled the outside of the Haldiburson world headquarters, the 54-story mirrored glass and aluminum phallic monstrosity that housed my day job. Since I started six years ago, the company practically ran the last five wars and won a no-bid for the next two in the queue. Las year, they sold Mount Rushmore to the Japanese, started an oil-drilling operation in the Grand Canyon, and angel-funded a restaurant chain that sold dolphin and bald eagle hamburgers. They were also involved with a Pixar remake of *Chitty Chitty Bang Bang*, which put them at the top of many a person's shit list.

"No Blood For Syrup!" chanted the unwashed masses at the edge of the parking lot. "Mad Cow is a Lie!" "End War (and give our vegan drum circle for hemp legalization money instead)!" The worst of it wasn't the signs, but that they were playing that Celine Dion song from *Titanic* over and over and over. And all of this effort was lost, considering the building was soundproof, and the execs either flew in on choppers or drove limos with pitch-black glass.

Last week, the media exposed that the recent mad cow epidemic came from Canada, and President Samuel L. Jackson started clamoring to strike down upon thee to the north with great vengeance and furious anger. Of course, Haldiburson made up the mad cow thing, planted it in the media, and paid Jackson to get things started. My job at the bottom of the food chain involved making stupid pie charts and PowerPoint decks that were factually useless but aesthetically pleasing. It wasn't bad for an art-school dropout; most of the other illustrators I knew were now sucking dick for crack. As long as I wasn't actually pointing the guns at peoples' heads, I could justify my meaningless life, sort of.

I parked in the underground garage and hoped the office would be sedate, so I could sneak to my cube and pretend like I'd been working for hours. A splitting headache tore through my brain, and I needed a handful of Excedrin and a few hours of Freecell to tune out the world. I got past the armed security guards and took the all-chrome express elevator to the 27th floor. Inside, it looked like the Cubs threepeated the World Series. Strippers and whores hung off of every suit, hundred dollar bills were scattered like confetti, and a dozen people were snorting rails off of the receptionist's desk. Empty bottles of Dom were stacked like the war dead in a cubicle. A huge sheet cake in the corner read "FUCK CANADA" in frosting letters. As I walked through the front doors, someone thrust a glass of champagne in my hand.

"We're rich! We're fucking rich!" yelled some loud-talking Ivy-league suit. "Fuck Canada! I'm buying a 200-foot boat and an SUV with no exhaust!"

"What the fuck are you talking about?"

"We got the drilling contract! After we nuke every fuckin' Tim Horton's on that French Iceland and make them crawl to us for mercy, we're going to tear down Montreal, drill for crude, and run a huge fucking pipeline south."

"Holy shit, that went through?" When the CEO announced the oil drilling bid at the last quarterly meeting, I assumed he was drunk and it was a joke.

"Fuck yeah it went through. We haven't done shit yet, and the stock's up to 387! If you've got any options and you're not covered by the SEC executive disclosure rule, you better get to a fucking phone and sell that shit!"

"Thanks for the champagne, um..."

"Baxter," he said. "Baxter Denslow, SVP Sales." he extended a cocaine-encrusted hand for a quick and firm handshake.

"Cliff Martin, production."

"Oh, are you the one that makes all of those charts for us?"

"Yeah, something like that."

"Well you better get to work. We're going to need as many win-win graphs as we can get for this war. It is going to be the sha-zizzle."

"Nice meeting you, Bax. I've gotta make a phone call."

I often contemplated wiping my ass with the 250 million Haldiburson stock options granted to me at $1.46 a share years ago. I would have preferred a cash bonus, or even a Fruit of the Month subscription. The big H wasn't public for the first two years I worked there, and then after the IPO, half of the executives went to prison for some elaborate insider trading fuckup that kept the price well below a dollar. It wasn't the stuff you'd use to fill out your retirement fund, although everyone did.

While my brokerage web page loaded, I tried to get a back-of-envelope figure. My calculator didn't have enough digits to figure out the math. 387 bucks a share, 250,000 shares, that's almost $98 million, minus my $365,000 exercise price. The page loaded, and I immediately clicked sell. The flip cleared instantly, since every trader in the world wanted shares before they hit the ceiling. I dumped ten million into my checking account, and left the rest in brokerage to... wait, do you pay taxes on this shit?

Tax, tax, tax... I dug through my address book and found the number of the one guy who could help me, Rudy Epstein. He was a lab partner of mine in Physics 201 in college, and was the most Jewish a Catholic could be. He never got laid in college, never drank a beer, never even left his dorm room. He sat around most nights playing solitaire with real paper cards and not a computer like everyone else would do later. But he pulled a 4.0 in b-school, blew through a law degree, and now drove a desk as a high-level tax attorney for the State Department. About once a year, he would roll into town, and when I reminded him that I did all of the damn lab work in that physics class and saved his ass, he'd drag me to Scores for hours, throwing money into strippers' cracks like a rap artist's drug dealer. He'd even end up expensing the whole thing somehow, so the fucking taxpayers covered our lap dances. He knew every single tax loophole in the book and had no morals whatsoever, so he'd be able to help me figure this one out.

My voicemail message light was blinking like a motherfucker, but I ignored that and dialed his number in DC, of course using the company phone so I didn't have to pay for the call.

"Rudolph Epstein, office of foreign missions tax department" he said.

"Hey Rudy, this is Cliff Martin in New York. What's up?"

"Cliff! I just left you a message. Looks like your stock is up — It's all over Fox News. I guess our next trip to Scores is on you, right buddy?"

"Looks like. Hey, I just exercised the options, and now I have a huge albatross hanging around my neck."

"Let me guess... does this involve me telling you how much tax you owe and how to get around it?"

"You're a mind-reader, pal."

"Let's see — no wife, no kids, no house, no business... you're pretty much screwed. How much did you clear?"

"97.3 million and change."

"Ouch. Well, 97.3 big minus $352,550... 35%... plus 97,653... That's roughly 34 and change that you owe Uncle Sugar. I don't have the NY schedule around, but they're going to hit you too."

"Thirty four fucking million dollars?"

"$34,029,278, to be exact."

"Jesus fucking Christ on a cross! I thought it would be like a hundred grand. I'm not giving those fuckers anything if I can help it."

"That is with the standard deduction, though. You might be able to cook something up. Maybe you could give some of it to a charity? Something tax-deductible, but get a receipt."

"Fuck charity. If I give anyone money, they will fucking call my house ten times a week for the rest of my life wanting more."

"No shit," he said. "I gave twenty bucks to Greenpeace back in '91 when I was trying to get in a girls pants, and those fuckers are still sending me letters."

"What if I buy some Russian chick right off the boat and marry her? What does that get me?"

"It gets you a lot of grief because, trust me on this, Russian women can be mean-hearted bitches. Tax-wise, it saves you like $6,660. And then when she becomes completely insufferable and splits, you lose half of everything."

"What if I buy a house? Isn't that what everyone does?"

"Everyone mortgages a house and deducts the interest. Showing up with a suitcase of money won't do a damn bit of good."

"How about I don't pay the money? I mean what if I just go Unabomber and head for the hills?"

"You ever hear of a guy named MC Hammer? Or Willie Nelson? Fuck man, the IRS will show up and take the fillings out of your god damned teeth."

"Any other suggestions? Anything I can buy, someone I can hire?"

"Lose a lot of money in the stock market. Incorporate a business that burns up a lot of cash. The only two schemes involve losing more money than they would take, or getting it out of the country undetected. I would tell you to wire it all to some shady offshore or South American bank, but that's the kind of thing we try to stop at my day job, and that kind of advice would get me fired, so of course you don't want to do that."

"Fuck fuck fuck, I don't want to give them anything."

"Look man, just take the hit. Dump the rest into the stock market and you'll be golden, especially if this Canada war starts. You're not against this war, are you?"

"No, no, I'm all for war. I hate Canadians. I have moral problems with paying for other peoples' education and welfare, though."

"I hear you. But the easiest way out is to get rid of the money, give it to a school or a foundation or something, like every other dying rich white dude."

"I'll see what I can do. I'd like to cause a hundred million dollars of grief before this is over. Maybe start a foundation of pain..."

"Hey Cliff," said Rudy. "What did you sell at?"

"Just over 387. Why?"

"I've got Fox News on mute here. It looks like they found out Haldiburson's got Bryan Adams on the payroll to juice the stock price. It's dropped down to 120 already. You might want to get the fuck out of the building, maybe buy some firearms, vanish into the jungles of Cambodia. Not official tax advice, though."

"Thanks for the heads-up. Catch you later."

"Good luck, guy."

I was in deep shit. I took the express elevator to my Honda, and tore out of the garage at light speed. Outside, it looked like Kent State redux; cops shooting tear gas, protesters torching cars, executives breaking out office windows and holding hostages at gunpoint. Apache gunship helicopters flew in a pattern over the area, waiting for the go-code to start strafing pedestrians. I pulled out of the garage, and tried to look for a path through the people running down the road on fire.

With a sudden crash, the front of my car slammed to the ground and the windshield exploded. It felt like my car got hit by a running deer strapped down with explosives. I kept my foot on the gas, and then saw through the spiderwebbed safety glass that it was Baxter's corpse on my hood, a mess of Brooks Brothers, blood, hair gel, and shattered bones, launched earthward from 27 floors above, straight into my Civic's A-pillar. I gunned the engine, still miraculously functional, then slammed the brakes to roll the useless sack of shit off of my hood. Then I punched out the pieces of my former windshield and headed home.

* * *

BEGIN TRANSCRIPT OZK008

F: You were describing a 'they'. Who are 'they'?

[20 second pause]

C: They. THEY. They made the Pinto explode. They engineered AIDS. They made Ralph Nader get into politics. They invented New Coke. Think of every bad thing that happened in your life, in the last century. It was them. They.

F: Is 'they' a group of people, an organization, a company?

C: I don't know! They! They! The devout they will only eat with his right hand, because his left is caked with lubricants and impacted fecal matter from repeated anal fisting. They made an animated snuff film so it would be legal. They killed the chick, storyboarded it, and sent it off to a Korean animation company. It took a couple of tries, because Koreans can't draw well.

F: Is this why you were in Korea?

C: I was in Korea because of the *Turner Diaries*. The *White Album*. Carlos Mencina. Just pick something so they can kill me! Unleash the fucking fury! Unleash the fucking fury!

F: [To orderly] Proloxin, 100mg. Help me hold him down.

END TRANSCRIPT OZK008

* * *

If you have never tried to withdraw two million dollars in twenties from your checking account after arriving at a bank in a car with no windshield and drenched in human blood, I wouldn't recommend it. But since it would take me about eleven years to withdraw it $500 a day from an ATM, desperate measures were required, and I had to slap around a few tellers before they finally pried open the vault and sent me on my way.

A hundred thousand twenty dollar bills weigh about a hundred pounds, take up as much space as the average coffin, and barely fit in the trunk of what was left of my car. Driving around in a thousand-dollar shitheap car with the average price of a used Learjet in the back can cause some anxiety in some people, and I found I was one of them. But I worried even more about what would be waiting for me at my apartment. I envisioned two lines at the door: one of stragglers asking for handouts, and the other a line of Treasury department employees that just got the red alert that someone took a shitload of money out of the bank. Both were bad.

Back at my one-bedroom shithole, the answering machine had 47 messages on it, so I took the phone off the hook. On average, I get about four messages a week, all wrong numbers. Now that I didn't want to hear from anyone, a million calls. I pressed play.

BEEP. "Cliff, this is your Uncle Jethro. I know we haven't talked for a while and maybe I called you a faggot or something because you took all of those fruity paintin' classes. But I heard about your company, and well, me and your aunt are having some trouble out here on the dirt farm and could use some help. Ever since your cousin Jamie went to prison for that meth lab, we're been having trouble with the bills, and then the dogs got sick..."

DELETE

BEEP. "Hey buddy. This is your old college hallmate Forest. You remember, I lived two doors down from you freshman year and sold pot out of my van. Anyway, I work for AustinLittleGreenfeld now, and manage an event-driven hedge fund that has been outperforming..."

DELETE

BEEP. "Hi Cliff, I don't know if you remember me or not, but I'm Cheryl Smith, and we dated a few times back in 1992, before I fucked your best friend. I guess I never got to apologize, but I was wondering if you were ever in Boston on business, I'd really, really like to see you again. I mean, I'm married, but I can be very discreet..."

(I distinctly remembered the quality of her blowjob, and wrote down her number before deleting.)

Every redneck relative, former babysitter, elementary school teacher, and distant neighbor called with a sob story. Every woman that ever dumped me and screamed "I DON'T WANT TO EVER TALK TO YOU AGAIN" at me, every former out-at-third-date who couldn't remember my name when I was inside them left a message suggesting their availability for sexual relations, married or no.

Before I could even stop to take a piss, they started knocking on my door. "Cliff! It's Vincent, your landlord. We're going to have to raise your rent to $40,000 a week. Come on Cliff, you signed a lease. We know you're in there! The lights are on!"

Good point; I shut off every light, used the Paris Hilton Cocksucking setting on my camcorder to pack a suitcase of vitals, then kicked out the bathroom window, crawled to my car, and drove fast to find a hotel where I could hide and regroup.

* * *

Aircraft Accident Report
Controlled Flight Into Terrain
Korean Air Flight 120
Boeing 747-300, HL7468
Wal-Mart Dunlap shopping center, Elkhart, Indiana, USA
August 6, 2009

NTSB Number AAR-00/01
NTIS Number PB00-910401
PDF Document (3.7M)
Related information from the Public Docket

Abstract: On March 16, 2009, about 0142:26 Indiana local time, Korean Air flight 120, a Boeing 747-3B5B (747-300), Korean registration HL7468, operated by Korean Air Company, Ltd., crashed outside Goshen, Indiana. Flight 120 departed from Kimpo International Airport, Seoul, Korea, with 2 pilots, 1 flight engineer, 14 flight attendants, and 237 passengers on board. The airplane had been cleared to land on runway 6 Left at O'Hare International Airport, Chicago, Illinois, and crashed into a Wal-Mart department store about 3 miles southwest of Elkhart, approximately 129 miles east-southeast of O'Hare, after a transfer of control to an unlicensed pilot during an armed hijacking. Of the 254 persons on board, 228 were killed; 23 passengers (including the unlicensed pilot) and 3 flight attendants survived the accident with serious injuries. 12 of the flight attendants and 22 female passengers were also found to have endured repeated and aggressive acts of sodomy, many post-mortem. The airplane was destroyed by impact forces and a postcrash fire. Flight 120 was operating in U.S. airspace as a regularly scheduled international passenger service flight under the Convention on International Civil Aviation and the provisions of 14 Code of Federal Regulations Part 129 and was on an instrument flight rules flight plan prior to the hostile takeover.

The National Transportation Safety Board determines that the probable cause of the Korean Air flight 120 accident was the unlicensed pilot's desire to run into a Wal-Mart at high speed in order to obtain an erection and become Jesus, fucking twelve hostage disciples with the body and blood of Christ. Contributing to this issue was the unlicensed pilot's total lack of flight training outside of the Ace Combat videogame series, the psychiatric condition of the unlicensed pilot, and his extreme fatigue after anally and vaginally raping over 24 passengers and crew members during the flight. Contributing to the accident was the inability of ground emergency crews to respond to the fire due to the season finale episode of the American Idol television program.

The safety issues in this report focus on flight crew performance during a hostage situation; air traffic control response, including controller performance; the adequacy of the Elkhart County fire and rescue response units; the amount of merchandise that immediately burst into flame after the collision due to poor quality and non-fire-retardant fabrics; and flight data recorder documentation. This report also analyzes the lyrics of the music album by the musical performance group known as "Inverted Bitch Fister", entitled "Fucking Crash a 747 into a Wal-Mart to Get a Hard-On" and the possible relationship between the album and the accident, given that the alleged pilot and hijacker, was a fan of the aforementioned music group, and the Jesus/disciple motivation was also depicted in a B-side single to their third album, entitled "I Am Jesus, Go Fuck Yourself."

[...]

* * *

The next morning, I woke in a shithole hotel just under the LaGuardia flight line. Between the landing jets rushing over my head and the usual nightmares about the Zionist Occupational Government and the Priory of Sion starting a nuclear war for the hell of it, I slept maybe ten minutes, and watched enough late-night TV infomercials to make me hate the world even more.

You'd think a sure bet in the stock market would be McDonald's. I mean, not a sure bet to make money, but even money that the company would fold. I popped out my laptop, fired up an MP3 from the extreme black metal band Inverted Bitch Fister, and bought just over two million shares of MCD, at $38 each. Ten seconds later, a trading floor employee called and asked if I was insane, to which I said "WIN OR LOSE I MAKE YOU MONEY NOW FUCKING EXECUTE THE ORDER! PULL THE STRING!" I knew McDonald's stock would soon hit the floor because of the Canadian mad cow thing, and also some doofus recently tried to film a documentary where they ate 10,000 calories an hour for 30 days at a McDonald's, and exploded. Of course, this was entirely the fault of McDonald's, and they were quickly boycotted by millions of people who never ate there anyway.

I took a long shower, got dressed, and considered various methods of leaving the country with a hundred pounds of cash. On the tube, CNN's scroller said "Mad Cow cured..." I flipped on the sound:

"...citing a new form of meat treatment that just finished phase three testing, the fast food chain has announced. The simple all-organic treatment regimen kills prions that cause bovine spongiform encephalopathy. The news has driven up the stock of the restaurant chain to over $200 a share."

God damn it! Is this going to be a real life *Brewster's Millions?*

"However, President Jackson has stated that the looming war with Canada will most likely continue, saying 'this shit's way too fun to stop. Snakes on a motherfuckin' plane!'"

It's harder than you'd think to tear out a hotel TV and throw it through a window, but my extreme anger certainly helped. I knew that Haldiburson made up all of the mad cow crap in the first place, because I drew their doctored charts. They probably cut Micky D's a check or maybe concocted some massive stock shorting operation so they could call off the threat and make money.

After my Keith Moon moment, I hauled the bags of cash down a service stairwell to my windshieldless Honda and drove at top speed to my next idea in wealth distribution, a Bentley/Lamborghini/Rolls Royce dealership. I e-braked my bloody windshieldless car sideways into three spots in front, and went inside, to find a group of horrified suits staring at me.

"I want to buy all of your cars," I said.

"Pardon me sir?" said a distinguished-looking gentleman with a slight British accent.

"Cars, cars, cars. I want to buy a bunch of fucking cars. Who's in charge? Can you sell me a car carrier truck, and just load it full of your most expensive models in stock?"

"Sir..."

"How much for the ugly blue one with the flat front?"

"That is the 2010 Rolls-Royce Phantom Drophead Coupe. It's one of the finest motor vehicles..."

"I didn't ask for a speech, Winston, just the pricetag."

"The base price is $410,000. That one, as equipped, is $620,000, plus tax, delivery, and other surcharges."

"Sounds good. You take cash?"

"Sir, I hardly think the refined craftsmanship brought forth and inspired by Sir Henry Royce would be appropriate for a person of your... caliber."

"Are you saying you won't sell me the fucking car?"

"Sir, I highly recommend the Saturn dealership two miles down the road..."

From behind me, a group of four security guards arrived to drag me out.

"I could buy five Saturn dealerships and still have enough cash to buy a Bentley for each member of the Portland Trailblazers, you fuck! It's people like you that made American Idol happen in the first place! I hope you Limey pricks are next in line after Canada! Princess Diana deserved it!"

They hauled me outside and dumped me on the ground in front of my Honda. It felt like someone was behind this, but I didn't know who. All I knew is I needed to buy a sledgehammer and knock out the windows of everything on their lot after they closed at night. Fuck!

* * *

FORENSIC EVALUATION DOCKET NUMBER CR S-96-259 GEB PAGE 6 (Continued)

In 1991, the subject contacted a campus psychiatrist, Dr. Robert Upton, concerning insomnia. Records indicate the subject reported nightmares and 'night terror' involving paranoid visions of totalitarian government and apocalypse. He indicates the doctor suspected he was depressed, but he was dissatisfied with his diagnosis.

Dr. Upton's notes indicate he suspected possible undifferentiated type schizophrenia (295.9/F20.3), but did not have the opportunity for further evaluation. Dr. Upton did prescribe a low dose (300 mg) of Neurontin, but the subject never returned and had no other mental health contacts prior to the period of his arrest on the current charges.

VII. THE DEFENDANT'S UNDERSTANDING OF THE CHARGES AND THE PROCEEDINGS AGAINST HIM

The subject does not acknowledge his custody situation and says that "this is all just something that they made up to sell more hamburgers" and "you're probably holding me next to the studio where they faked the Iran war". The subject refuses to provide any descriptions of the roles of court functionaries, and his paranoid delusion makes the basic understanding of general legal procedure impossible. When confronted with or questioned about the possible consequence of a guilty verdict, the subject repeatedly states "why don't you just get Celine Dion to shit down my throat until I die?"

VIII. MENTAL STATUS EXAMINATION

The subject was agitated, unresponsive, or uncooperative during the examination. Personal hygeiene was not a factor as he was kept in full restraints. Speech was incoherent, unintelligible, or delusional. Mood ranged from uninterested to extremely violent. There was constant evidence of suicidal ideation and suicidal intentions. Observed emotional tone was completely inappropriate. He constantly referred to a conspiracy group or movement simply called 'they' that ran all of modern man, and would cause its demise. The subject also demonstrated an irregular belief that if one ate a large number of Little Debbie Zebra Cakes, their excrement would taste like the undigested product, and this was evidence of a higher conspiracy.

Aside from possible depression from injuries caused in the crash, there was no evidence of organic impairment of mental functions. The subject's actions could not be ruled out as Limbic psychotic trigger reaction, but partial history dictates a longer-term underlying condition, due to psychosis observed during examination.

[...]

* * *

I bought the fucking Saturn. I actually bought two, because when they didn't want to take away my decapitated Honda, I took out the tire iron and beat the shit out of a car on the showroom floor, and you break it, you buy it. So now I had a $32,000 car, $1,933,000 in twenties, and $120,000,000 in the bank. And the Saturn Sky was no Rolls-Royce, either. It was like GM's subtle way of telling America that Japan should have won the war. It drove like a car sold by Ikea that you had to assemble yourself with a tiny allen wrench, and the money barely fit in the trunk. But thank baby Jesus it had OnStar. I pressed the little blue button every two minutes and tried to initiate phone sex with the agent, until they disconnected my service and gave me a stern reminder that I should not try to masturbate while operating a motor vehicle.

On an aimless drive through the city, I thought about buying a huge apartment for ten or twenty million, but they all required board approval, and boards don't like to hear things like that you work for Haldiburson, or that your first redecorating project will be building a *Silence of the Lambs*-style death pit, throwing all of the board into the hole, and screaming "THEY PUT THE LOTION IN THE BASKET" while dancing around the apartment to the song "Goodbye Horses" with your dong hidden between my thighs. I also tried to write the Catholic Church a check for $25,000,000, earmarked for pro-abortion rallies, but they hung up on me.

I rolled to a stop at a red light, next to a freeway cloverleaf, six lanes meeting six lanes. A second later, a tapping on my passenger door greeted me.

"Hey man," said a guy that resembled the cover of the Jethro Tull album *Aqualung*, but much smellier. "I ain't gonna bullshit you, I need a drink. You got any money? I was in 'Nam, man" He looked like he just took a strong pull from a bottle of PVC pipe adhesive, and began his rehearsed tale of woe.

"Really, where were you stationed?"

"Da Nang, Khe Song, Cambodia, secret missions north of the DMZ, all over the place. And I fucked your mom."

"What? What the fuck did you just say?"

"I was a Lieutenant Colonel in the Green Berets and we trained with the SEALs and did Lurp patrols. They paid me to fuck your grandmother in the ass. I served under John Kerry. We double-teamed your mom, and nine months later, you popped out. You got any change?"

I swore that's what he said, even though it made no sense. I still had my Wal-Mart sledgehammer in the front seat, from the Saturn dealership debacle. I vaguely remember someone at Wal-Mart not selling me a gun or knife, so I stole the sledge. I jumped out of the convertible with the hammer of Thor and rushed the bum.

"What the fuck is your problem? What did I say to you? I just asked for change! Are you crazy?"

"You work for them! You fucking work for them!" I clearly watched the hammer in my hands swing like it was a freshman-year trig problem. It connected with his skull, and it exploded in a cloud of red and grey. I hit him 16 more times in the head. I counted. I watched his face turn into dog food. A hundred people in the intersection were honking their horns for me to get the fuck out of the way.

I dropped the hammer, got in the car, and gunned onto the highway going west. My head really hurt, and I needed more Excedrin. And I really craved Tom's Burgers, this chain out in LA. I figured I could get there in a few days. Maybe I'd need a car with different plates and no blood. And an iPod. And a machine gun. I'd figure that out later.

* * *

BEGIN TRANSCRIPT OZK122

F: What is the last thing you remember before the plane crash?

C: I remember being in LA, and then nothing...

[20 second pause]

C: Then everything smelled like shit.

F: On the plane?

C: No, Korea. Have you ever eaten Kimchi? It smelled like straight-up fermented shit. It was everywhere.

F: Why were you in Korea?

C: KAL 007. KAL 858. KAL 801. I thought I'd hit for the cycle.

F: I don't follow.

C: GOD DAMN IT GET A COMPUTER AND LEARN TO USE GOOGLE! Korean Air 007, shot down by Russians in 83. Flight 858, bombed by crazy North Koreans. Flight 801, flew into a mountain because of a stupid pilot.

F: You don't remember the drive across the country? Planning the hijacking? The practice run at LAX? The plastic guns?

[15 second pause]

C: One of the orderlies said a couple dozen people lived.

F: 22 passengers, 3 attendants. And you.

C: And me. They probably planned that. That's my point.

[30 second pause]

F: What's your point?

C: I can't change anything. They run everything. If you let me out of here tomorrow and I wanted to kill another thousand people, they would stop me, unless they wanted those thousand people dead. They control everything. If you put a gun in my hand and pointed it at my head, it would miss, if they wanted me alive. The only reason I haven't killed you with your own pen is that they don't want me to.

F: The only reason you haven't killed me is you're strapped to a bed in ten-point restraints.

C: BUT THEY STRAPPED ME TO THE BED! IF THEY WANTED YOU TO BE DEAD, I WOULD KILL YOU IN A HEARTBEAT! THEY! THEY! THEY! THEY ARE YOUR GOD!

F: [To orderly] Proloxin, 500mg. Quickly...

END TRANSCRIPT OZK122

* * *

Seat 24A. The plane pushes back in ten minutes. They didn't catch his fake passport. They didn't search his carry-on. It's the older airport in Seoul, and there's so much traffic, so many people. Wear a suit, smile, you can get through with a Stinger missile and a suitcase full of crank. No problems.

Before he left LA, he found a guy who completely retrofitted Glock 17s, replacing the barrel, slide, and all metal parts with carbon-fiber or polymer. It used a caseless ammo that contained no metal. He bought two of them, and found a gym bag that enabled him to take the slides and magazines off the pistols and hide them in shoes and shampoo bottles. He also bought three military-grade ceramic knives, strapped to his socks.

He watched the flight status on the LCD screen. He would wait until everyone was asleep, an hour or two before O'Hare. He would fly at a thousand feet, until he saw a fucking Wal-Mart. Maybe even one right by a Saturn dealership. He would prove that they couldn't control everything.